The Amorous Adventures of

AUGUSTUS OF SAXONY

The Amorous Adventures of

AUGUSTUS OF SAXONY

containing

Several Transactions of his LIFE, not
mentioned in any other HISTORY

Together with Diverting
Remarks on the ladies of the Several
Countries thro' which he travell'd

by

KARL LUDWIG VON PÖLLNITZ

*Translated from the French by a
Gentleman of Oxford*

WILDSIDE PRESS

FIRST PUBLISHED ABOUT 1750

CONTENTS

CHAPTER I

7

9

ILLUSTRATIONS

CHAPTER I

Of the Splendor of the Saxon Court in the Reign of the Elector John-George IV. Of his Mistress, Marriage, Disputes with his Brother, Attempt to stab his Electress, how his Brother hinder'd him, reprov'd the Elector's Mistress, and of Frederick-Augustus's *Departure from Saxony on that account.*

No part of Germany could ever boast of more Gallantry and Splendor, than the Electorate of Saxony, whose Magnificence was more particularly conspicuous in the Reigns of John-George IV, Elector, and Frederick-Augustus, chosen King of Poland. This latter was a polite, graceful, and amorous Prince, and though several of his Passions were innate, yet did he by the continual ardency of his Love, seem to be but lately enamour'd. No Court was ever adorn'd with such beautiful Ladies, and no less accomplished Gentlemen; Nature seem'd to have delighted in placing the most exquisite of her Beauties in a resort of Persons of the greatest distinction. The Princes of the Electorate exceeded all others, and the charms of the Princesses were not to be equall'd.

John-George IV was very young when he succeeded his Father. His natural qualifications would have render'd him amiable, had he not given himself over to the conduct of an imperious, haughty, revengeful, and always incensed Mistress, who, sacrificing all to her own Ambition and Interest, esteem'd nothing sacred. Such was

13

AN UNWORTHY MISTRESS

Mademoiselle Neitsch, whose Command over this Prince was so absolute, that some Persons have accus'd her of having made use of supernatural means in the attainment of it.

Prince Frederick-Augustus was extreamly perplex'd to see the Regard his Brother had for so unworthy a Mistress. He pleas'd himself with the hopes of diverting his Fancy from her, by persuading him to marry a Princess; and though such a persuasion was disadvantageous to himself, yet did his generous disposition not suffer him to neglect it: thus he postpon'd his personal Advantages to the Welfare of the Common-wealth, and to Honour of his Family.

The great influence Mademoiselle Neitsch had over the Elector's mind did not impower her to undertake a dissuasion from consenting to what was propos'd; and the Advice of his Ministers induced him to make choice of Eleonor of Saxe-Eisenach, Widow of the Marquis of Brandenburgh-Anspach; a Princess, whose excellent accomplishments gain'd a great Veneration, and beautiful Person the Admiration of all that saw her. Her Husband was the only Person insensible of her Merits: though by her Agreeableness, Obliging Carriage, and an uncommon Patience, she endeavour'd to obtain his Favour, yet could she not untie that fatal knot, which ally'd him to Mademoiselle Neitsch; she would have been happy, had this arrogant Mistress been contented with attracting a

Heart that was her own, and not occasion'd the Abuse of the Person she had already injur'd.

Frederick-Augustus was sensibly touch'd with the Perplexities of the Electress; for, had she not been his Sister-in-Law, common Generosity would have induc'd him to lament her. He frequently comforted her, and made as frequent intercessions with the Elector in her favour; but those endeavours prov'd ineffectual: for his Advice was rejected, and he forbid interposing in his Brother's Quarrels with the Electress. 'Was it Your fate 'to lead a conjugal Life, (said the Elector) I should not 'interrupt your method of governing Your Spouse; why 'may not I insist upon an equal Privilege? How can I 'prevail upon myself (reply'd the Prince) to be a Spectator 'of such Injustice? my Concern for your Interest is so 'peculiar that I cannot but represent to you the Injury 'your Reputation suffers by your inhuman usage of an 'amiable Princess, to please a Mistress so little worthy 'of you. I presume not to prescribe you Rules, and should 'be heartily sorry to find I had in the least deviated from 'the Respect I owe you; but think myself capable of 'telling you, that you have a Lady, whose Birth, Beauties, 'and Virtues ought at least to gain your Respect.' The Elector, being insense'd with these Reproaches, and Mademoiselle Neitsch having by several Insinuations persuaded him to believe, that the Prince and Electress were unlawfully acquainted, he look'd upon his Brother

15

with Eyes inflam'd; 'Alas! (said he in a threatening tone) 'I perceive your vile affection for my Unworthy Wife, 'but shall soon be capable of ridding myself of you 'both.' He then left his Brother precipitately, and directed his Course to the Electress's apartment, giving himself over to the great Rage, that had taken possession of his Heart, he approach'd the Lady's Bed, and had certainly stabb'd her, if his Brother, acquainted with the Violence of his Passion, and suspecting his Design, had not pursued and disarmed him. 'By no means, dear Brother, '(cry'd he when he deprived him of his Sword) it shall not 'be reported that an Elector of Saxony was the Murderer 'of his Wife;' and when the Elector attempted to draw nearer to the Princess, threatening to strangle her, the Prince seiz'd him with that extraordinary force, which he only was famous for, and carry'd him to his Chamber. The Elector, being highly exasperated, spoke whatever Words his Anger supply'd him with; but the Prince, not ignorant of his furious Temper, and assured, that the sentiments of his Heart differ'd a little from the Words, his Rage induced him to utter, suffer'd him to give vent to all his Fury, and did not leave him till his Passion was cool'd.

As soon as he had left the Elector, he went to Mademoiselle Neitsch; and found in her Apartment the Countess of Rochlitz, her Mother and her Unworthy Confident. 'I am very glad, Ladies, (said he with an Air,

Augustus of Saxony

Engraving by Kruegner

'that show'd a Contempt of them) to find you together, 'for I design to treat with you about some Things, 'relating to you all. The Elector has just now been venting 'the effects of those vile Maxims you have infected him 'with. The Respect that is naturally due to him from me, 'permits me not to take any Revenge; I have besides so 'good an Opinion of my Brother, that I am persuaded he 'will one day be acquainted with the Snares you have 'laid for him, and punish you for having so highly abused 'the Confidence he has repos'd in you. In the mean 'while I shall prevent the perpetration of a piece of 'Injustice, and, if possible, deprive you of the means of 'slandering the Virtue of the Electress. In order thereto 'I am resolved to retire from hence. But you may be 'assured, that whilst I let you have the free use of your 'Speech upon that subject, I shall have a watchful eye 'upon your pernicious schemes, and be capable of pre-'venting the execution of them; you are now acquainted 'with my intention of making you responsible for the 'Fate of the Electress. I command you to let her quietly 'enjoy the Honours, She is here entitled to; and if my 'Brother should so far injure himself, as to abuse her 'in my absence you shall be applied to for Satisfaction. 'You know me (added he in a threatening manner) and 'you may be assured that my Promises shall be performed.' He did not wait for any Answer from them, but went home to give Orders for his Departure.

FREDERICK-AUGUSTUS DEPARTS

The Elector hearing of his Resolve of quitting Dresden, was heartily sorry for it. His Anger ceased, and Passion gave way in his Heart to the Affection he had for his Brother. He intreated him not to depart, but the Prince desired him so earnestly not to be displeased with his removing from thence for some time, that the Elector could not longer refuse his Consent. He even gave him all the Retinue, requisite to make him appear in foreign Courts with a Grandeur becoming the Brother and Heir apparent of one of the most potent Electors of the Empire.

Europe at that time enjoy'd so profound a Tranquility, that all Countries were open to satisfy his Curiosity. He undertook to view the most celebrated States and Provinces. His excellent Aspect, Strength, Address, Splendor and Politeness caused universal Admiration. Being persuaded that Grandeur is sometimes obnoxious to Pleasure, never conducive towards it, he determined to travel incognito, and took upon him every-where the Title of Count of Misnia, which was a shelter from tedious Ceremonies, and sufficient to procure him a handsome Reception. Whilst he retained this Name he met with several Adventures, of which those shall be mentioned here that will seem most agreeable to the Publick. After having travell'd thro' all the Courts of Germany, he went to Holland, from thence to England, and at last to France. He had in all these several Countries various

Amours; but as these were only the Attendants of
transient Flames, in which the Heart had a less share
than that intriguing Spirit, which never suffered him
to be idle, I think it most proper to pass by them
silently.

CHAPTER II

Of Prince Frederick-Augustus's *Voyage to Spain, his Adventure at a Bull-Feast at Madrid, Reception at the Spanish Court, Amour with the* Marchioness of Manzera, *ill success in this Amour, the* Marquis of Manzera's *Order to assault the Prince executed, the Marquis's Barbarity to his Spouse, her Murder, and the Prince's Departure from Spain.*

THAT same courtly mind induced him to undertake a Voyage to Spain. The Description he heard of the Beauty of the Spaniards and of their courtly Behaviour occasioned his Visit to the Country, as a Place deserving his Presence. He arrived at Madrid the evening before a great Bull-Feast, which King Charles II gave to entertain his new-married Spouse Mary-Ann of Neuburg, Princess Palatine. When he was informed that an Entertainment was preparing for the next day, 'Behold, (said he with 'that charming Grace, that accompanied his Discourses, 'when he addressed himself to the Lords his Attendants) 'an Opportunity of signalizing ourselves, and of acquiring 'a Reputation here: let us wrestle and sacrifice some 'Bulls to the Honour of our Mistresses.' The Courtiers approved of the Project, and the manner of putting it in execution was next consulted upon.

On the Day of the Entertainment the Prince and his Retinue went richly dressed to the place called Majose, one of the greatest and finest Theatres in the World.

ADVENTURE AT A BULL-FEAST

Scaffolds and Amphitheatres were erected, which contained an infinite number of persons next to the first Rank. The Balconies, of which all the Windows that border upon that place are beautify'd, were adorned with rich Carpets. An infinite number of Ladies was seen there, who by their Beauty and splendid appearance formed an admirable prospect.

If the Prince of Saxony was surprised to find there so many beautiful Ladies, all the Spectators were in no less Amazement to see him; for he spared no Expence or Pains to appear in a Stately manner at such a Solemnity; the Richness of his Dress, and that noble Air, with which he presented himself, drew the Eyes of all the Spectators upon him. They omitted no enquiry after the Quality of the Stranger, and soon after the King and Queen made their appearance. Their Majesties took a seat in a Balcony shining with Carpets and Squares embroidered with Gold. The King's Trumpets, Fifes, Hautbois and Drummers gave the Signal; the Gentlemen appeared, the Bulls were let loose, and the Battle begun. The Prince was for some moments a Spectator, but soon became an Actor, the Sight was new, and the manner of the Battle agreeable to his Fancy. He was soon as skilful at it as any that were in the Career, and quitting his Balcony, mounted on Horse-back, and presented himself at the Bar, which was soon opened unto him; he then entered the Career, and there shewed his surprising Dexterity and Strength. He struck the hinder-part of the Neck of one of those furious Animals with such Force with his Hanger, that he had almost deprived it of its Head, and caused its final Fall. The Spaniards could not sufficiently admire him, nor could they be persuaded that a Man, not a Spaniard born, was master of such Strength and Dexterity.

The King was greatly astonished, and desirous of knowing who this Stranger was, her Majesty seeming as curious, the Marquis of los Velos Gentleman of the Golden Key, was ordered to enquire after it. This Nobleman thought he could be no better informed, than by addressing himself to the unknown Person. He accosted the Prince very gracefully and said, 'Your 'extraordinary Aspect, Sir, your Dexterity, and the 'invincible Courage you just now discover'd, have 'deservedly attracted an universal Applause, and justly 'obtained the Regard of their Majesties. By their Order 'I take the Liberty of asking you, who that Person is, 'whom our Gentry acknowledge to be their Superior, 'and whom we cannot cease admiring?' The Prince replied modestly, 'That he could claim no Right to the 'Praises, they would feign honour him with: as for his 'Name, he doubted whether that was a fit place to 'discover it to their Majesties; but since they seemed 'very eager after the Knowledge of it, he begg'd they 'would pardon the Boldness of the Prince of Saxony in 'appearing before them, without having previously had 'the Honour of an Audience from them.' The Marquis of los Velos having reported his Answer to their Majesties, they were extreamly surprised, that a Prince of so eminent a Birth had ventured to enter into mutual Combat with the Bulls, and sent him a Congratulation thereon. The King, by reason of the Ceremonies, not capable of seeing him that day, acquainted him by a Messenger with his being welcome to his Country and his Court, and that he was heartily glad to see him. The Queen, less inclined to submit to those Ceremonies, invited him to an entertainment the same Evening, and to be introduced to her by the private Stair-case.

The Prince was at the entry of the Queen's Apartment receiv'd by the Countess of Berlips, her Majesty's Favourite, who conducted her into Germany. The Queen was standing, leaning against a Table upon a Canopy, at some distance from her Majesty stood on the Right-hand Side, the Chief Lady of the Bed-chamber, Catherine of Macade-Arragon, Spouse of the Duke of Fernandine. On the Left-hand Side were the Ladies of the Palace; and a little more backwards were the Chamberlains. The Prince approaching the Queen, intended according to Spanish Custom, to Kneel on one Knee and to Kiss her Majesty's Hand: but She would not suffer it. He intreated to be permitted to pay that Homage to a person of her Beauty and Distinction; whereupon the Queen presented to him her Hand, to which he gave so respectful a Kiss, that That Princess, who had been extreamly pleas'd with his Dexterity and Courage, was no less with his Politeness. The Pleasure with which she received him, the extraordinary Honours she conferr'd on him, the marks of Benevolence and Esteem she shewed him, cannot be Verbally express'd.

Whilst she was entertaining herself with the Prince, all the Ladies fix'd their Eyes on him, and view'd him with as much Admiration as formerly the Followers of Statira did Alexander.

Among these Ladies that surrounded the Queen, the Prince observ'd one, that seem'd to him to exceed all her Comrades in Beauty. He could not but shew some particular regard for her, which the Lady took notice of. The Prince had the pleasure of seeing her Eyes fix'd modestly on him. The Satisfaction he was sensible of in seeing her, induc'd him to exceed the common limits of a Visit; it was of a tedious length, and had not the Queen finish'd it by saying it was late, and the King's Supper-hour approaching, the Prince would probably have staid longer.

Tho' he only address'd himself to the Queen, yet he saluted the Ladies in so graceful a manner, that they were charm'd with it; they could not be weary of admiring him. The Queen was highly pleas'd in hearing the gesture of a Prince of her Nation applauded, nor could she sufficiently praise him. 'Alas! (said she to the Countess

'of Berlips) how do these Princes differ from those of
'our Nation.' Perhaps she meant the King her Consort,
who, being of small size, tender and sickly constitution
and disagreeable temper, could certainly not be an
amiable Object. During Supper time she diverted the
King with a description of the Prince of Saxony. 'His
'Mind and Politeness, (said she) equal his fine Aspect;
'you cannot but esteem him: my Women are all taken
'with him, and have tir'd me with commendations of
'him. I suspect that even the Dutchess of Fernandine
'(continu'd she laughing and looking at that Lady) has
'such Regard for him, as she has hitherto not been
'sensible of for her Spouse.' 'Women of my Age (replied
'the Dutchess with a grave Air that was appropriate
'to her) are incapable of raising suspicions of that kind,
'and I am fully persuaded, that your Majesty is only
'pleas'd to divert yourself in accusing me of having been
'smitten with the Prince's Merits; nevertheless I protest
'before your Majesty that I find him design'd to imprison
'Hearts, and if our young Ladies will hearken by my
'Advice, they'll shun his acquaintance.' The Dutchess in
speaking these words incessantly look'd on the young
Marchioness of Manzera, her Daughter, Lady of the
Court, and the same Person whom the Prince had taken
so particular a view of. She observ'd that the Marchioness
did just lift up her Eyes and looking on her Mother
precipitately changed colour. The Dutchess needed no

more to confirm her Suspicion. She thought the Prince
of Saxony had left an impression on her Daughter's
Heart, by her manner of looking at him, and because she
was the sole person that omitted praising him. She
resolv'd to watch her Daughter and if possible, to
preserve her from the precipice of Love. Vain Projects!
that fatal Star which sometimes determines the Heart to
engage itself for the remaining part of Life, had so
powerful an Influence over the Marchioness that her
Destiny was inevitable, and the preservation from it
impossible to the Dutchess.

In the mean while the Prince of Saxony desperately
in Love with the Marchioness, strove diligently to be
inform'd of her Quality, and to find some means of
acquainting her with his Tenderness for her.

By the Superiority she seem'd to have near the Queen
in Rank he conjectur'd that she was one of the first Ladies
of the Court. The next morning he found himself not in
the least mistaken; by the account some young Lords,
who came to pay him a Visit, gave of her, he was informed
of her Name, and that her sole dependence was upon a
very jealous Husband, and as severe a Mother; so that
she was thought to be inaccessible.

This News would have mortify'd any one except the
Prince of Saxony, for his intrepidity in Amorous adventures, equall'd that in the middle of a Slaughter in war,
the more difficult the Conquest of the Marchioness was,

the more he esteem'd her worthy of himself; for some Days he could not attain at the happiness of the sight of her.

The King being indispos'd the Night after the Bull-Feast, confin'd himself to his Chamber: the Queen did not leave him, and the young Marchioness being serviceable to both, remained in the Anti-Chamber, where the Prince could not appear, not having yet visited the King.

In this interval of Time he was told, that the Marchioness had a Chamber-maid in whom she greatly confided; he knew that she was an old Maid, who had several Nieces, that were supported by the Generosity of her Mistress. He despair'd not of gaining this person's Interest, and making use of her to procure him a good reception with the Marchioness. His only Obstacle was the almost impossibility of conferring with her; he could not be admitted into her House, nor was he master of the Spanish Language, and she whom he design'd for his Confident could apparently speak no other but that Tongue. But what can be an Impediment to Love? After having well consider'd of the execution of his Project, he resolv'd upon entrusting a Brother Mendicant, Friar Recollect, Italian by Birth, and a bare-fac'd intrepid Intriguer. He went every Day, and procur'd some Salads and Flowers, which he brought to reap the effects of the Prince's Bounty. To him the sentiments of an amorous

Heart were discover'd, he was charged to speak with
Freedom in the House of the Marchioness; and the
officious Friar obey'd his Orders so zealously, that he
perceived Donna Lora (which was the Confident's
Name) was a person of such mercenary Views, that a
Refusal of the Prince's Liberality was inconsistent with her
temper. He boasted much of the Presents he had receiv'd.
'He gives me more (said he) in one day than all the
'Gentry of Spain do in a month.' He described the
graceful appearance and uncommon Strength of the
Prince, of which latter he related such Prodigies, that
she was astonish'd at and charm'd with it. Old Lora
reported all this to the young Marchioness, who heard
her with the utmost attention and pleasure. When
Donna Lora had no News to tell her, she said with a
sorrowful Countenance 'how now! have you nothing to
'relate of the beautiful Stranger?' That was the Denomination given the Prince by the Ladies of Madrid.

The King being recover'd, the Prince appear'd in
publick at Court by the appellation of Count of Misnia,
and was introduced there by the Count of Benavente.
He saw in the anti-chamber the Duke of Montalte and
several Lords, that attended him. The King receiv'd
the Prince in his Closet, He was standing cover'd and
leaning against a Table, having a Chair of State at his
right Hand. He uncover'd his Head at the second Bow
the Prince made him. His Majesty was addressed in

Italian, answered in Spanish; but afterwards they both made use of the Italian Tongue in their Conference. The Prince was desired to be covered, and those that were present, and the Officers of the Court was ordered to pay him the respect due to a Prince of the Blood. He was at last intreated to go to pay his Compliments to the Queen, who impatiently waited for him. The Prince return'd thanks to his Majesty for the great Civilities receiv'd at Court, and the Count of Benavente went to inform the Queen of his coming.

All the Lords that were in the King's Apartment accompanied the Prince to that of Her Majesty, who in the Reception she gave him testified the same Esteem, that she had honoured him with at the first Visit. The Prince whilst his Discourse was directed to the Queen, sought for the Marchioness of Manzera whom he easily distinguished in the crowd, which was the only Advantage he could that Day gain, a Conference with her being yet impracticable. On the Prince's departure from the Queen he went to the Palace of the Queen Mother, Mary Ann of Austria, Widow of King Philip IV. That Princess demonstrated an uncommon esteem for him. She remember'd an acquaintance with the Elector John-George III at Vienna, and was pleased to see his Son at Madrid.

The Day after the Prince had been at Court, the Queen Regent, young, beautiful and loving diversions, persuaded the King to give a Ball; to which the Prince of Saxony was invited. He appeared there in a Dress that set off the charms of his Aspect. The Queen and he opened the Ball, his Majesty being unwilling to Dance; and leading the Queen back to her place, he asked her, which Lady she was pleased to Chuse for his next partner; She replyed, that she was unwilling to constrain him, and desir'd he would make choice of her that seem'd to him most Beautiful. Upon this answer he bowed very gracefully, and without hesitation applied to the Marchioness of Manzera; addressing himself respectfully to her. 'Madam, (said he) the Queen has enjoined me to Dance 'with the most Beautiful Lady in this Assembly, I doubt 'not of her Majesty's Intentions to recommend me to the 'Marchioness of Manzera.' 'I believe Sir, (replied the 'Marchioness) the Queen will not approve of your 'Choice, and I fear her Majesty will be displeas'd to see 'you have so little regard to her Orders.' 'Madam, (replied 'the Prince) her Majesty has too much Discretion not to 'allow you to be the most perfect Lady in these King-'doms, and was she not to do you that Justice, it would 'not obstruct my Opinion of your being the most 'accomplish'd Lady in the World, and the most deserving 'of a respect equal to that which is paid the Gods.' The Marchioness understood the Prince's words very well, tho' she pretended to be ignorant of what he said. She continued to Dance towards the End of the Room with a Grace that transported the Prince with amasement,

and forgetting the place where he was; 'Good God!
'(cried he) couldst thou possibly joyn such Graces to
'such Beauty.' This Transport changed the Marchioness's
Colour, and was observed by the Dutchess of Fernandine
her Mother. The old Lady was solicitous about the
matter, for she foresaw, that, if the Prince made any stay
at the Spanish Court, her Daughter would be exposed
to his pursuits. But the Prince's Expressions rendered
the Marchioness's condition more deplorable. Her
Husband was from that time extreamly jealous of her,
and accosting her, desired plainly that she would desist
dancing with the Prince. The young Marchioness
knowing his perverse humour, was not at all surprised
at this Order; she obeyed it, and placed herself behind
the Chair of State all the Evening; but could not deny
herself the pleasure of beholding the Prince in a manner
that assured him, that his Expressions were not at all
disagreeable to her. He was desirous of speaking to her,
but she so carefully avoided his Addresses, that he could
not approach her.

In the mean time his above-mentioned Words produc'd
all the desir'd Effect, and entirely convinced her of his
Passion; for the Prince's Actions were so agreeable to
his words, that she had no reason to doubt of his Sincerity,
she did not endeavour to love him, but to keep him
ignorant of her tender Affection for him, which was
no very easy Undertaking, but she not being acquainted

The Nymphs' Bathing Pool in the Zwinger

Engraving by Poeppelmann

with the difficulty of it, thought the only means of succeeding therein would be to avoid his Company. A slight Indisposition served for some time as a pretence to remain at home, and shun all those places, where she was in fear of meeting her Persecutor. Moreover, she ordered Donna Lora to make no farther mention of the Prince. 'It is an Idea which my Heart (said she) is unwill-'ing to retain.' But Donna Lora being by several presents already engaged in his Service, thought it improper to obey her Mistress. She spoke of him incessantly, and the Marchioness was incapable of silencing her Servant. The Prince, informed of what passed at his Mistress's, undertook to write to her, and charged the Brother-Recollect to deliver his Letter to Donna Lora. This Woman directly made great Difficulties of the matter, she said her Mistress had given her strict Orders not so much as to mention the Prince to her; and that she dared not, without venturing her Fortune, give her a Letter. The Monk perceived the Deficiency; he offered her a fine Diamond with which she was so dazzled, that she determined to deliver the Billet.

The same Evening she told the Lady Manzera that her retired Life and long Silence could not discourage the Prince from Adoring her, and that he had got a Monk to give her a Letter, which she was charged with. At these Words the Marchioness's Colour changed. 'Will you ruin me, Lora, (said she) and will you be the

C   33

THE MARCHIONESS'S RESOLUTION

'Cause of my forgetting the Obligations I am under to
'Lord Manzera? Can you not foresee what perplexities
'and miseries I shall be expos'd to, if I engage in the
'Correspondence you endeavour to persuade me to?
'No, I am resolved to have no reason to blame myself,
'speak no more (continued she shedding some Tears) of
'the Prince of Saxony, my Heart is too full of him.' 'Thus
'Madam, (said Donna Lora) do you refuse his Letter?'
'Yes (replied she) I refuse it, return it to him that has
'undertaken the Care of it, and enjoin him from me, to
'depart from my House and never to return hither again.'
Donna Lora was not a little surprised at this Resolution.
'You will cause the Prince's Death (said she) or else he
'will take to some Extream of which you will ever repent.'
'Let me alone, Lora, (replied the Marchioness) the
'Refusal is almost intolerable to me; but I do my Duty,
'which must not be postponed to any private Satisfac-
'tion.' At these Words her Eyes were covered with
Tears. Donna Lora thought that a lucky minute to open
the Prince's Letter. 'Madam (said she prostrate at her
'Feet) do not, I beg of you, refuse me to read this Billet.
'The Prince will be persuaded that you slight him; and
'how can a Gentleman of his Rank put up with such
'usage?' 'What is it to me? (cried she) let him suffer me to
'enjoy my desired Tranquillity, that is all I demand of
'him.' Her Heart was so burdened with Grief, that she
could no longer contain her Sighs. Lora studied all her

A SUCCESSFUL STRATAGEM

Mistress's motions, and continued to press and propose to her numberless motives to open the Letter. The Marchioness seeing that she did not cease perplexing her, arose precipitately and retired to her Closet. Donna Lora, having promised to see the Letter accepted, was desirous of keeping her Promise, and not being able to prevail upon the Marchioness to receive it, opened it herself, took off the Cover, and put the Letter between some Embroidery, at which the Marchioness used to employ some time after Dinner. This Stratagem succeeded. Some hours afterwards the Marchioness being come to finish a Nosegay, which she had begun, found this Letter. She could not help reading it, when Donna Lora surprised her at this Employment; she continued to intreat her to answer it, but the Marchioness constantly refused.

Donna Lora related to Brother Stephano what had happened. He found Virtue and Tenderness in Lady Manzera's Proceedings; could not help lamenting her, and would feign have persuaded the Prince to disengage himself from her Mistress, or else to look for another Commissioner. At present he desisted not intreating Donna Lora to make some fresh Attempts to obtain a Line or two of her Hand. She renewed her Reasons and Intreaties; but the Marchioness displeased with her Importunities, threatened to acquaint her Husband with these Persecutions. And consequently the Friar could be of no further service there, but returned to his Patron.

A SECOND LETTER

The Prince was at the Window, when his Confident was coming, knew him at a distance and could not patiently stay, but ran to meet him, and desired to know what Answer Lady Manzera had made? But the Friar, having brought none, begg'd he would hear him patiently. The Narrative he heard threw him into a deep Melancholy. He fancied himself more unhappy than he really was, and imagined that Donna Lora, induced by Interest, had composed all those flattering Conferences, which she insinuated to have had with her Mistress; but that she however was but indifferently inclined to him, because he had not a line from her. This Opinion he retained so deeply in his Heart, that his Pain began to grow extream.

Thus he passed three Days, desiring sometimes one, sometimes another thing, and at last determined to send Stephano again to the Marchioness, and to write a respectful and lamentable Letter that might affect her. The Friar told him, that he should succeed no better in the second, than he did in the first Negotiation. The Prince reproached him for the little Regard he seemed to have for his Orders, and for his Ingratitude, and obliged him to perform his Commands. Donna Lora's Alacrity was soon renewed by a Present of an hundred Pistoles from the Prince. She gave the second Letter to the Marchioness, who was then so weak, as to peruse it. This revived Donna Lora's Eloquence, and occasioned her to endeavour to persuade her Mistress, that Justice

THE MARCHIONESS REPLIES

would not permit her to refuse her Compassion to a Person, that adored her. She praised the Prince's Merits to the Skies. 'I am positively assured, (said she) that 'any Woman in the World besides Yourself, Madam, 'would think herself happy in such a Man's Affection.' In fine, this dangerous Confident vexed, and troubled the Marchioness so much, that, notwithstanding the Resolution she had taken not to write to him, she could not prevail upon herself to be Silent. The Prince having always kept the Letter, and not communicated the Contents of that, which he writ to the Marchioness, to anybody, the Reader will find himself disappointed, if he expected to read them here. All the Intelligence that could be had from one of the Prince's Confidents, is, that the Marchioness answer'd him to this purpose. 'That 'she was sensible of his Love; that she would feign 'acknowledge her present and promise a future and lasting 'Affection for him, but that was all she was capable of 'assisting him in: that she begg'd he would be contented 'therewith; hoped he did not expect to speak to her, 'because it could not be done except either one or the 'other of them was exposed to the greatest Dangers'. This Letter fed the Prince with so many Hopes, that he would proceed further. The Danger did not dishearten him; nor was it a motive to induce him to desist. He pleased himself with the Thoughts of escaping them by the means he was going to make use of, and had a

THE PRINCE MEETS DONNA LORA

Conference upon this Subject with Donna Lora, who met him for that purpose, under pretence of taking the Air, at the Casa del Campo, a Royal Palace, the Gardens of which look out upon the River Mancanares. The Prince was accompanied by Stephano, and passed for the Friar's Italian Friend. He had covered his brown Chestnut-colour'd Hair, with a Light Wig, which perfectly disguised him. Donna Lora had one of her Nieces with her, whom she without any Difficulty left with Stephano, whilst she turned into a Walk with the Prince alone. When they were together he emptied his Pockets filled with Pieces of Gold, and gallantly begg'd her to accept of them, as Witnesses of his Acknowledgment, assuring her that that should not be all, and that, if she continued to be favourable to him, he would promote her Fortune and that of her Nieces. He conjured her finally to procure him an Opportunity of conversing with the Marchioness. Though he said all these Things in scarce intelligible Spanish, yet Donna Lora understood him very well: but an Offer of Gold for her Niece rendered her more tractable. 'I wish to God (said she) I was the 'Marchioness! You should see me, if I was to die the 'moment afterwards.' The Prince thanked her for the Good-will she testified for him, and continued to entreat her, to invent some method of conferring with the Marchioness. After several Projects, they agreed, that, if her Mistress still refused to receive him, Donna Lora should

introduce him into her Chamber. 'You are to fall down
'at her Feet (said Lora) ask her Pardon, and I am almost
'assured she will grant it. But you are not to leave her
'(added she) till she promises to pardon me for the Fraud
'I shall have put upon her.' These Matters being thus
concluded upon, both Parties were sworn, and the
Prince on Departure conjured his Confident to hasten the
Execution of it. Donna Lora being returned to her Mistress, told her, 'That she had been at the Casa del Campo;
'that she had there seen the Prince, who had directly
'moved her Pity, he was so changed. But (added she) I
'could not contain myself from crying, when he told me,
'that his Love for you had almost killed him. He threw
'himself at my Feet, and conjured me to procure him a
'Moment's Conversation with you. I found myself
'compelled to promise him to propose the matter to
'you; and really, Madam, your Conscience must oblige
'you to speak to him, since you know it will save his
'Life. See him, and tell him, that his Hopes are ill-founded.'
'What do you persuade me to, Lora, (answered she) you,
'that know the deplorable Condition of my Heart? and
'how can I alter it!' 'But Madam, (replied the dangerous
'Woman) can you prevail upon yourself to see him die?
'for, if you persist in refusing him Admittance, I cannot
'insure for his Life. By the manner in which he spoke to
'me I have Reason to fear his Despair. What Harm will
'there be in suffering him to come and telling him that

'his Hopes are unnecessary, and that he cannot too soon
'endeavour to recover? When you have escaped his
'memory, I doubt whether you will retain him in yours.'
'God send I may not! (cried the Marchioness shedding
'Tears) but I fear the Reverse. However, that you may
'have no Reason to blame me, I consent to it: Contrive
'some quarter of an Hour for me to see him.' Pleased
with the Permission, Donna Lora informed the Prince
that he might come instantly.

He extreamly satisfied with this News, dressed himself
neatly, and at the Hour appointed, being covered with a
Cloak, he took Mr. Fitztuhm Gentleman of his Bed-
Chamber, who had long since been accustomed to his
nocturnal Gallantries; and was at the Garden-Door of
Lord Manzera's House, as he had agreed with Donna
Lora.

His Undertaking was so rash that he dared not to
consider of it. He was subject to the Discovery of a
Jealous Husband and a Watchful Mother. The dire
Effects of their Resentment, if he had been discovered
would have been intolerable, and nothing was more
probable: The Marquis of Manzera and the Dutchess of
Fernandine lodged in the same House, and the Windows
of their Apartments were towards the Gardens. Thousand
unforeseen and unfortunate Accidents might easily
happen. Nevertheless his natural Intrepidity and his Love
permitted him not to look upon these Dangers in any

other than a bold manner; he ran thither without Hesitation. Everything was so luckily prepared, that he found the Garden-Door open, and the officious Lora waiting for him. He ordered Mr. Fitztuhm to stay for him, and followed Donna Lora, who conducted him through a private Staircase to the Marchioness's Apartment. I do nor relate here the Satisfaction with which this enamoured Couple met, nor can I repeat their Words; for the one may be as easily imagined, as described; the other is a Mystery never revealed to any one. However they did not probably tire each other, for they remained together three Hours; and notwithstanding the Resolution the Marchioness had taken not to see the Prince, but to discharge him, she could not keep it.

A Sickness that perplexed Lord Manzera favoured our Lovers for some time. He kept his Chamber and Suffered not his Lady to lye there. But this very Circumstance, that seemed so favourable to their Designs was also the Cause of their Misery. Lord Manzera's Distemper deprived him of Rest; he got up almost every Night and took a Walk in a Balcony that had the prospect of the Garden. One Night an excessive Heat obliged him to open a Window that was cool, when by Moon-light he perceived a Man led by a Woman, coming from the Lady Manzera's Apartments, and having crossed the Garden going out at a Door that led him to the little Street. He saw the Woman return, and knew her to be Donna Lora.

THE MARQUIS'S DESPAIR

As her Age clear'd her of the Suspicion of having
Followers, he doubted not, but the Person that he had
seen was his Wife's Lover; and recollecting at the same
Time the Prince's Transport at the Ball, became the more
suspicious. No Man could ever be in greater Despair
than was at that time the Marquis. The Treachery of a
person whom he loved as a Mistress, and the Shame of
being thus deceived by a Woman gave him so great an
Uneasiness, that it almost deprived him of the Use of
his Reason. He was a long while determining what to
do in this Affair. His first Emotion had almost caused
his going to stab his Wife and Donna Lora. Afterwards
reflecting, that by such an Action his Shame would be
publish'd, and the Author of it remain unpunished, he
proposed first to sacrifice him to his Fury, and afterwards
to demand Reparation for the Treachery of his Spouse,
for whom he thought no Torment great enough. Day-
light surprised him in his Despair, with which he would
not acquaint his Domesticks; but laid down and feigning
to be more indispos'd than he was before, he refus'd to
see anybody, not even the Marchioness herself, who had
since his Indisposition passed the Afternoon with the
Dutchess of Fernandine. One of his Domesticks remained
with him who was a Servant in whom he could confide.
The Marquis discovered the Sentiments of his Heart to
him, and consulted with him upon the manner of reven-
ging himself. The Death of the Prince of Saxony, or of the

ASSASSINATION RESOLVED UPON

Marchioness's Lover, whoever he might be, was in this wicked Conference resolved upon. The Valet de Chambre undertook the Execution of it, and promised to procure three Men, who, without knowing upon whose Destruction his Design was formed, were to kill every Man, that dared to present himself at Night at the little Garden-Door.

Whilst the Marquis entered into this Combination, the two Lovers being entirely occupied in their Amours, were far from thinking of the Evil that was preparing for them. The Marchioness went to her Husband's Chamber-Door, and Refusal of Admittance did not at all surprise her, because she was accustomed to it: The Marquis was subject to violent Head-Aches, and when they tormented him he commonly shut himself up, and none, but one Valet de Chambre, dared to approach him. She supposed that the same pain perplexed him still, and that he was only on that Account desirous of Solitude. The Valet de Chambre not being able in less than two Days to compleat the proposed number of Assassins, acquainted his Master that all Things were ready and that only the Victim was wanting to be sacrificed. The Marquis not doubting, but that the Object of his Hatred would be present there that same Evening would not delay his Revenge. He gave the Assassins Orders to present themselves in the Dusk of the Evening in the small Street, where the little Garden-Door was, and there to assault every Man that dared to walk there. The Execution of the project answered the Design of it. The four Assassins (at the Head of which was the Valet de Chambre) did not wait a long while in the little Street, before they saw a Man advance towards Manzera's Garden-Door, covered with a Cloak, and who was going with a Key to open the Door. They assaulted and gave him several Blows, before the Prince (for he was the Person) could put himself in a posture of Defence. But having pulled out the Pocket-pistols, with which he was provided, he broke that person's Head, that seemed most forward to kill him. The Shot came to Fitztuhm's Ears, who had waited at the Bottom of the Street, and hastened up. He found the Prince with Sword in Hand in Opposition to three Men, and joined to his Assistance, whereupon the Fight became obstinate: Another Assassin lost his Life, and a third was mortally wounded. The fourth took to his flight, that neither the Prince nor Fitztuhm could overtake him. The Prince, well satisfied with having escaped the Danger, notwithstanding the pain the Wounds gave him made all possible Haste to get to his Lodging. This Care preserved him from the Affront of being seized by the Watch-men, who at the Sound of the Shot ran to the place from whence it proceeded. These Officers of Justice lifted up the dead and wounded Bodies. The Latter of which desired the Benefit of having a Confessor, to declare in the presence of the Constable and other Witnesses, that the Marquis of Manzera's persuasion first engaged him in the Assault, a little while after which Confession he expired. In the mean Time the Prince having reached his Lodgings, sent for a Surgeon to visit his Sores, which seemed not to be mortal, by the Assurance the first Surgeon gave him, that if he would keep his Bed three or four Days, he needed no longer keep his Room, but would be able to go out. The Prince enjoined him Secrecy in this Affair, as he did Mr. Fitztuhm, whom he begg'd not to mention the Adventure; seeming careful to preserve the Marchioness's Reputation, whose Fate gave him more Uneasiness than his own Wounds, for he doubted not, but that the Condition he was then in was only to be imputed to the Marquis of Manzera. He supposed her subject to the Effects of her jealous Husband's Rage, and foresaw the sad Event of this Amour. He told Fitztuhm, that he pardon'd the Marquis for having designed Ill upon his Life, but, if he attempted to take away that of his Spouse, he should never be forgiven; and, was he to be so unfortunate as to commit an Action of that Kind, it should be resented in a manner, that might be reported throughout Spain. Whilst he was thus disquieting himself, Confusion, Grief, and Horror had taken possession of Manzera's House. The Marquis being informed that his Antagonist the Prince of Saxony had escaped his Vengeance, and that the Assault had reached the Magistrate's Ears by the Declaration the wounded person made, thought himself utterly ruined; but was resolved that a Satisfaction from his Spouse, should precede his perdition; pursuant to which Resolve he took a Dagger in one Hand, and a fine Cup full of Poison in the other; with these dismal Arms he hasten'd to his Wife's Apartment, whom he found with Donna Lora struck with Fear and Trembling. They had heard the Pistol-shot, and not seeing the Prince dreaded what had happened, and at the same time thought their Death inevitable. The Idea of which had possessed their minds and so terrify'd them, that they forgot to shut their Chamber-Door. The Air with which the Marquis made his Entry, and the Dagger and Cup he had in his Hands soon signified to them the imminent Danger, it so startled Donna Lora, that she swooned away. 'Oh! thou Monster of Iniquity (cried he) thy 'Death is most certain, but it shall be hasten'd by my 'Hand.' At the same Time he stabb'd her, and turned about to the Marchioness, casting an incensed Eye upon her, desired she would chuse either Fire or Poison. 'Dear 'Sir, (cried she lifting up her Hands) have Compassion 'upon an unfortunate Woman, whose Actions have not 'been so criminal, as you imagine. Allow me at least a 'small space of Time to recommend my Soul to God.' The unmerciful Husband was not at all moved. 'Your 'Sentence is pronounced, (answered he in a terrible 'Tone) you must die. I give you your Choice of Fire, or

46

'I AM POISONED!'

'Poison, which is more than you deserve.' The Marchioness not being able to prevail upon her Husband to wait, determined to take the Poison, he remained there to see her take it, without looking any other Way, reproaching her severely till he thought the Poison had sufficient Effect to render all further Assistance ineffectual; then he left her alone, with Donna Lora lying at her Feet. As soon as he was gone the Marchioness would have called her Servants, but could not. She fell into a great Chair and would have died there unknown to any one but her barbarous Husband, had not a little Dog, that was her Favourite, scratched at the Door of the Ward-robe, when a Chambermaid, opening it, saw her Mistress sitting and Donna Lora lying on the Ground. She called her Companions, and instantly acquainted the Dutchess of Fernandine with the miserable Condition of her Daughter. The distressed Mother ran to her Daughter's Assistance, and found her sitting in a Chair. Her fine eyes, formerly full of Fire, sparkled no longer, she was extreamly pale, spoke nothing, and sighed constantly. Sometimes she cried, *I am poison'd!* all her Servants wept, The Dutchess was in Despair; she conjured her Daughter to let her know what had happen'd to her, though she was too sure of it. Donna Lora breathless, her Daughter dying, and Lord Manzera not appearing, when they call'd him, assured her sufficiently of his being the Author of this misery. She sent for the Physicians, who told her, that the Marchioness had but few Hours to live. Her Death could not be prevented, because she would not take any Remedy; and a little while afterwards she died in her Mother's Arms. Whilst this deplorable Scene was acted in the unfortunate Marchioness's Chamber, the Marquis suffered the most dreadful Torments in his. No Despair was perhaps ever so violent; he was struck with Horror and called Death to his Assistance, and in fine not being able to resist the Aggravation of his misery, he was taken with the Fever, that same Day, and other Circumstances instantly shewed his Disease to be incurable. And seeing that his Life was almost ended, he sent to the Dutchess of Fernandine and begg'd of her not to refuse him the Comfort of seeing him; she went directly to his Apartment and the Marquis desired her by Signs to sit down at his Bed-side; when in a sad and mournful Tone, he related to her all that a furious Jealousy had induced him to commit, testifying an inexpressible Sorrow, intolerable Checks of Conscience, a sincere Repentance for what he had done, and an earnest desire of pardon, by which he so moved the Dutchess that she could not help deploring his Condition. The Dutchess's presence had caused such an Emotion in Lord Manzera, having strove with might and main to speak to her, and the Remembrance of all that he had done shocked him so, that when he had done speaking he swooned away, lost the Use of his Senses; and his last moment seemed

Augustus of Saxony

Engraving by Bernigeroth

to approach. The Dutchess unwilling to be a Spectator of such a horrid Sight, left him among his Domesticks, in whose Arms he expired soon afterwards. The Quality of the Marquis and the Share he had in the King's Friendship, occasioned the Magistrates not to proceed against him, whilst he lived; and the King, hearing of his Death, forbid any one to stain his memory; so that perhaps we should have been ignorant of all these Circumstances, had not the Dutchess of Fernandine related them to one of Donna Lora's Nieces, who informed the Prince of them by his Confident Stephano. The Prince hearing of these unfortunate Catastrophes, was sensibly touch'd with them. He has been heard to say, even upon his Death-bed, that he had never loved any Woman more tenderly than he did Lady Manzera, and had never been afflicted so, as he was for her Loss.

In the mean while, being perfectly cured of his Wounds, he looked upon Madrid as a place too mournful for him to make any longer Stay in, since the Death of the Marchioness of Manzera. Wherefore he gave Orders for his Departure, and went to Court to have an Audience of Leave of their Majesties, where he was received with all the Tokens of Esteem and Benevolence, he could desire. They begg'd, he would reside some time longer there, but he excused himself, saying, matters of great Importance occasioned his Return into Saxony. The King gave him four saddled Horses, eight Mules, and a

Sword enriched with Diamonds. The Queen gave him two Suits of Hangings of an admirable Taste and uncommon Sort, a large Quantity of Indian Rarities, and besides all this her Picture set in Diamonds. And in short, had he not been still afflicted with the Death of his dear Marchioness, he would have left Spain with great Satisfaction on Account of the Honours he had there received, and of the obliging Behaviour of the Spaniards. He directed his Course through the Kingdoms of Valencia and Catalonia to Barcellona, where he stay'd some Days; the Count of Corzano, Governor of the place, honoured him in an extraordinary manner. This was the same Nobleman, that some Years afterwards held out a Siege of two months against the Duke of Vendosme, to whom he was at last obliged to surrender the place, seeing himself forsaken by M. de Velasco, Governor of the Principality. From Barcellona the Prince went to Perpignan, the Capital of Rousillon. He there observed with Amazement the great Fortifications Lewis XIV had raised about that town. At length passing through Provence and Languedoc he arrived in Italy.

CHAPTER III

Of the Prince of Saxony's *Voyage to* Venice, *the Honours shewn him there, his Love of* Lady Mocenigo, *her Refusal, his amorous Adventure with a Widow, her Infidelity.*

As time lessen'd the Prince's Grief, and all imaginable dispositions to Gallantry, and the Qualities requisite to gain good Success therein, were innate to him, he had several new Amours there, which at last made him forget the unfortunate Marchioness of Manzera. Venice and Rome having always been the most noted Cities in Italy both for Politicks and Gallantry, they were the places at which the Prince made the longest Stay. The Senate of Venice to do him Honour, mitigating of that severe Statute which forbids Noblemen to converse with Strangers, permitted them to see him, and chose three Noblemen to attend him, and to shew him the Curiosities of the Town. They permitted the Ladies to make use of their Diamonds and to wear colour'd Habits during the Prince's Stay at Venice. Since Henry III King of France and Poland no Prince received greater Honours of the Republick. Every particular Nobleman was eager to entertain the Prince of Saxony. There was nothing to be seen every Day, but Balls, Treats, Concerts, and several other Diversions; which together with the Ceremony of the Sea-Nuptials, the Celebration of which was soon after

the Prince's Arrival there, drew together a large number
of Strangers. Never was Venice so magnificent. The
Doge performed the Ceremony of espousing the Sea on
one of those fine days, on which the Sun is so hid, that
neither Wind nor Heat are inconvenient. The Number of
Boats was infinite, and they were filled with numberless
masqued People of both Sexes. The Prince was in one
of the Pleasure-Boats with his Attendants and several
young German Noblemen, all dressed after the Spanish
manner. As he was extreamly well-shaped, this Dress set
him off more advantageously; and drew on him a shower
of Sugar-plumbs, which the Ladies threw at him, as a
sign of Applause. He observed, that among all the
masques only two neglected to do him that Honour.
These were two Women dressed in Spanish Cloaths, and
who, by the quiet posture in which they sate in their
Boat, seemed rather to have come thither for the Benefit
of the Air, than to partake of the pleasure of the Entertainment. One of them seemed to be very well shaped,
her Neck was of a dazzling white Colour, and gave
reason to think that that which was covered with the
Masque was not less admirable. Her Dress was plain,
but perfectly neat, and an exquisite Taste appeared all
over her person. The Prince, to whom she appeared
charming, not being able to know of the Water-men,
who she was, ordered them to pursue the Boat in which
were the two Spanish Ladies. They landed at the place

of St. Mark, where all the Masques meet on the day of
that Solemnity. The Prince stepp'd out of his Boat about
the same Time, that they did out of theirs. Whilst he
endeavoured to address them, though he knew them not,
he was himself accosted by Lord Mocenigo; 'I beg your
'Highness's permission (said he) to present you my
'Spouse. She is yesterday returned from a journey to
'Loretto, and has consequently not yet been able to pay
'you her Compliments.' The Prince, who at any other
Time would have been glad of an acquaintance with a
person of so great Quality as Lady Mocenigo, was then
thinking of an Excuse to dispense with it; but Lord
Mocenigo giving him no Time to answer, cried 'Madam,
'Madam!' The Prince, who had all the while eyed the two
Spanish Ladies saw them turn at Lord Mocenigo's Cry,
and come back instantly. When they came to the place
where he was; 'Come, Madam, (said the Nobleman to
'her, whom he had chiefly observed) pay your Respects
'to the Prince of Saxony, and assist me in acquitting
'myself, if possible, with him, for the Honours I was
'heaped with at Dresden by his Father the Elector.' The
Lady quitted the Arms of Lady Cornaro who accompanied
her, and having taken off her Masque, advanced towards
the Prince, who being likewise unmasqued prevented
and addressed her with that polite Air and noble Loftiness, which signalizes persons of his Rank. Lady
Mocenigo addressed him in her Turn with a pleasant and

53

modest Air, no less agreeable to the Prince, than the
Beauty he observed in her person. She entertained him
in a very obliging manner, with an Account of the
Satisfaction Venice was sensible of in seeing him within
its Walls, and of what she had heard of his extraordinary
Qualifications. The Prince answered her so politely and
with so much sense, that Lady Mocenigo was soon convinced, that his Merit exceeded all the Reports that had
been spread of him. After the first Compliments she
presented to him Lady Cornaro, one of the most beautiful
Ladies of Venice. The Prince addressed her with all the
Respect due to her eminent Birth. The two Ladies, the
Prince and Lord Mocenigo having put on their Masques
again, they walked together. The Prince entertained them
with numberless pleasant Discourses and their Conversation was the most agreeable and better supported, than
any other in the place. They were so much delighted
with it, that they had almost been the last Masques
remaining in the place. Lady Cornaro was the first that
took Notice of it, and said it was Time to retire. Whereupon Lord Mocenigo, addressing himself to the Prince,
told him that his Lady and he had invited some Friends
to dine with them; that he dared not take the Liberty to
beg of him to honour the Company with his presence:
But if they might be bless'd with that Favour, he should
be received at their House with a Respect due to him.
Lady Mocenigo here interrupted her Husband to tell

him: that he was mistaken, in inviting the Prince to so slight a Dinner as theirs; but he replied, 'That he took 'the Liberty at all Hazards to offer his Dinner to the 'Prince: that he relied upon his Kindness in excusing 'him if he was not served as he ought to be; and that he 'would endeavour to supply the deficiency of his Dinner, 'by a Repast, which he would presume to beg his High- 'ness to accept of at his House; that then he would use 'him as Count of Misnia, but at another Time he should 'shew the Esteem he had for the Prince of Saxony.' The Prince thanked him, and offering his Service said, 'That 'he desired his Friendship both as Count of Misnia, and 'as Prince of Saxony, and assured him of his Esteem; 'that he took the obliging manner with which he enter- 'tained him, as a great Favour; and that if he knew that 'his presence would not be disagreeable to Lady Moce- 'nigo, he would gratefully accept of the Offer he made 'him.' Lady Mocenigo replied, 'That his presence at their 'House could not but please her, and when therein she 'so directly opposed her Spouse, it was out of Fear that 'her Dinner would not be agreeable to him.' The Prince in a gallant manner answered, 'That he preferred the 'Honour of being near her to any other Satisfaction,' and then he handed her into her Boat, into which Lady Cornaro went after her; and he followed with Lord Mocenigo in another Boat. At the Palace of Mocenigo he met with the Ladies Foscarini, Pesero and Nani, together with the Lords Justliniani and Grimani—All these Persons were related, and had erected among themselves a Society, at which few others were admitted. They were all amazed to see the Prince of Saxony come; that free manner of inviting another Person to Dinner, which Lord Mocenigo had made Use of not being customary in Italy; and though they did not remain under the Constraint of their Society, yet had they not sufficiently laid aside that prejudice of their Education, to be persuaded that Strangers ought to be used with Familiarity. The Prince excused himself so politely for having entered into their Company, and begg'd with so much Grace and Condescension, that they would put him upon a Level with them, that they at last thought themselves obliged to Lord Mocenigo for having brought him to his House. They laid aside the troublesome Constraint they should have been under, and perhaps no Repast at Venice could ever boast of having seen an equal Satisfaction more generally diffused. After Dinner the whole Company agreed upon diverting themselves in a Pleasure-Boat in the great Channel Murena, after that they went to the Place of St. Mark, and from thence to the Opera. They returned to Supper to Lord Mocenigo's and did not depart from thence till the next Morning, when Day-light begun to appear.

Lord Mocenigo's Presence was the only Obstacle that hindered the Prince from declaring openly to that

A GALLANT DECLARATION

Gentleman's Spouse the Impression she had made upon his Heart. But he had made her Signs enough to be understood, and she had comprehended them very well. Lady Mocenigo was in Respect of her Character the finest Woman in the World. She easily perceived the Prince's Sentiments, and they occasioned no little Uneasiness in her. She loved and esteemed her Husband, and since the Beginning of the six Years after their Marriage she had not in the least disagreed with him, but now feared that the Prince designed to set them at Variance; she resolved however to behave herself in a manner that might deprive him of all Hope, and preserve her future Quiet. In pursuance of this Resolution she would not shun his Presence; for her Opinion was, that the Difficulties a newly enamoured Lover at first meets with, serve only to inflame his Passion the more. Thus did she, without flying or searching for him, propose to live in her usual manner. The Prince utterly impatient to acquaint her with the Condition of his Heart, was at her Door when he expected to see her. Though the Lady Mocenigo was by herself, when he desired to speak to her, yet was he not refused. Their Conversation was directly very indifferent; she spoke of what had been done and discoursed upon the Night before; but the Prince made her at last attentive to what concerned him. He made so gallant and so polite a Declaration of Love, that any one besides Lady Mocenigo would have been taken with it. She quietly heard him, and suffering him to express at his Ease whatever his native passion inspired him with, did not answer till he had quite done speaking: 'I have with 'Attention heard all the fine Things you have been 'pleased to divert me with (said she with a gay and 'charming Air) and do not conceal from you that the 'excellent Turn you have given it, and easy Manner in 'which you expressed yourself in our Language, have 'extreamly pleased me. I am besides all this very much 'obliged to you for the Expression you have made of the 'Sentiments of your Heart concerning me. But as I 'neither can nor will answer them, I beg you would 'change your Love into Esteem; and then you may be 'assured of my Gratitude.' 'Dear Madam! (cried the 'Prince) you deserve quite different Sentiments and——' 'I beg, Sir (replied she) you would not interrupt me; I 'have permitted you to speak whatever you pleased, 'suffer me to speak in my Turn. Hitherto God be thanked 'my Virtue has not been stained. Several Men have 'declared a passion for me, but their Discourses have 'neither affected, nor troubled my Mind; being per-'suaded that Virtue is not solely consistent with Austerity, 'I have not answered their Sentiments, and then they 'ceased to be Lovers. As I am resolved to act in the same 'manner with you, I hope you will follow the Example 'of others; and that will be the most acceptable mark of 'your Esteem you can shew me. I dare even say, that is

'the only Thing you can do; for what can you after all
'pretend to? I am not free; and if I was I know too well,
'that Fortune would not be sufficient to procure me a
'Sovereignty; and I am more sensible that it would be
'inconsistent with my Virtue to be your Mistress. Judge
'then, Sir, since I am married to the most worthy Gentle-
'man of the present Age, whom I love, whom I esteem,
'and who has for me a very tender Affection, whether I
'can, without running precipitately into Ruin, be sensible
'of any other Flame—No, Sir, nothing shall induce me
'to neglect my Duty to my Spouse and myself. If I can, I
'will deserve your Esteem, which I cannot do without
'preserving my Virtue. I believe you are too subtil a
'Lover, to be capable of loving a person, whom you
'cannot esteem. What Advantage shall I reap then by
'answering your Sentiments? I shall be guilty of a great
'Crime to the best of Husbands, forfeit your Esteem, and
'that of Consequence a little while after your Love; and
'then I shall pass the remaining part of Life covered with
'Shame, for having been so weak as to comply with your
'Desires. I tell Your Highness (continued she) what
'another person would have perhaps concealed from you
'for some Years; but I shall at least enjoy the Satisfaction
'of not having perplexed you with deceitful Hopes.
'Believe me, (added she laughing) lose not your Time;
'there are numberless Ladies here that far exceed me in
'Beauty, and will perhaps not be displeased to see you

'attach'd to them. You may find there a more lucky
'Destiny.' The Prince had given Lady Mocenigo an
extreamly impatient Audience, and the respect he had
for her silenced him. When she had done speaking he
endeavoured to confute her Reasons. He told her all, that
he thought would affect her; and at last threw himself at
her Feet. 'You give yourself too much Trouble, Sir (said
'she lifting him up again) hitherto I have taken all your
'Words for meer Gallantries, but I see that the matter
'begins to be serious, and that I must speak seriously to
'you. I beg of you (continued she) if you are unwilling
'to oblige me to leave you, to cease mentioning Love to
'me. Let me tell you once more, that you must address
'yourself somewhere else; for I neither will nor can I
'hearken to your proposals; if you still continue these
'Discourses, you will give me the Trouble of retiring to
'some remote Village during your Stay here. That will
'cause great Uneasiness in Lord Mocenigo; and I dare
'say that the Respect and Value he has for Your Highness
'deserve to have so great a Grief spared on your Hands.'
This Discourse supported by a noble Loftiness, had
almost deprived the Prince of all his Gallantry. He saw
that he had nothing left to hope for; but could not be
pleased to give up a Coquette, who he thought was his
own. He would feign continue his fine Expressions, but
Lady Mocenigo pretended not to hear him; she proposed two or three Questions to him, which utterly

frustrated his Measures. He had at the same Time the good Luck of seeing Company come in, which gave him Time to recover from his Disorder. They offered him a party at a Game, called Milchiade, which he accepted of, but play'd so distractedly, that he knew not what he did; whilst Lady Mocenigo was in the merriest Humour imaginable. That occasioned his Despair. When this Game was finished Lord Mocenigo, who was come in, when they play'd, would have kept the Prince to Supper, but he said he had some Letters to write, that required Expedition, and obliged him to return home. When he stepped out of his Boat his first Waterman gave him a Billet. The Prince could not think who it came from; he opened it and read it at the Bottom of his Stair-case, and found it to be an Appointment to meet him at Mid-night; he was invited to come singly, and told, that his Waterman would inform him of what he had previously to do to get into the Arms of a Person, who dared think of herself worthy of him. The Prince, delighted with Adventures of that kind, and desirous of driving away the Melan-cholly, his ill Success with Lady Mocenigo had caused, instantly resolved upon undertaking what had been pro-posed to him: he ventured the Honesty of his Waterman, of whose Fidelity he had Intelligence of one of the most eminent Bankers of Venice. Midnight was near, and seeing that he had no Time to lose, he wrapped himself up in a Cloak, furnished his Pocket with Pistols; and entered into his Boat, without knowing where he was row'd to. The Waterman, that had given him the Billet, left the management of the Boat to his Comrade, and placed himself at the side of the Prince. 'Your Highness '(said the Man) is a handsome Prince, and well deserving 'of a beautiful Mistress. I am going to procure you one, 'that is a Lady of eminent Birth, and cannot be equall'd 'in Beauty. She is but sixteen Years of Age, and never 'lov'd a Man besides you.' The Prince smiled at the Preamble; pressingly asked the Name of the Lady and how the Billet she sent, came to his Hands; in short, how he, as a Waterman, came to be acquainted with her, but his Curiosity was scarce at all satisfied. 'As for the Lady's 'Name, (answered the Waterman) I am forbid mentioning 'it, and nothing shall induce me to discover a Secret I 'have been entrusted with. The Billet was given me this 'Morning at the Church where I heard Mass; an old 'Woman, covered with a long Cloak, came near and 'beckon'd to me, whereupon I followed her; she led me 'into a Lane, and there, giving me the Billet I deliver'd to 'you, told me that her Mistress loved you and should be 'glad to see you. I agreed with her to conduct you at 'Mid-night to the Windows of the Lady's House; that 'she should be there to tye a Ladder of Rope, by which 'you should go up into the House; that she should lead 'you into her Mistress's Chamber; and that when you 'are got in, I should retire with my Boat; that at Three

A TRUSTY WATERMAN

'o'Clock in the Morning I should come to fetch you
'back; that you should again descend by this Ladder,
'and return into your Boat, and I see you home.' The
Prince found this Project very well managed without his
Knowledge; but the Execution of it seemed a little
dangerous to him. He recollected his Adventure of
Madrid which so intimidated him, that he considered
some moments whether it would be better to hazard the
Adventure, or to return home. The Waterman seeing
him thus dubious, persuaded him to fear nothing; that
he would insure for any Misfortune that should happen
to him; that he might confide in him, who was a Man of
Honour and incapable of deceiving any Person. The
Prince, ignorant of what Fear was, had almost been
enraged against his Waterman for suspecting him to be
subject to it. He told him that Fear did not hinder him
from engaging in the Adventure; but that he appre-
hended the Lady not deserving of his Pains. The Waterman solemnly protested that she was the most beautiful
Woman of Venice. In short, the Prince satisfied with
the Reasons he alledged and besides little accustomed
to long Invitations ordered him to row towards the
appointed place. After several turnings the Boat landed
in a narrow Channel. All necessary measures were taken
so carefully that the Ladder was found prepared. The
Prince stepp'd up and having entered the Window, he
felt himself taken by the Hand, and heard some-body say

to him, 'Fear nothing, Sir, you are here in Safety, follow
'me; who am going to make you happy.' Her Voice
signified her to be a Woman. She conducted him through
several dark Chambers, and at last he arrived at a Door,
by which he enter'd into a large, light and magnificently
adorn'd Apartment; they then crossed a Chamber richly
furnish'd, and at last arrived at a little Closet, which
equall'd the others in Splendor. His Guide begg'd he
would not be displeased at her leaving him for a small
space of Time to go and acquaint her Mistress with his
presence. She left him; and directly afterwards he saw a
Lady enter, whose Beauty, graceful Appearance, and
extraordinary fine Dress struck him with Amazement.
He thought he was in an inchanted place; 'It is impossible,
'(said he to himself) that this should not be a Woman of
'great Birth: her noble Air, and the Grandeur that sur-
'rounds her, are sufficient proofs of it.' He complimented
her respectfully. The Lady took him by the Hand and
led him to a Sopha desiring him to sit down. 'What I am
'now doing (said she, looking modestly on him) plainly
'convinces you of the present State of my Heart, pardon
'then the possession of a passion, whose Ardency I have
'for a whole Month in vain resisted; and pity an unfor-
'tunate Person, that is ready to die for Shame of what
'she is doing, but could not longer have supported her
'enamoured Soul, had she still denied herself the pleasure
'of your Conversation.' The Prince took her Hand and

kissed it in a Transport, and having thank'd her for the
Esteem she had testified for him, he told her he should
reckon that the most delightful Night of his Life-time,
and himself in her Embraces the happiest of mankind.
His Thoughts at that Time exactly corresponded with
his Words. The unknown Beauty, having already caused
the Oblivion of Lady Mocenigo, appeared incomparably
charming to him. He could not comprehend how she
could be hid from his Sight during the three months he
had been at Venice, and how he arrived at that pitch of
Happiness to be beloved by her. The Lady explained
those Mysteries to him in giving him an abridged
Account of her Life. She told him, 'That her Parents had
'given her away in Marriage very young, and against her
'Consent to Lord N—— who being a superannuated
'old Man had kept her under Constraint, and confined
'her for six Years together; that he at last died two
'Months ago, and had left her possessed of great Wealth;
'but what she esteemed far more excellent than the
'Possession of these Riches, was an unusual and inesti-
'mable Liberty, that the Custom, that confined Widows
'at home the three first Months of their Widowhood, was
'the occasion of her living then so retiredly; that conse-
'quently she could not yet frequent the Assemblies. I go
'no-where (said she) but to Church, where I at first saw
'you about a Month ago; since that my Mind has retained
'a painful Idea of you, and as I could not deny myself the

E   65

AN UNJUST REQUEST

'Pleasure of seeing you, determined to trouble you with
'a Billet, and therein humbly to desire that Satisfaction.
'Moreover (continued she) pardon the Precautions I
'took to introduce you. I pretended to conceal my Name
'from you, and even my Abode, till I knew how agree-
'able my Person would be to a Prince of so exquisite a
'Taste. My Happiness I find to be at present so great,
'that I presume I flatter myself, with having some Return
'from your Hands, and your Presence here will be very
'acceptable whenever you shall think proper to honour
'me with it.'

The Prince returned kind Thanks to the beautiful
Widow for all the endearing Expressions she had made
use of in her obliging Address; he assured her, that he
was very sensible of her Passion, and his Affection for
her should never cease. The Widow believed all his
tender Assurances and kind Promises, for Women are
naturally inclined to believe what they wish for; and her
Lover took no small Advantage of her Credulity; for he
refused to depart when the Widow's Confidant gave
him Notice that his Servants waited for him, and begged
the Lady's consent to supply the vacant Place of the
Deceased. She soon made some Objections to that Proposal, but afterwards postponing Virtue and Reason to
Love, did not refuse her Compliance with his unjust
Request. The old Woman sent the Servants away, and
desired they would not return again; this proved after-

wards no useless Precaution; for the enamoured Pair were so delighted with pleasing each other, that they remain'd together three Days. The old Woman supplied them with Diet, and the Prince wore the Deceased's Linnen. Whilst thus they gave themselves over to all kinds of amorous Pleasures, his Servants were highly surprised at his long Absence. Mr. Fitztuhm intended to imprison the Watermen to know which Way they carried him. The first of which, who had negotiated the whole Matter, begg'd he would not be in the least uneasy on the Prince's Account, who he protested was then in a very safe Place, and readily offer'd to remain imprison'd in the Palace, and to be that same Evening, if the Prince did not appear, deliver'd into the Magistrate's Hands. This was the Day after the Prince had disappear'd, whereupon Mr. Fitztuhm accepted of his Offer. The Waterman as willingly consented to execute his Proposal, as he had offer'd it, he laughed, sung, and drank merrily: but when he saw the last Hour of the Day approach and the Prince not yet returned he was so mortified that he had almost lost the Use of his Reason by it. He cried out incessantly, *Io sono ingannato, Io sono tradito,* I am deceiv'd, I am betray'd! At last he had the good Luck to see the Prince come in at the same Time that Mr. Fitztuhm resolved earnestly to seize him. The Waterman was so transported with Joy at this, that not being Master of his Passion, he embraced the Prince and almost tired him with Demonstrations of Joy. The Prince ordered him to be presented with six Zechins, which soon alleviated the Trouble his Master's Absence had caused. Since this Time the Prince paid frequent and publick Visits to his beloved Widow, whereby all the Inhabitants of Venice were informed of his tender Affection for her. Lady Mocenigo was heartily glad that he was otherwise engaged. She jested with him sometimes upon his inconsistency; but the Prince told her, that he was not of so fickle a Disposition, as she imagined him to be; that she should be always the Object of his Worship, and that he only look'd upon the Widow as a Confident, to whom he disclosed the Sentiments of his Heart concerning Lady Mocenigo. 'I am very willing, 'Sir, (replied the Lady Mocenigo) that you should all 'your Life-time love me in the manner you now do, 'provided that you be satisfied with only declaring your 'Passion to your Confident.' In the mean while the Prince continued to love the Widow, and thought her Love to be Equal to his. But how impenetrable is a woman's Heart! Whilst she testified the most lively and most tender Affection for the Prince, she deceiv'd him. He happened one Day to go to her at an unusual Hour, and the Servants who already esteemed him as Master of the House, giving no Notice to their Mistress of his coming, he directly went up towards the Widow's Apartment. He met upon the Stair-case the seemingly faithful old

THE WIDOW AND THE FRIAR

Chamber-maid, who being forbid to admit him, begg'd he would not go to her Mistress's Bed-Chamber, because finding herself slightly indisposed, she was gone to Bed to take a little Rest. The disordered Look of the old Woman caused the Prince justly to suspect the Widow's Fidelity, and therefore hastened to her Chamber, to Surprise her in an Action he feared her to be too guilty of. But his Surprise was greatly increased when he found her in the Enjoyment of a Dominican Friar's Embraces. These two Lovers were so eager in the Fruition of their Pleasures, that the Prince was at the Bed-side before they knew of his Entrance. The Widow first saw him, and cried out loud, which together with her Endeavours to push the Fryar from her, made him fall upon the Bed, in which they were mutually engaged in this amorous Combat, and when the Lady was rising, she unfortunately intangled one of her Feet in the Fryar's Gown and fell upon him. This Accident increased their Confusion. Whilst they were rising again, the Prince reproached her severely, and the Fryar content with taking his Hat and Cloak, went out holding his Breeches in his Hand. The Prince pursued and caned him so, that he cried out, *I am a Priest, and if you strike me, you shall be excommunicated;* but the more he cried the more the Prince beat him, and the poor Saint, finding no Boat to run into, leap'd into the River, and would infallibly have been drowned, had not one of the Widow's Domesticks run out to his Assistance, and saved his Life. This noble Scene well worthy of the Italian Stage, finished the Prince's Correspondence with the graceless Widow; and the Adventure filled her with so much Shame and Confusion, that she some Days afterwards retired into a Convent, in which she passed the remaining part of her Life, and having gained the Reputation of a pious Woman, died there some Years ago.

CHAPTER IV

Of the Prince's acquaintance with Trompettina, *his Intrigue with* Signora Mathei, *and a Nun, his departure from Venice.*

THE Treachery of a Person in whom the Prince had so greatly confided, mortified him extreamly, but the Melancholy it had occasioned in him could not obstruct his desire of an acquaintance with Trompettina, a Lady of Pleasure. He commonly supped at her House with the brightest young persons at Venice. Debauchery was practised there in the greatest degree, which proved prejudicial to the Health of several of them, but His remained unchangeable. However, though as he said himself, he was a Don Quixote in Gallantry, yet had he but little success there. He received several Billets, with appointments where to meet him, and went, but found they were only Ladies of Pleasure, whose chief design was upon his purse. During the Prince's stay at the City of Venice, his faithful Waterman was of no small assistance to him, for to him was all his master's good fortune to be duly ascribed. He one Day brought his Prince a Billet, which was really writ in an exquisite style, the Prince was therein desired to come to the assistance of an unfortunate Woman, whose passion for him was so excessive that she despaired of her Life; among several fine expressions in this Letter were these, 'that the only

'reason why she desired to see him was to tell him that
'he was adored by her, that it was the only weakness she,
'that was in expectation of him, was guilty of, if it might
'be called a weakness to adore a God.' The Romantick
Style of this Billet raised the Prince's curiosity to know
who writ it, but sent word in the mean while, that he
should be at the appointed place. His Waterman told
him, that the person, that expected him, was the Wife of
a Merchant, called Mathei, that she lived in Mercer's
Street, and that he would not find a Window open to
receive him, for the Lady had agreed with the Waterman
to leave her House door open, and that there his Highness should meet with an obliging reception from her
Hands. But they were both deceived in their expectations.
For Mr. Mathei, who was to have gone to Parma, was
by some affairs detained at Venice, and consequently his
House-door was found shut. The Lady was at a Window,
and excused herself for not performing her promise in a
sorrowful manner. The Prince was obliged to return
home, not a little dissatisfied with having been put to so
much unnecessary trouble. Some Days past after that in
which he heard nothing of Mrs. Mathei. One morning,
when he was in his Bed still, Notice was brought, that a
Woman, who was unwilling to discover her Name, and
had her Face covered with a Veil, desired Admittance to
him; he gave Orders to admit her, and desired his
Servants to leave him alone with her. The unknown

THE VEILED LADY

Lady being entered, the Prince excused himself for having received her so freely, and begged of her to sit down, and let him know in what manner he could be serviceable to her. The Lady having taken a Seat, sighed and addressed him in a very low tone, 'Your Highness, '(said she) has been pleased to give yourself the trouble of 'coming to my House some Days ago; I could not have 'the honour of giving you a reception, and am for that 'reason come to excuse myself, and, if possible, to make 'you amends for that incivility.' By this Address the Prince perceived her to be Mrs. Mathei. He assured her of his pleasure at, and grateful Acknowledgment of, the Favour she did him, and begged that she would pull off her Veil, and not refuse him the satisfaction of seeing her. But he was amazed to hear Mrs. Mathei say that nothing in the World should oblige her to pull off her Veil; that it was not the effect of any Woman's prudence, to appear in a Man's Chamber with her Face uncovered, especially when he is in Bed; that he should see her at her House after she should be convinced of the sincerity of his Love, which she assured him required more time than one Day. The Prince did his utmost to persuade her to it, but could have no other answer. She staid two Hours with him, repeating some passages out of *Tasso*, and at last left him, after having agreed to meet him at her House the next Evening. The Prince went, and found her Face covered as it was before. She conducted him to

THE LADY FORSAKEN

a lower Room, adorned with excellent pieces of Painting, where a Collation was served up very nicely. Mrs. Mathei seemed extreamly glad to see him, and sung an Ode, which she said, she had made on purpose for him. But the Prince could not prevail upon her to pull off her Veil. That manner of Courting not being agreeable to his Taste, and suspecting that the beautiful Lady had some secret cause, perhaps little for her own advantage, to be so obstinate in persisting to hide herself became very indifferent, which she soon perceived, and made her tremble. 'I see (said she in a languishing Tone) that 'your Will requires Compliance with it. Look on me 'then (continues she lifting up her Veil) and give Your 'Sentence either for my Life or Death.' The Beauty of Mrs. Mathei surprised the Prince so, that he could not conceal his amazement. She, on the other hand, saw with inexpressible satisfaction the speedy effect of her Charms, and losing the command over her Passion, fell upon his Neck, and called him her Caro, her Angelo; in short she finished the affair much sooner than she had proposed to do, and than the Prince hoped she would. He continued to visit her during the time that her Husband remained at a proper distance; but the difficulties he was afterwards troubled with to get into her Company, and the Natural inconsistency of his mind induced him to break off that Correspondence, and forsaking Mrs. Mathei, to enter into an intrigue with a Lady who led a Monastick Life

74

FAREWELL TO VENICE

in the Convent of —— to which none but Noblemen's Daughters can be admitted, who enjoy numberless extraordinary Liberties. The Prince found himself reduced to a regular method of Courtship. The Lady obliged him to shew the greatest and most tender fondness he was capable of, before she admitted him to an enjoyment of the effects of all his pains. During the course of these Intrigues he passed whole Days at the Church of —— at the Door of the Parlour. This raised a report throughout Venice of his having embraced the Roman Catholic Religion, and the Monks mentioned his Conversion as an evidenced and Miraculous Fact. The pious persons admired the goodness of divine Providence in thus having guided a strayed Sheep to the bosom of the Church. They had almost made a Declaration of the pious Nun, and the rest of Mankind, who were not of the Vulgar Opinion knew the whole project. The Prince freely disregarded popular Opinion, and pursuing his own way, thought of nothing but how to satisfy his eager desire of pleasure. Thus did he pass a year and a half at Venice, enjoying the Love, Esteem and Respect of all Mankind. The excess of Gallantry is not reckoned Criminal there, and on account of the Prince's Youth, it was overlooked in him. He at last quitted that Town to take a turn through Italy.

CHAPTER V

Of the Prince's Journey to Bologne, from thence to Florence, his reception at the Grand Duke's Court, his Challenge to the Duke of Mantua, *and the Duke's answer, his Journey from Florence to Sienna, and an Adventure, wherein the Prince shewed his uncommon Generosity.*

BOLOGNE was the first Town, that was honoured with the Prince's stay after his departure from Venice. The Nobility of this place, famouse for obliging strangers in a manner to accept of the civilities they are fond of shewing them, honoured the Prince of Saxony in an extraordinary manner. The Pope's Legate, Cardinal Buoncompagno,[1] gave him a grand Entertainment; but all these uncommon Civilities would not detain the Prince any long while at Bologne, for he soon set out from thence for Florence. He had the pleasure of seeing Cosmus III, Great Duke, and of contracting an inviolable Friendship with the Great Prince, who had espoused the Sister of the deceased Electors of Cologn and Bavaria. He was charm'd with the sight of this Princess, whose Beauty rendered her the chief Ornament of the Tuscan Court, and whose polite and engaging Deportment and uncommon Modesty occasioned all Italy to look upon

[1] This Cardinal was Uncle to Cardinal Buon Compagno, Arch Bishop of Bologne, in whose Presence the Electoral Prince of Saxony, since Elector, and Crowned King of Poland, professed the Faith of the Roman Catholic Church.

77

and hear of her with Admiration. Pleasure, Grandeur and the concomitants of these were her chief Delight; Her Spouse and herself strove to procure their serene Guest the Prince of Saxony all the Diversions that were capable of publishing his Dexterity and of exposing to publick view the Splendour of their Court. Preparations were immediately made for the most magnificent Balls and Comedies imaginable; but these Diversions the Grand Duke thought to be too private for he was desirous of some, whose Pomp might be more signal. He therefore resolved upon a Military Entertainment, at which all Persons of eminent Births might be admitted as Actors, and all the Common People as Spectators of so uncommon a Sight. The Prince, whom few, if any, could equal in exercises of that kind, joyfully approved of the Great Duke's project, and proposed that there should be four Troops of Horse, to represent the four Monarchies, which should be commanded by the Prince of Saxony, the Great Prince, the Dukes of Mantua and Guastalla: that there should be besides four Generals, to command; and those Gentlemen who best exerted their Valour, should receive a Prize, the value of which should be left to the discretion of those that were to be appointed Judges; that all the Gentlemen, as well as those of Florence, as Strangers, should produce some proof of their Nobility before an Officer of Arms, without which they should not expect Admission. Matters being thus

ordered and concluded upon, the Princes and Lords
employed most of their Time in giving Orders for whatever seemed requisite for them to appear with Grandeur,
and in putting something into their Cyphers, the Gallantry of which might relate to the objects of their Love.
The Day of this Martial Exercise at last appeared. The
Great Duke, the Cardinal de Medicis his Brother, and
the great Princes, placed themselves in those Galleries
and Scaffold that had been appointed for them. The four
Commanders appeared with their Troops at the Career,
followed by a large Number of Horse and Livery-men,
which formed the most magnificent Sight, that was ever
seen at Florence. The Prince of Saxony was at the Head
of his Men: whose Liveries were of a white and blue
Colour, being equal to those of the Great Princess, with
which he designed to honour her, not having had a
Mistress at Florence yet. The Prince's Dexterity was
such, as never was seen nor heard of. Tho' the Great
Prince was the best Horseman of all Italy, yet did it seem
dubious to which of the two the Preference was due.
All the Prince's Actions were accompanied with so agreeable a Grace, that they could not help deciding it in his
Favour; and the Ladies testified an inexpressible Joy,
when he had luckily run the Race. He gained the first
Prize, and would not have failed of any of the rest, had
he not been apprehensive of mortifying the other Gentlemen too much. The Duke of Mantua, who thought his

DISCRETION BEFORE VALOUR

Dexterity not inferior to any other, impatiently suffered the Superiority the Prince of Saxony carried over him; he happened in his envious Rage to slip some Words, by which the Cause of his Uneasiness was perceived. These were the next Day reported by some very indiscreet Person to the Prince of Saxony, who was directly in search after Revenge. Soon afterwards he resolved to write a Billet to the Duke, in which he challenged him to a Duel and gave him his Choice of Weapons. Rose,[1] Gentleman of the Bed-Chamber, carried this Challenge instantly to the directed Person. The Duke of Mantua, who did not aim at an immortal Renown for valiant Deeds, trembled at the perusal of this Billet. He told Rose, 'That he could not remember any Action by which 'he thus disobliged the Prince; that he begg'd his Pardon, 'and that rather, than fight the Duel, no submissive 'Excuse should be thought of, that he was not ready to 'make to His Highness.' Rose answered him, 'That he 'believed his Master would be satisfied, if His Highness 'would write a Declaration and sign it with his own 'Hand, therein to acknowledge, that his most Serene 'Highness the Prince of Saxony had challenged him to a 'Duel; but that not trusting to his Courage, he dared not 'undertake a Combat with so valiant a Prince.' The Duke of Mantua embraced Rose, and thanked him affectionately for having invented Means to escape the Battle. He wrote

---

[1] He was before he died Lieutenant-General in the Saxon Service.

Magdalene, Countess Rochlitz

Engraving by Schenk

AN ADVENTURE AT SIENNA

a Billet conformable to those Particulars Rose had proposed to him, and after having signed, he sealed it with
his own Seal. The Prince, when he saw this Billet, lifting
up his Shoulders, 'Is it possible (said he) that a Prince
'should be guilty of so much Cowardice, as to sign such
'a Declaration!' In the mean Time the Duke of Mantua
had some Reason to fear, that the Prince was not yet
satisfied, took a private Post, and retired to the Capital of
his Estates. Some days after this Adventure, the Prince
departed from Florence, extreamly well pleased with the
Honours he had there received. As he had been at little
Expense during his Stay at this Court, because the Great
Duke defray'd his Charges, he gave splendid Presents to
all the Officers and other Servants of that Prince. He
resided some days at Sienna, where an Adventure happened, in which he so discover'd his uncommon generosity, that he drew upon him the Veneration of all that
had any Pretensions to common Honour. The Adventure
was this: When he was at Florence an Abbot, Native of
Sienna had mentioned a young Lady of his Kindred, as
the most beautiful Woman in Italy, and had promised
that on his Journey to Sienna he should be bless'd with
the Sight of her. The Prince, as soon as he was arrived at
this Town insisted upon the Performance of the Abbot's
Promise; whereupon the Abbot conducted him the same
Evening to the Great Church, where she was waiting for
the Blessing. The Prince found the young Person to be

exceeding charming and conjured the Abbot to procure
him a private Conference with her. The officious Priest
directly made Answer, 'That the Execution of his Desire
'was not utterly impossible, but that it would not only
'cost him very much pains, but also a very large Sum of
'Money.' The Prince replied, 'That, as for the Trouble
'he should esteem it but little; and in Regard to the
'Expense, he should never grudge that, and, provided he
'could but obtain his End, he was ready to disburse
'whatever Sum should be required of him.' The Abbot,
furnished with these ample Ingredients without Hesitation undertook the Matter: he went to the Young
Woman's Mother, and found her more pliable than ever
he expected. This inhuman Woman consented to sacrifice
her Daughter for a Thousand Pistoles, to be paid at the
Delivery of the innocent Victim. The Project being thus
agreed upon, she spoke to her Daughter, whom she found
very unwilling to comply with her Request. The young
Woman was deterred from consenting to this proposal,
not only by the Horror of being exposed to publick
Dishonour, but also by an Amour between her and a
young Man, who had promised her Marriage, and of
which Match her Mother refused her Approbation. She
threw herself at her Mother's Feet, and conjured her not
to compel her to an Action which would infallibly cover
her with Shame and Infamy. The Mother, deaf to her
Intreaties, threaten'd, that if she did not obey, Imprison-

ment in a Convent should be her Fate ever afterwards. These Threats made the unfortunate Daughter tremble; but her Despair suggested to her some means of preventing a Prostitution. She hid her Intention from her Mother, and feigning to submit totally to her Will, told her the Prince of Saxony might be admitted. The Abbot, well satisfied with this Answer, introduced the Prince to his Cousin. The Mother gave him a very kind Reception, but the Daughter cast down her Eyes and spoke not a Word. So cold an Entertainment did not at all surprize the Prince, for he imputed it partly to the last Endeavours of departing Virtue and partly to the Mother's Presence. He impatiently desired to be alone with her, when the Abbot and Mother left them. But how great was his Surprize, to see the young Woman fall down at his Knees, full of Tears, embrace them, and with a lamentable Voice intermixed with frequent Sighs and Groans conjure him to have Pity upon a young Woman of Quality, who was then by a barbarous Mother sacrificed to vile Interest! 'Great Prince (said she to him) I am now wholly in your 'Power, and my only Hope is placed in your generosity; 'which I implore, and am persuaded to be in Greatness 'not inferior to your Birth. Abuse me not, I beg of you 'in the Name of God, in this miserable Condition, to 'which my Mother has reduc'd me.' A Shower of Tears interrupted her Voice; and obliged her to desist. The Prince, touch'd with the Misery, which he saw this young Woman subject to, lifted her up. 'Fear nothing, 'Madam, (said he when he raised her) I am so far from 'abusing the Authority your Mother has given me over 'you, that I will even protect you against that same 'Mother; only tell me, what you desire me to do.' A condemned Malefactor, to whom Pardon is declared at the last Approaches of Death, could not be sensible of a greater Joy, than was at the Time this virtuous young Woman. She again threw herself at the Prince's Feet; but was incapable of producing a Word; and continuing to embrace his Knees, seem'd to adore him, as her Guardian Angel; but the Prince raised her up, and after having given her Time to regain her Senses, he desired to know, why, since she refused to satisfy his Desires, she had consented to be left alone with him. She related to him all that had passed between her Mother and herself, and concealed not from him, that the Fear of being deprived of a Lover, who was very dear to her, had induced her to consent to her Mother's Orders. 'I pleased 'myself with the Hopes, Sir, (said she) that my Miseries 'would touch you, and if I had been deceiv'd in my 'Expectation, (continued she, pulling out a dagger) this 'should have prevented my Infamy; for I should have 'plunged this Dagger into my Breast.' The Prince was astonish'd and charm'd to find so much Courage in a person not seventeen Years of Age. 'Madam, (said he) I 'admire your Beauty, and cannot but respect your Virtue.

84

THE PRINCE'S GENEROSITY

'I am heartily glad that I am capable of contributing to
'your Happiness, and shall even endeavour to obtain
'your Mother's Consent to your Marriage with that
'person to whom you have promised Fidelity; and fully
'to convince you of my Esteem, be not, I beg of you,
'displeased at my settling upon you an annual Pension
'of a Thousand Crowns for Your Life-Time.' These
generous proceedings enliven'd the young Lady with
Gratitude, and she gave the Prince fresh Assurances, that
her Lover and she should for ever gratefully acknowledge
his Munificence. 'May Heaven, (said she to him) endue
'you with greatest and best of its Blessings.' The Prince
answer'd that his Obligations to her for those Wishes,
were exceeding great, and begg'd she would call up her
Mother, and leave him alone with her. This Woman had
no sooner enter'd the Room than she was loaded with
the Prince's Reproaches for the great Injury she had
done her Daughter. He continued to persuade her to
consent to her Daughter's Marriage, which if she refused,
she must not expect him to perform the Contract he had
made with her for the payment of a Thousand Pistoles.
'You must (said he when he saw her irresolute) consent
'to my Demands, or else be content with being shut up
'in a Convent. I intend to ask that favour of the Great
'Duke, and am well assured that the Share I have in his
'Friendship will not suffer him to deny it me. For I tell
'you again that I shall not consent to let your Daughter

'remain with you.' The mention of a Convent put the Mother in a Fear, equal to that, which she had put her Daughter in before, wherefore she submitted to the Prince's Desires. A Notary and the Bridegroom were directly sent for, the Marriage-Contract was drawn and sign'd the same Hour. The Prince paid the Thousand Pistoles to the Mother, and settled the promised Pension upon the Daughter. This generous Act being thus ended, the Prince departed from thence for Rome.

CHAPTER VI

Of the Prince's Arrival at Rome, his Reception and Entertainments there, he gains the Affection of the High-Constable's Wife, several other Amours, his Voyage to Naples, from thence to Sicily, his happy Deliverance of the Ship in the latter Voyage; his Journey to Germany, his Campaign on the Rhine; his Marriage of the Princess of Bareith, *Death of* Mademoiselle Netsch, *of the* Elector of Saxony, *of the* Countess of Rochlitz, *and of the new Elector's Fidelity to his Spouse.*

THE Prince of Saxony arriv'd at Rome, the Metropolis of all the World, at a Time, when it was visited by Strangers from all parts to attend their Devotion and to satisfy their Curiosity. Anthony Pignatelly was then possessor of St. Peter's Chair, by the name of Innocent XII. The Prince paid his submissive Respects to the Pope, and though he made his Appearance there as Count of Misnia, yet did he receive Honours from the Pope equal to those that are paid to a Prince. He entertain'd him a long while with an Account of his Voyages, the State of the Spanish Court, and the deplorable State of the Catholick Religion in Saxony. His Holiness recommended those that adhere to the Doctrines of that Religion, and the Prince promised to protect them as far as it was in his power. The Pope, transported with Joy, embrac'd his Guest, and, as if he had been inspired with a Spirit of Prophecy, 'God will retaliate your Virtues

'(said he) he will cause your Return to the Bosom of the
'True Church, and bless you with a long Series of Pros-
'perities.' At every Ceremony in the Holy Week, the
Pope gave careful Orders that the Prince might be con-
veniently placed. He gave him splendid Presents, and
sent every day a Cameriero d'Honore to enquire into
the State of Augustus's Health. On Corpus Christi day
His Holiness perceiving the Prince at a Window of the
Palace Occoramboni, gave him the Benediction of the
Blessed Sacrament. All the Inhabitants of Rome were not
a little displeased at this Action, Pasquin said that His
Holiness was become Lutheran, and the Prince of Saxony
a Papist. The Cardinals imitated the Pope, and remitting
of their haughty Ceremonies, were eager to pay him all
due Civilities. The Nobility in imitation of their example
were no less forward in procuring him Pleasures of all
Kinds. They vied each other in entertaining him, he
was constantly diverted at Frescati, Tivoli and Albano.
No House in Rome laid the Prince under greater Obligations for their Civilities than that of Colonna, which he
also frequented more than any other. The High-Constable's Lady could not boast of very great Beauty; but
possessed an Air of Majesty, and so charming a Genius,
that it procured her a much larger Number of Adorers,
than those whom Nature has endow'd with more in-
chanting Attractions. She was more skilful than any other
person in retaining her Lovers; and without giving any

John-George IV of Saxony

Contemporary Engraving

particular sign of preference to any one, amused them all with equal Hopes. Her House was at the free Use and ever ready for the Reception of all Persons of Distinction of either Sex. That free and unconstrained Behaviour once introduced by the Lady High-Constable Mary Marcini was still practised there. They entertained all Rome with frequent Concerts, Balls, grand Feasts, and Diversions of all kinds. The Prince of Saxony spent almost every Evening there: the great Pleasure every one that frequented that Place received in the Lady High-Constable's Company, induced him to go thither, who was no less pleased with her delightful Conversation, than she with the Delicacy of his Expressions. She discharged all her other Adorers, to have the more Leisure to entertain herself with him; and was so little capable of hiding her Sentiments in Regard to him, that the High-Constable soon perceived them. His jealousy permitted him not to consent to his Lady's further Residence at Rome, at least not whilst the Prince of Saxony was there: he pretended that Affairs of some Importance called him to Naples with Speed, obliged the Lady to accompany him, and then retired with her to one of his Estates.

The Prince was easily comforted at the Departure of the Lady High-Constable, for his Sentiments for her were limited within the Bounds of a common Esteem. His Heart was determined in Favour of Madame Monti, who was then reckon'd the greatest Beauty in Rome.

LEISURE FROM AMOURS

The Prince made his Addresses to her, and she gave a willing Ear to them; it is even said, that his Victory would not have been very laborious, but the Flame of his Passion was almost as suddenly extinguished as it had taken Rise, for the dull and insipid Deportment of Madame Monti occasioned the Loss of her Conquest.

The Prince's Heart, now at his own Disposal, roved for a considerable time from one Beauty to another, nothing was capable of fixing it upon one amiable Object. He took no small Advantage of this Leisure-Time his amorous Disposition allowed him, for he employed the greatest part of it in viewing the antient and modern Rarities, which Rome is so well known to abound with. In this Interval he acquired that exquisite Taste in Painting and Architecture, that uncommon Knowledge of Antiquity, and that solid Judgment, which enabled him to act and speak so judiciously of all the polite parts of Learning.

His Curiosity being thus fully satisfied he departed for Naples, and made as long a stay there as was requisite to see the Rarities of a Town whose situation renders it so singular and renowned. From thence he embarqued for Sicily, and though the Wind seemed at his Departure to favour him, yet did they undergo a horrible Tempest, which lasted five Days, and deprived the Sailors of all Care and Resolution and the Passengers of all further Hope. The Pilot almost positive of the Impossibility of

FROM PLACE TO PLACE

a Deliverance, tired with the hard Labour he had been at, and terrified at the Danger they were in, had left the Helm, and given up the Ship to the Mercy of the Winds and Waves. The Prince seeing the Disorder the Ship's Crew seemed to be in, undertook the management of the Steer; and by performing the Pilot's Office during the space of a Day and a Night, had the good Luck of saving the Vessel and arriving at Palermo.

His stay in this Place and in all Sicily was very short; but his Curiosity would not suffer him to neglect the Sight of the Principal Towns, it even carried him as far as Mount Ætna, the fatal Grave of the proud Giant Typhœus, and the Cavern where the unmerciful Vulcan resides. He was at length at Messina, from whence he embarqued to pass the Streights, and land at Reggio. He crossed Calabria, reviewed Naples, and at length returned to Rome. The Pope admitted him to two or three Visits before his Departure from them to Venice. He was heartily glad when he arrived at Venice, to see himself returned to a Place, where he had before led so pleasant a Life, and the Inhabitants of that City were overjoyed at his Presence. He again proposed to spend Some Time there, but being informed that Lewis XIV had declared War against the Emperor Leopold and the whole Empire, he forsook the Pleasure prepared for him at Venice, and undertook for his future Employment the Acquisition of Glory. He made his Appearance at the

Army and signalized that intrepid Valour, which in all
Emergencies he was capable of making use of, and was
even the Admiration of his professed Enemies.

The Campaign ended, the Prince designed to return
into Italy, but the Electress his Mother,[1] and his Brother
the Elector were so earnest in their Intreaties for his
Return into Saxony, that he could not possibly refuse
them that Comfort. He passed in his Journey through
Nuremberg and Bareith, and was in this latter Town
detained by the Margrave of Brandenburg, who gave
him a very splendid Reception. He saw at this Court the
Princess Eberhardine Daughter of the Margrave. This
Princess's Beauty seemed to him to exceed all that he had
seen in his Travels: He became more enamoured with
her, than he had yet been with any other of his Mistresses,
and resolved here to stop the Course of his roving
Amours, and to secure the Possession of her, which
seemed to him the greatest Felicity imaginable.

The Princess of Bareith was in Reality one of those
Persons the Sight of whom causes a delightful Admiration. The Fairness of her Complexion, and her beautiful
dark-brown Hair set off her whole Person in a manner
that was never seen, but in her. Her Features were all
regular, her Face and Person were full of Graces and
Charms. A certain Modesty and Goodness of Nature
rendered her Company exceeding pleasant. All the Blame

[1] Ann Sophia, Daughter of Frederick III, King of Denmark.

she was subject to, was for more Gravity, than was commonly experienced in a Lady that had not yet attained the fifteenth Year of her Age.

The Prince of Saxony studied to please her and when he thought his Endeavours in that Respect were not displeasing to her, he offered her his Fidelity. The Princess answer'd, that she was at the Disposal of a Father and Mother, and should make no Choice without their Approbation; but that she would submissively accept of the Husband they should present to her. The Prince therefore applied to the Margrave and of him demanded the Princess in Marriage; she was promised to him, the Ceremony of betrothing was performed, and a little while afterwards the Nuptials were celebrated with all the Grandeur and Magnificence usual on the like Occasions.

The Prince conducted his Spouse to Dresden, where they were received by the Mother Electress and Elector with all the Marks of a most lively Tenderness. During some Months nothing was heard of but Treats and Rejoicings. The Saxons, who lov'd the Prince far more than the Elector, did their utmost Endeavours to testify their Affection for him and the Joy his Return had caused.

All these publick Rejoicings were soon after changed into Sorrow; for Mademoiselle Neitsch, whom the Elector always lov'd with an Ardency not to be equall'd, fell sick of the Small-Pox and died. The Elector was hereat in a Despair, not to be appeased. He could not be persuaded to leave the Body of the Deceased; but continued to embrace her, and express himself in numberless affectionate Terms to her, and called Death to deliver him from a Life which was tedious to him, since the Decease of his Mistress.

Every one imputed the Elector's Despair to some supernatural Cause; and as the Saxon Court of Judicature was not of an equal Opinion with the Parliament of Paris, which admits of no Sorcerers, they doubted not, but that Mademoiselle Neitsch had employ'd some magical Art in gaining the Elector's Love. A Report was thereupon industriously spread, that a Cloth dipp'd in Blood and in it a Piece of Paper, on which were writ very singular Characters, had been found under her Left Arm, and that, as soon as this Paper was taken away from her, the Elector had been pacify'd, and had recover'd his Reason, which he seem'd before to have lost. I cannot assert the Reality of this Fact, but it is very well known, that the Elector's Obstinacy in refusing to leave his Mistress gave him the Small-Pox about five days afterwards, of which he died the seventh day. He was less regretted by his Subjects than he would have been, had any other except Frederick-Augustus succeeded him.

The Condition of the Countess of Rocklitz, Mademoiselle de Neitsch's Mother, may be easily imagin'd. The Prince suffer'd her not to approach the Elector during his Illness, and sent to her to demand that Prince's Seals and Jewels, which had been committed to her Care. She asked whether the Elector was dead, and when she was answered in the Negative, 'I have no other Master 'than him, (answer'd she) and no one shall oblige me to 'deliver up that, which his Confidence has deposited in 'my Hands.' John-George was no sooner expired than the Elector imprison'd the Countess, and prosecuted her according to the utmost Rigour of the Law. She was not so unfortunate as to survive her Sentence, which was given the same day on which she died. This Sentence condemn'd her to be drawn on a Hurdle, then to be hang'd, and her Body to be expos'd without any Burial. But the Elector mitigated the latter part of it, and permitted her Kindred to inter her. He said his Reign should not begin with putting so grievous an Affront on a noble Family.

Frederick-Augustus's Promotion to the Electorate entirely Changed the Face of the Saxon Court. That Prince gave the Command of the Army to the Field-Marshal Schoning; the Management of the Exchequer, together with the Great Seal, was given to Mr. Beichling, Mr. Hauchwitz was nominated Great Marshall; he discharged all his Brother's Officers, and retain'd no others, but those who had been faithful in the Service of the Elector his Father.

The Funerals of the deceased Elector were solemnized

in an extraordinary pompous manner, and his Corps was carried to Torgau the Place appointed for the Burial of the Electors of Saxony. Frederick-Augustus was present at the Ceremonies of the Funeral, and seem'd more sensible of his Brother's Loss than those commonly are to whom by Right of Inheritance the Supreme Power devolves.

The new Elector liv'd in perfect Unity with the Electress his Spouse; he was ador'd by her, and lov'd no other Person but her; and that Princess esteem'd herself the happiest Person on Earth. The Courtiers doubted not but that she had for ever fix'd the inconstant Heart of Augustus upon one Object, and even that Prince himself thought he had now renounced all Gallantry, but the Event proves their great Mistake, and that his Heart was never design'd for Constancy.

CHAPTER VII

Of the Elector of Saxony's *Intrigue with* Mademoiselle Kessel, *his Visit to her, the Electress's Jealousy, the happy consequences of it, and* Mademoiselle Kessel's *Marriage.*

THE Elector's Mother, who by reason of her eminent Birth, being Daughter of Frederick III, King of Denmark, was distinguished by the Title of Royal Highness, had among her Attendants a young Lady named Mademoiselle Kessel. This Lady induced the young Elector to break the Promise of Fidelity he had made to his Spouse. The Chancelor Friese's Lady gave the first Rise to this Passion, by raising in the Elector a Curiosity of seeing and knowing Mademoiselle Kessel by the Commendations she gave him of the young Lady's Genius and Merit. This good and virtuous Woman designed by praising Mademoiselle Kessel, to perform an Act of Charity, I mean to procure her a Pension; she being born very poor, and incapable of maintaining herself at Court with the Salary of a Maid of Honour. The Elector had indeed before been pleased, but never yet conversed with her.

One Day he went to pay a Visit to the Electress his Mother, and met in the Anti-Chamber Mademoiselle Kessel; he spent a considerable Time in her Company, and was so charm'd with the Excellencies of her Mind,

that he instantly felt a Passion for her. He staid but a very
small space of Time with the Electress, return'd thither
the next day and proceeded thus for a whole Month.
The Courtiers were of opinion that some affairs of great
Importance call'd him so frequently to the Electress's
Chamber to ask her Advice. But during this Time he
had but few opportunities of speaking to his Beloved;
for this virtuous Creature perceiving his Tenderness for
her, and not thinking of making any Answer to the Signs
of it, carefully avoided him. The Elector, not willing to
lose his Time writ her the following Billet. 'Tho' my
'regard to Madame Friese's Recommendation is very
'great, yet I beg you would not attribute to her the Two
'Thousand Crowns of which I here send you a Bill. It is
'to yourself you owe this Token of my Esteem; and be
'persuaded that it is not the only Kindness I design to
'do you. Shun me not therefore, as you have done, nor
'refuse me I beg of you the great Pleasure of your Con-
'versation; perhaps when you are better acquainted with
'me, you'll not continue to refuse me your Esteem, the
'Acquisition of which can only make me happy.'

Mademoiselle Kessel thought it improper to answer
this Billet. She desired Fitztuhm, the Bearer of it, to tell
the Elector, that she was full of the most grateful Acknowledgment, and that she would not fail to return
him Thanks for his excessive Goodness. Fitztuhm
endeavour'd in vain to persuade her to write a line or

two; but she excused herself by saying it would look much more respectful to shew her Gratitude to the Elector by Word of Mouth.

The same Evening the Prince came to Supper to the Electress his Mother, and was met by Mademoiselle Kessel. 'Your Electoral Highness has given me so 'infallible a proof of your Magnanimity, (said she to 'him) that I am dubious what Terms to make use of to 'express my Acknowledgment of it. Permit me, Sir, to 'shew it by a respectful Silence, and to be contented with 'wishing sincerely that you may for many future Years 'cause the Admiration of those that Approach your 'noble Person, and be the Delight of all your Subjects.' 'The Favour I have done you, Madam, (reply'd the 'Elector) is so trivial, that it scarce deserves your Notice. 'I beg your Acceptance of it, as proceeding from one, 'that is desirous of doing Justice to your Merits, and who 'valueth his Supreme Power for no other Reason but 'because it enableth him to oblige you.' The Electress appearing at the same Time, the Prince was obliged to discontinue a Conversation, in which he was only engag'd to express the Sentiments of his Heart.

For two days after that he could not meet with any favourable Time to tell her some particular Things. He saw her at the Apartment of the Electress his Mother, and the more frequently he saw her, the more he became enamour'd with her. These two days seem'd to him to exceed the length of an Age. His Impatience at last induced him to consult with Mr. Beichling (who was at that time his chief confidant) about the means of procuring a Meeting with the Person only, for whom he had conceiv'd so great a Tenderness. Beichling overjoy'd at the Confidence the Elector reposed in him, made so many Enquiries, that he was at last informed that Mademoiselle Kessel was for some days to retire to a Country Seat belonging to Madame Friese, about two Miles Distance from Dresden. The Elector went out to hunt to a Forest adjacent to one of Madame Friese's Grounds, feigned to lose his Way there with Beichling, and unexpectedly to find himself near the House of Madame Friese in which was Mademoiselle Kessel; and as if Fortune delighted in favouring him, he met his dear Beauty diverting herself in a long Walk before the House. He alighted as soon as he saw her, and having tied his Horse to a Tree, he saluted and gallantly ask'd her whether she was not apprehensive, that some Gentleman acquainted with her Merits should come to take her away. She answer'd him, That she had no Reason to be in Fears of Adventures of that Kind; and especially in Saxony, under the Reign of a Prince whose Subjects, in Imitation of his Example, scorn'd to commit any Violence. The more attentive the Elector was to her Words, the more he delighted in hearing her. He enquired after Madam Friese and was told that she was alone.

'YOUR HEART IS ALL I DESIRE'

When he drew nearer to her House, Madame Friese, looking out of her Closet-Window, was not a little sur-priz'd to see Mademoiselle Kessel with the Elector. She ran down to meet them and begg'd of the Elector to come into her House. This Prince engaged himself in his beloved Lady's Company, whilst Beichling was con-versing with the other, or she giving Orders for a Repast, which she design'd to treat the Elector with. Mademoiselle Kessel's Aspect was more agreeable to the Prince than her Words, for she accompanied all her Discourse with so much Modesty that he could not help blaming her for being so little sensible of it. She excused herself for having given Occasion to this Blame by the Esteem she had for His Electoral Highness. 'O! (cried 'the Elector) Your Esteem would flatter me, was I as in-'different as you are. Your Heart, Madam, is all I desire 'and the longer you refuse me the Affection of it, the 'more unhappy you will make me. How! is it offensive 'to you, adorable Kessel, to tell you, that your Merit 'causes my Inability of living any longer but for you; 'and that, if you please, you will by loving me, find a 'sincere Lover, and a submissively respectful Sovereign?' 'Sir, (said she) I cannot so far flatter myself as to be per-'suaded, that Your Electoral Highness speaks seriously.' 'Yes, I protest before you, (reply'd the Elector in falling 'down at her Knees) that my Words express the real 'Sentiments of my Heart.' Mademoiselle Kessel lifting

him up, 'For God's Sake, Sir, (said she) rise up; what
'would be Madame Friese's Opinion of me, was she to
'find you at my Feet?' 'She'll think, (reply'd the Elector)
'that I adore you, and perhaps I shall be more capable of
'moving her pity than yours.' 'How unjust, (answer'd
'she, changing her Colour) is Your Electoral Highness's
'Opinion of me! Could you but penetrate my Heart, you
'would find it touch'd with the most lively Acknowledg-
'ments, and——' Madame Friese enter'd the Room the
same Minute, and the Elector begun to talk of several
indifferent Things. As he was in Fear of her perceiving
too early the pleasure that detain'd him at her House, he
rose up to take his Leave of her; and having joined a
large number of Courtiers, who had been in Search after
him, he could not help frequently mentioning Mademoiselle Kessel as being far the most beautiful of her
Sex, and they were in Reality, without being prevented
by his Commendations, obliged to own that she was
exceeding amiable. She was tall, beautifully brown, her
Eyes were exceeding bright, and agreeably weak, her
Complexion was charming and the Beauties of her Mind
incomparable, tho' she was a little Melancholy.

Three days after this meeting Mademoiselle Kessel,
being returned to Court, the Elector had a Meeting with
her, in which he told her all, that a tender and violent
Love could inspire a Man of Gallantry and one subject
to that Passion with. Mademoiselle Kessel desisted to be

any longer reserved; she owned, that her Heart was sensible of his passion for her. The Elector transported with Joy thought he could not sufficiently repay an Acknowledgment, which was solely conducive towards his Happiness. He had no sooner left her, than he sent her Jewels to the Value of a Thousand Crowns, several pieces of Silk, and in short a Collection of the most magnificent Presents. These acquir'd him that Favour, which is the greatest degree of Happiness a Lover can enjoy.

Mademoiselle Kessel begg'd he would conceal his Conversation with her, and told him that she had great reason to fear the Resentment of the Electress. He was desirous of drawing her away from his Mother, but she refused her Consent to that; thus was he constrained to see himself deprived of the Enjoyment of his Mistress's Company, which renders the Lover's pleasure more disagreeable. In the mean while the Young Electress perceiv'd that the Elector had not so great a Regard for her as he formerly had, and, highly mortified at it, she endeavoured a long while to conceal her Grief, not knowing where to expect any Assistance; but one day when the Elector's Birth was celebrated at Court, she saw Mademoiselle Kessel enter in a Dress equal in Richness to that of a Queen and shining all over with Diamonds. She easily conjectured that so splendid an Appearance could come from no other but the Elector's Hands, and unable to overcome her Jealousy, she asked who had presented her with all that she saw? Mademoiselle Kessel was in great Confusion for want of a proper Answer. Her Disorder confirmed the Electress's Suspicions; 'I see (said she) from whom you received 'this magnificent Apparel; but you may be assured that 'your Boldness to me to appear thus in my presence 'surprizes me.' Upon these Words she left her there and went to the Electress her Mother-in-Law to communicate her Suspicions and Uneasiness to her. The two Princesses after having consulted well about the matter resolved upon examining Mademoiselle Kessel with all possible Rigour. They sent for her, and after having obliged her to confess that the Elector was enamoured with her, they reprimanded her severely, and the Elector's Mother threatened to cause her to be shut up in a House of Correction. The poor Girl retired shedding numberless Tears and her Heart filled with Despair. In this Condition she happen'd to meet the Elector, who pressed her to acquaint him with the Cause of her Affliction. She instantly told him that she had been ill-used by the two Electresses. The Elector went in Rage and Fury like a young Lion to the Apartment of the two Princesses. 'Every one, (said he at his entrance) endeavours to 'offend me, but I shall make Use of proper means to 'render all my Subjects submissive to the Person I love.' The Electresses were troubled to the very Heart and began to weep bitterly; the young one especially was

Eberhardine, Spouse of Augustus of Saxony
Engraving by Schenk

nearer to Despair; 'How! Sir, (said she, overwhelmed in
'Tears, and casting a tender Eye upon him) dare you tell
'me that you love any other Person but me?' The Elector
'looking at her disdainfully, 'Madam (said he) you are a
'very talkative Woman; by whom you have been in-
'structed I know not, but it would be far better (con-
'tinued he, looking at his Mother) if every one observed
'his own Affairs.' He was going to leave them when he
had finished these Words, but the young Electress stopt
him, and throwing herself at his Feet, 'Dear Sir, (said
'she) either return me your Affection, or ease me of my
'Life; I love and shall never cease loving you.' 'Pity your
'Spouse, (said at the same time, the Electress his Mother),
'remember how much you disapproved of your Brother's
'Esteem for Mademoiselle Neitsch, and will you imitate
'an Example that was once so hateful to you?' The
Elector sensibly touch'd with these Reproaches, rais'd up
the Electress, and embracing her, said, 'Yes, Madam, I
'do and ever shall love you, and am now in great Despair
'for having caused this Grief in you. Tell me in what
'manner you require me to give you ample Satisfaction.'
'Marry Mademoiselle Kessel, (replied the Electress) and
'remove her to a place far distant from Court for ever.'
'Very well, (answered the Elector, being put to a Stand)
'you need only procure her a Husband, I am not ac-
'quainted with any.' The Mother-Electress promis'd to
procure her one. The Elector answered not a Word, but

retired to his Chamber, his Eyes full of Tears. A little
while afterwards he ordered his Coaches to be got ready
and set out for Mauritzburgh, taking with him only
Beichling and Fitztuhm, his two Favourites. Before he
went away he writ to Mademoiselle Kessel, asking her
pardon for forsaking her; and conjured her to submit to
the Fates' Will, and accept of whatever Husband the
Electresses should offer to her. 'This (said he) is the only
'method of preserving you from the incessant persecu-
'tions of the Electresses.' Mademoiselle Kessel was ready
to die with Grief at the perusal of this Letter. 'O, the
'perjured Traitor! (cried she). Yes, I will marry; but to
'no other person but him, that will have sufficient Courage
'to plunge a Dagger into the unfaithful Man's Breast.'
At these Words she swooned away, and her Servants
recovered her again with great Care and Pains. Madame
Friese came to see her, whilst she was recovering, and
officiously counsel'd her to the utmost of her power; she
put her in mind of her former Innocence, Religion, and
her Reputation. Mademoiselle Kessel submitted to her
Intreaties, and though she did not forget the Injury the
Elector had done her, yet she prevailed upon herself not
to shew her Resentment of it. She petition'd the Mother-
Electress by Madame Einsiedel Maid of Honour to that
Princess, for Leave to retire from Court. Her Request
was easily granted, and Madame Friese, who did not forsake her during her Distress, took her to her own House.

SEEKING A HUSBAND

The next day the Electresses sent her several Offers, but Mademoiselle Kessel made Answer, That she could not make any particular Choice, but would accept of him for her Husband, whom the Elector would be pleased to nominate as such. The Electresses very much troubled sent Monsieur Miltiz to the Prince, desiring him to name the Person whom he designed to present with the possession of Mademoiselle Kessel; but the Elector refused to chuse any, and replied, That the Electresses ought to be satisfied with the Liberty he had already given them in that respect; but that he should be much obliged to them, if they would not too forcibly resist Mademoiselle Kessel's Inclinations.

The Princesses little satisfied with this Answer, knew not what method to take to. The Mother-Electress went at last to Madame Friese, and having sent for Mademoiselle Kessel: 'You know, Mademoiselle, (said she) 'that I have always given you the preference to any of 'my other Attendants, and have frequently intimated, 'that I desired no greater Happiness, than to see you 'fortunately disposed of. You have since that time given 'me some Reasons to disapprove of your Conduct, but 'all those shall be buried in Oblivion, provided you will 'instantly chuse a Husband. I have made several advan- 'tageous Proposals to you, but you have refused them 'all; can you think of any other? If you can, I comply 'with your Desire. But speak, Mademoiselle, for I am

'resolv'd not to leave you till you have given me a posi-
'tive Answer. Please not yourself with the Hopes of my
'Son's protection; for he has forsaken, and is resolved
'never to return to you. Be persuaded by me, let all the
'Court be sensible that, though you have departed from
'the path of Virtue, yet you have found it again. The
'Electress my Daughter-in-Law and I have agreed to
'return you our Esteem, and shall be so far from remem-
'bering what is past, that we shall even contribute to that
'Person's future Welfare, whose Happiness it will be to
'be chosen your Spouse.'

Mademoiselle Kessel, who had remained silent, and as
it were petrified, during the time that the Electress had
spoke to her, answered at last in a trembling Tone, That
she was so little acquainted with those that had been
offer'd to her in Marriage, that she could not herself
determine which to chuse; she would however make
some Choice, but required a month's time to consider of
it. The Electress in Fear of offending her Son dared not
refuse her. 'I comply (said she) with your Request; but
'if, when that time is past, you still think to amuse me,
'be assured that I shall find some means of making you
'repent of your Obstinacy.'

The Space of Time, that had been allowed to Mademoiselle Kessel was almost expired without her having
yet made any Choice. She, like a second Penelope,
expected the Return of her dear Ulysses. She pleased

herself with the Hope, that the Elector, who liv'd
retiredly and mortally grieved, at Mauritzbourg, would
at length return and deliver her from the Tyranny of the
Electresses. Madame Friese, seeing that she deceived
herself with these vain Hopes, undertook to cure her of
her foolish Passion. She so excellently described the
ridiculous and horrible nature of it, spoke with so
much Eloquence and so much Judgment, and gave her
so advantageous a Character of Monsieur Hauchwitz
Marshal of the Field in the Elector's Service, that the
Young Lady was at last persuaded to determine to take
him for her Spouse. Madame Friese went directly to
report the News to the two Electresses, who were
equally rejoiced at it as if she had informed them of some
Victory carried by the Elector. The Mother-Electress
was at the Expense of the Wedding, and helped the new-
marry'd Lady with Presents and Endearments. Some
days afterwards Monsieur Hauchwitz conducted his
Lady to Wittemberg of which he was the Governor. He
had so great an Affection for her, that he gained her Love,
and caused her to forget the Elector. This Prince returned
to Dresden, soon after Madame Hauchwitz's Retirement
from thence. Grief was easily perceived in his Face, but
he did not in the least blame the Electresses. Time at last,
which blots out the Memory of all Things, caused the
Oblivion of his Mistress, and him to recover his Liberty.

CHAPTER VIII

Of the Arrival of the Countess of Koningsmark *at the Saxon Court, her Character, the Elector's Intrigue with her, and several Consequences of this Amour.*

THE Elector did not long enjoy the Benefit of his Liberty, for the Heart of Frederick-Augustus was by Fate designed never to be free from Passion. A young Beauty come from the furthermost part of the North was capable of perplexing it again, and inflamed it more vehemently than it had ever been before. This was Aurora Countess of Koningsmark, who to an eminent Birth joined the most exquisite parts and all the bodily Graces imaginable. Her size was moderate, and her Shape free and easy. An unparallel'd Delicacy and Regularity were seen through the Features of her Face. Her Teeth were so nicely placed and of so beautiful a Colour, that they could scarce be distinguished from a Row of Pearls. Her Eyes were black, bright, full of Fire and Tenderness. Her Hair, that was of the same Colour set off most exquisitely her beautiful Complexion, where an exceeding fine Carnation was seen sparkling. Her Neck, Breast, Arms and Hands were of a Whiteness, whose parallel was never seen. In a word, Nature seemed to have exhausted all her Charms in this Lady's Favour. To all these uncommon bodily perfections she joined as uncommon Faculties of the Mind, she had an engaging Address, her Jests were diverting, her Banters pleasant, she had lucky Sallies, a bright and lively knack either in describing the Character of, or ridiculing a Person; uncommon Ideas expressed in an uncommon manner; was incomparably gallant; no Instance of Generosity or Disinterestedness could be produced equal to her; she possessed a benevolent Mind, also ready to serve, and never thought herself too much troubled; no Animosity, no Spleen could ever take place in her Heart; she forgave and forgot all Offences; was humble, modest, and no way prepossessed in Favour of her extraordinary Merits. She spoke the French, Italian and German Languages as well as she did the Swedish; was not even ignorant of the Latin Tongue, and had a fortunate knack at Poetry; she loved Musick, publick Shews, Grandeur and Diversions; delineated exquisitely, was well acquainted with History, no less with Geography, and understood all the Fables and Fictions of antient Writers; in short, she was Mistress of that which may properly be called polite Literature. The World, I presume, will be no longer surprised, that she captivated the Heart of Frederick-Augustus. This amorous Prince conceived instantly a great passion for her, for when his inconstant Disposition induced him to forsake her, he never lost the Regard he had at first expressed; and she was the only one of all his Mistresses, for whom he seemed to have always retained a great Esteem.

A LOST FORTUNE

The young Countess of Koningsmark had quitted
Sweden with her two Sisters the Countesses of Lowenhaupt and of Steinbock. They were come into Germany
to take possession of an Estate left them by an only
Brother, who died some Months before at Hannover.
This Nobleman had deposited considerable Sums of
Money into the Hands of the Lastrops Merchants at
Hamburgh. As the Count's Treasure had been privately
carried away soon after his Death, his Sisters could produce no other proofs of this Depositum, than the frequent
mention their Brother had made of it both by Words
and Letters; and as soon, as they heard of his Death they
demanded their Funds. The Lastrops informed, that they
had not the Receipt, which they had given the deceased
Count, denied their possession of any other Effects,
belonging to him, but Diamonds to the Value of Forty
Thousand Dollars. They offered to remit these to the
Countesses, provided they would prove the Death of the
Count, and that he had not signed any Will before his
Death. One of their Clerks betrayed them, and told the
Countesses that the Lastrops had Four Hundred Thou-
sand Dollars, the property of the deceased Count of
Koningsmark. The three Sisters applied to the Magis-
trates of Hamburg, but the Reputation of Messieurs
Lastrops, well known to every Member of the Senate,
was far prevalent above the just Cause. The Countesses,
not daring to address themselves for certain good

H   113

Reasons to the Directors of the Circle of Lower Saxony, went directly to Dresden to implore the Protection of the young Elector. They had been presented with Letters of Recommendation by the King and Queen of Denmark to the Mother-Electress. This Princess gave them as kind a Reception as can be imagined. She was easily acquainted with the Merit of the three Sisters, but perceived that Aurora, who was the youngest deserved the Preference; and both she and the young Electress entered into an inviolable and most affectionate Friendship with that Lady. The Elector was at the Fair of Leipzig when the three Sisters arrived at Dresden. At his Return he made some stay to divert himself with the Chase at Meissen, and consequently the Princesses could not make their Complaints to him till a Month after their Arrival. When he was returned to Dresden the Mother-Electress presented them to her Son. 'Behold, my Son, '(said she) I present to you three Sisters of the House of 'Koningsmark, who are come to implore your Protec-'tion; of which both their Merit and Birth render them 'deserving. I join with them in intreating you not to 'neglect any thing, that may in the least contribute to 'their Satisfaction.'

The Elector was really amazed at the Beauty of the three Countesses; but his Eyes were instantly fixed upon Aurora. He made his first Address to her, and she for that Reason spoke for her Sisters. 'Your Electoral High-

'ness (says she) see three Sisters of the Count of Konings-
'mark, whom you have honoured with your kindnesses,
'and Company in some part of your Travels. We are
'come, Great Sir, to implore your Assistance, in pro-
'curing us Justice against some Merchants at Hamburgh,
'who undertake to deprive us of the Funds, which our
'unfortunate Brother has intrusted them with. Those
'that approach you are sensible of your great Munificence,
'the nature of a Refusal is utterly unknown to you: What
'may not we hope for then, we, who are come from the
'furthermost part of the Universe to crave your Aid?'
'You may be persuaded, Mademoiselle, (answered the
'Elector) that I shall see your Case proceeded with
'according to strict Justice; and if I am so unfortunate as
'not to succeed in my Undertaking, I shall resent any
'Injury the Senate of Hamburgh will dare to do you. In
'the meanwhile I beg you would be pleased with your
'Sisters to reside in my Court. I shall give proper Orders,
'that you may be served according to your Merits, and
'by my own Example shall teach my Courtiers how to
'respect you.'

The young Electress's sudden Entrance into the
Room made an End of that particular Conversation, the
Elector made some polite Addresses to the Ladies of
Lowenhaupt and Steinbock, and after that they conversed
about general Matters. Every one admired the exquisite
Wit Aurora seemed to possess: She could have no

AN INFLAMMABLE HEART

Sounds round about her, but what were caused by the Courtiers' Praises of her. She heard and received them with so noble a Modesty, that she seemed not even to hear them. In regard to the Elector he was so affected with her Beauty and the modest Air, which he had observed as a Concomitant of all her Actions, that from that moment he conceived a great Passion and an extraordinary Esteem for her.

His Impatience for an Opportunity of expressing his Love was extream. The next day he paid a Visit to the Countesses but could find no method of procuring a private Conversation with Aurora, the Countesses of Lowenhaupt and Steinbock being always present. His Eyes could not resist his great Desire to express himself, and Aurora soon perceived the Effect her Person had upon the Heart of Frederick-Augustus. The Countesses of Lowenhaupt and Steinbock observed it not less than she, and bantered their Sister on that Account, after the Elector was retired. 'We are compared to the three 'Graces (said jestingly the Countess of Steinbock) nor is 'that Comparison altogether unjust. It is however not 'the Prize of Beauty we are in search of, and the Paris 'that decides it, ought at least to wait until we desire him 'to give his Opinion of us.' Aurora blushed at her Sister's Railleries; she looked at her and said not a Word. 'You 'blush, dear Sister, (replied in the same manner the Lady 'Steinbock) you seem more humble than Venus, in not

'triumphing at your Conquest and our Abasement. But
'when you become a little more proud of it, I doubt
'whether my Sister Lowenhaupt and I shall not be as
'much perplexed at it, as were formerly the two God-
'desses.'—'As to that (answered the Countess of Lowen-
'haupt) I assure you, dear Sister, that I shall never be in
'Competition with you for Beauty, and if a Paris was to
'present me with the Prize, as your Superior, I should
'have but an ill Opinion of his Taste and Judgment.'—
'I beg, Sisters, (replied the young Lady Koningsmark)
'you would desist speaking thus allegorically. What have
'I done, that you should thus insult me? Of what Paris
'do you speak, and what Conquest can I boast of?'—
'How! (said Lady Lowenhaupt) is it not sufficient that
'we give way to you without Jealousy, do you pretend
'further to oblige us to name the Person, who gives you
'so notorious a Preference before us? By no means,
'Sister, our Kindness shall not extend to that degree; we
'cannot name, without praising him, and we are seldom
'eager in praising those that abase us.'—'I assure you
'(answered the Young Lady Koningsmark) I shall be not
'a little displeased, and forgetting the Deference I owe
'you, as my eldest Sisters, I shall impose your Silence.'—
'If you are displeased at our Discourse, dear Sister,
'(replied Lady Steinbock) you will undoubtedly silence
'us; But you cannot hinder us from thinking of what
'you have observed no less, than we, I mean, the Prefer-

'ence the Elector has been pleas'd to give you in re-
'gard to us.'—'I know not in what you have been capable
'of observing it, (answered Lady Koningsmark) for he
'seemed to give us all an equally gallant Reception.'—'I
'own he did, (replied Lady Lowenhaupt) but did he give
'us all an equally respectful Look?'—'You are more
'capable of making Observations than I, (answered Lady
'Koningsmark, with a serious Air, by which she shewed
'her Dislike of Conversations of that kind) and as you
'are both married, and your Husbands have been Lovers,
'I suppose you have been joined together by the Lan-
'guage of the Eyes. I, who have never yet been
'enamour'd, cannot comprehend, that I am loved, if I am
'not told so by the enamoured Person.'

Some Persons of Quality, that came to visit the Countesses made an end of the Discourse. They went in the
Evening to the Mother-Electress's Court; the Elector
came thither, and after having spoke some Words to the
Electresses he went to Mademoiselle of Koningsmark's
Seat, and giving himself over to the Violence of his
Passion; 'I know not, Madam, (said he) whether it will
'not be offensive to tell you, that your Merit has so affected
'me, that I can no longer live, but for you, and shall be
'the most unhappy of all Mankind, if my Respect, En-
'deavours, and Homage prove disagreeable to you.'—'I
'pleased myself in coming hither, (answered she) with the
'Hopes of having nothing to boast of but Your Electoral

CONFUSION AND PERPLEXITY

'Highness's Generosity; and never expected, that your 'Kindnesses should make me blush. I humbly beg there-'fore, that you would abstain from Discourses of that 'Kind, which can only lessen my Gratitude and the 'Great Esteem I had conceived for your Person.' After this she called her Sister, the Lady Lowenhaupt, who was not far from her. 'The Elector is asking me some 'Questions (said she) relating to the Court of Sweden, to 'which you are more capable to returning Answers, than 'I.' The Confusion and Perplexity of the Elector was such as cannot be imagined. In the mean while, thinking himself capable to conceal it, he propos'd some Questions to Lady Lowenhaupt before he retired from thence.

When he was alone in his Chamber with his Favourite, Beichling, he could not help saying, 'That if ever any 'Person's Condition was deplorable, he was well assured, 'his was. I adore, (said he) an ungrateful Beauty, who 'hates, and perhaps despises me; and believe, I shall 'never cease loving her.' Mr. Beichling perceived his Master's extream Passion, assured him, that his Fears were groundless, and addressing him with the Freedom he had himself acquired: 'Must you, Sir, (said he) because 'a Lady of Quality complies not with your first Desires, 'instantly begin to despair? By no means, Sir, Made-'moiselle of Koningsmark, does not at all deserve your 'Blame; her Answer to you was such, as well became a 'Lady of her Birth. It was the only Method of inducing

'you to join Esteem to your Love. What would you have
'said, if she had surrender'd herself to you at your first
'Address? you would have despis'd, and perhaps no
'longer lov'd her.'—'No, (cried the Elector) I should have
'loved her more, if such a Thing was practicable. But
'endeavour not to justify a cruel Woman; invent for me
'some means of convincing her of my Love.'

After this the Master and the Confidant consulted
together, and the Result of their Conference was, that the
Elector should write to Mademoiselle of Koningsmark,
and Mr. Beichling should carry the Billet. The Project
was executed the next Day. Mr. Beichling went to the
Countesses at a Time, when he knew, that Persons of
the greatest Distinction at Court were there. As his
Favour with his Master procured him a Passage every-
where, he found it an easy matter to place himself near
the Countess of Koningsmark. He conversed with her
for a considerable time about several indifferent Things,
and insensibly fell into a Discourse concerning Poetry.
I mentioned before that she delighted in that Art, and
compos'd Verses herself. Mr. Beichling happening to be
very expert in that respect, as well as she, repeated her
an Ode of his own Composition; and when he saw her
pleased with and attentive to them, he told her, that he
was utterly impatient to shew her a Copy of Verses he
had made on the Elector's Amours with Mademoiselle
Kessel; but that he could not shew them except they

Aurora, Countess of Koningsmark

Engraving by Schenk

were together in some private place. She rose directly and retired with him to the Chamfretting of a Window. Having actually repeated some Verses he had made on that Subject, he took Occasion to mention the Elector's Passion, and gave her so lively and moving a Description of it, that Mademoiselle Koningsmark seemed to be moved at it. Mr. Beichling made use of this happy Minute to present her the Billet. She took it and having put it into her Pocket, told him he might wait for an Answer. She then returned to the Company, but a little while afterwards went to her own Chamber, and there read the Elector's Billet; the Contents of which were these:

MADAM,

If you was in the least acquainted with my Despair, I am well assured that whatever your Aversion be to me, the natural Benevolence of your Heart would not suffer you to refuse me your Pity. Be persuaded, Madam, that no Person's Affliction can be equal to mine, in daring to declare that I adore you. Permit me to expiate the Crime I have committed at your Feet; and since you desire to hasten my Death, refuse me not the Comfort of hearing my sentence pronounced by your Mouth. The Condition I am in suffers me not to give you any further Account of it, believe Beichling's Words; he is my second Self; he can truly tell you, that my Life and Death are in Your Hands.

Mademoiselle of Koningsmark found herself very much moved after the perusal of this Letter; she knew not what method to take, whether to be pliable or severe would more become her; that fatal Ascendant, which drew her away against her Consent, occasioned her to make the following Answer:

SIR,

It is so little becoming a private Person, to give their Judgment concerning Sovereigns, that I know not what Means to take in Regard to Your Electoral Highness. We cannot easily condemn the Persons we esteem, much less can we desire to hasten the End of their Lives. Judge, Sir, whether I am capable of acting thus by you, I, who join to my Esteem, a grateful Acknowledgment and due Respect.

Having finished this Billet she returned to Mr. Beich-ling, and giving it to him, 'Here (said she) are the Verses 'you desired to see. I beg you would shew 'em to no 'other Person.' She had no sooner done this, than numberless Thoughts perplexed her. The Company being inconvenient to her, she feigned Sickness, retired to her Chamber, and went to Bed, where, having reflected upon what she had done she blamed herself for it, as if it had been a Crime. 'I am overcome, I am conquer'd by an 'Inclination that had drawn me away to do a Thing 'against my own Consent (cried she) all my Resolutions 'are vain and useless. I have not been capable of refusing 'a Billet sent to me, nor of resisting my Desire to answer 'it; can I ever prevail upon myself to conceal my Passion? 'I must retire from this Place, and return into Sweden;

SELF-TORMENTING

'and if my Sisters persist in refusing me that Satis-
'faction, to be informed of my Reason, I can do no
'otherwise than acquaint them with it.' She retained
this Resolution, and passed the rest of the Day and
Night in resisting a Passion, of which she was no
longer Mistress.

Whilst she was thus afflicting herself the Elector
enjoy'd no greater Tranquility. He was not at all pleased
with the Lady Koningsmark's Billet; the Word Respect
which ended it, perfectly shock'd him. 'It was that
'Respect, (said he to Beichling) which she thinks due to
'my Rank, that caused her to receive my Letter, and has
'procured me this cold and disagreeable Answer.' Some
Minutes afterwards he took the Billet and kiss'd it
tenderly, because it was writ by the Countess of Koning-
mark's Hand. At length, after having for a long time
tormented himself, Beichling prevailed upon him to rest
satisfied till the next Day and to go himself and learn
how Fortune designed to favour him.

The next Day the Lady Koningsmark knowing that
her Sisters were risen, desired them by a Servant to pass
the Morning in her Bed-Chamber; she told them that
the Air of Dresden was so little agreeable to her Constitution, that she could not help begging they would
depart instantly; she moreover insisted upon it, because
she thought their Presence at the Saxon Court would be
useless, since the Elector could be of no further Assis-

tance to them, than by interceding with the Emperor to oblige the Senate of Hamburgh to do them Justice in regard to the Treachery of the Lastrops. The Countesses of Lowenhaupt and Steinbock were much surprised at their Sister's unexpected Request; they told her, that they could not be persuaded, that the Preservation of her Health was the Motive, that induced her to remove from Dresden, since she had never before been indispos'd there; and pressed her to confess the real Reason of so precipitate a Resolution. 'Is it not rather, dear Sister, '(said Lady Steinbock) what my Sister and I truly con-'jectur'd some time ago, I mean that you are appre-'hensive of the Elector's Presence?' The young Countess would willingly have made a Reply; she was very desirous of confessing sincerely the State of her Heart; but a Torrent of Tears interrupted her Voice, and her manifest Grief sufficiently explained her Mind. Her Sisters shewed a sincere Concern for her Trouble; they renewed their Intreaties, and begg'd of her to acquaint them with the Cause of her Grief. 'Force me not (said she) 'to tell you a Thing which I have not Strength, tho' Will 'enough to declare. Consider only that Prudence will not 'permit a Person of my Age, and one, that is at her own 'Disposal, to remain exposed at the Head of this Court.' The Countess of Steinbock sensibly touch'd with her Sister's Misery, told her that she was very ready to depart from thence instantly; and begg'd she would

AN OBLIGING COURTIER

Conceal her Grief. 'Let us, if possible, deserve the same 'Esteem, that has been hitherto shewn us by the Saxons.' The Countess of Lowenhaupt spoke not a Word. Her Heart was at no more Ease, than that of her Sister Mademoiselle Koningsmark; the Thought of departing from the Saxon Court entirely shocked her. She was entered into inviolable Engagements with the Prince of Furstemberg, who was next to the Elector the most amiable Gentleman at Court. He was tall, graceful, his Deportment was extreamly noble, no one exceeded him in Gallantry and Politeness; his Taste was exquisite, his Expressions fine, and he had the happy Art of persuading whomsoever he pleased: He would certainly have been an accomplished Gentleman, had Sincerity accompanied his bodily Graces, and had he been more scrupulous in his Amours. He had no sooner seen the three Countesses make their Appearance, than he was enamoured with Mademoiselle Koningsmark; but his penetrating Genius soon discovered that the Elector's Heart was captivated by that Lady's Charms. He was too obliging a Courtier to become his Master's Rival; Love gave way to Reason; and as he was not inclined to any other Lady at Court, he was enamoured with the Countess of Lowenhaupt. She was well acquainted with his Merit, and they were soon united by a strict Alliance. Their amorous Intrigues were just begun, when the young Lady Koningsmark intended to return into Sweden. The Countess was far from consenting to her Sisters' Demands, though she promised them to be at any time ready for Departure; but she resolved not only upon staying, but even upon persuading them to stay. Mademoiselle Koningsmark was more satisfied, when her Sisters promised to conduct her into Sweden. She rose and was the remaining part of the Day in her Deshabille, as if she had been indisposed. The Heaviness that appeared in her Eyes, gave her a weak Air, which did not in the least diminish her Charms. The Countesses received the whole Day the usual Visits of the most polite Persons of the Court. The Elector went in the Evening to see them; at his Entrance the Countess of Koningsmark retired to write a Letter. He was apprehensive that she designed to avoid him, and his Heart was in great Uneasiness about it; he was scarce capable of making his Addresses to the Ladies. The Countess of Lowenhaupt soon knew the State of Augustus's Heart; she drew near to his Person, and in a low Tone addressed him, saying, 'You are at present shunn'd, Great Sir, but 'you would not be thus avoided was you an Object of 'Hatred.' These few Words supplied the Elector with Hope. 'How, Madam, (answered he) have you been informed of the Perplexities I am under?'—'Your Grief 'is utterly unnecessary, Sir, (replied she) you are beloved, 'confide in me; and I shall be serviceable to you with 'the utmost of my Power.' Mademoiselle Koningsmark appeared in the Room, as soon as her Sister had ended these Words; her presence and Lady Lowenhaupt's last Words gave the Elector so great a Joy, that all the Courtiers were instantly sensible of it. The young Countess, ignorant of that Prince's Arrival, seemed to be at a Loss, whether she should see him or not; She coloured and paid him all due Respects, without daring to look at him. 'You appear so beautiful, Madam, (said 'the Elector when he embraced her) that I cannot believe 'I had any just Cause to fear your Indisposition, at the 'News of which I was greatly troubled. I now imagine 'you designed to make a Trial of your Friends, by this 'pretended Distemper. Can I, if my Conjecture proves 'true, be so fortunate, as to be one of that number? I dare 'undertake to say, that I am deserving of such a Prefer- 'ment, by the Misery I have been in since the first Report 'of your Sickness.'—'I am too sensible, Sir, (replied the 'Lady) of my Duty to your Highness, to presume to place 'you among my Friends, the Person, whom I ought to 'respect as my great Sovereign, and reverence as the sole 'Protector of my Family. I am nevertheless incapable of 'Ingratitude for your Electoral Highness's Pleasure to be 'concerned for my Indisposition.'

The Courtiers knowing the Elector's Delight in private Entertainments with the Ladies and more particularly those, whom he was enamoured with, retired most respectfully. The Prince of Furstemberg pleased himself with Lady Lowenhaupt's Company, and Chan-

celor Beichling discoursed with the Countess of Steinbock, about their Differences with the Lastrops.

The two Lovers in the full Enjoyment of the Liberty
of discovering the true Sentiments of their Hearts to each
other, made an advantageous Use of it. The Elector's
Expressions were so tenderly persuasive, that the Countess of Koningsmark experienced the Impossibility of
retaining the Resolution she took before to conceal her
tender Affection for him. They mentioned numberless
pleasant Things, that were equally Agreeable to both,
and at last promised a constant Love to each other. The
enamoured Lady required her Lover to acquaint no-body
with their future Correspondence, and especially to hide
it from the Countess of Steinbock, whose rigorous Virtue
she was very much in fear of. The Elector told her, what
he had heard the Lady Lowenhaupt say, and they resolved
to repose all their Confidence in her. At last they parted
extreamly satisfied with so fair an Opportunity of
conversing together.

Before the Elector retired he spoke to the Countess of
Lowenhaupt; informed her of the great Success he had
met with in his new Amour, and begg'd she would
endeavour to promote his Interest in that respect, and
prevail upon Lady Koningsmark to consent to his pro-
fessing a publick Adoration of her. She made fresh
Assurances of her Integrity in serving him, and he
retired with all the Satisfaction imaginable.

A READY APPROBATION

The Countess of Lowenhaupt laboured so effectually for the Elector, that she removed all her Sister Konings-mark's Doubts and Fears. She informed the Elector of the Success of her Negotiation, and in a private Meeting between them assured him of the Infallibility of his Conquest; But one Objection was still remaining to perplex them, which was, that he could not see his beloved Lady without the knowledge of Lady Steinbock. The Elector, who never wanted Expedients in his amorous Intrigues, told her, that she must persuade her Sisters to retire with her to Mauritzbourg, that he could there procure an Apartment for the Lady Koningsmark, in which they could converse together without any knowledge of the Countess of Steinbock.

The Confident-Lady gave a ready Approbation of the Project, she proposed it to her enamoured Sister, who directly made some Objections to it, but at last submitted to her Sister's Desire and the Elector's Intreaties, who came to visit them at the same time, that they were consulting about the Journey to Mauritzbourg. The Elector never appeared more satisfied, than at having obtained the Lady's Consent to depart from thence; and in the same Conversation they promised each other upon Oath an everlasting Affection, and the Pleasure Mademoiselle Koningsmark's Company gave him was by reason of her charming Addresses so great, that, whilst he was with her, he employed all his Time in renewing all the Protestations of a most tender Passion. They at last quitted the Room, and the Lady Koningsmark took an affectionate Leave of her Lover, and left him the most enamoured Person on Earth.

The Countess of Steinbock was highly displeased at the Promise her Sister had made to depart for Mauritzbourg. She represented to them the Injury such a Proceeding, which the Electresses were undoubtedly averse to, would do them in regard to their Friendship with those Princesses. 'Whilst I thought (said she to the 'Countess of Koningsmark) that you received the Elec-'tor's Passion for you with a Coldness, that becomes your 'Birth and Virtue, I never made mention of it in your 'Presence; I acquiesced in your Prudence: but now am 'sorry to find that you forget the Austerity you at first 'proposed to yourself; I think, dear Sister, my Duty 'obliges me to advise you of the Precipice you are going 'into. Your Inclinations are certainly at free liberty. I 'pretend to no Authority over you, but am persuaded 'that your Virtue guides your Actions, and let me conjure 'you never to resist its Injunctions. Consider even the 'Obligations you are under to youself, and consider that 'you are going to sustain the irreparable Loss of the 'Reputation you have hitherto so justly acquired. Let 'your former Courage and Vigour appear, and let us, 'dear Sister, depart from hence for Sweden; follow me, 'and fear not to undertake too austere and hard a Task;

'for however difficult it may at first appear, you will soon 'afterwards find the Effects of it far more convenient than 'the Misfortunes Amours are constantly subject to.'

The Countess of Koningsmark was instantly overwhelmed with Tears, and made no Reply to her Sister, but embraced her tenderly, and went to shut herself up in her Chamber; the Lady Lowenhaupt follow'd her thither, and, like a dangerous Confident, found it an easy matter to withstand and surmount all those Emotions of Virtue, which the Lady Steinbock had but just before rais'd in her. She represented the Elector submissive, respectful and amorous, the Despair he would be in, was she to forsake him, and the just Cause he would have to complain, if, after their Promise to go to Mauritzbourg, they were not to perform it. 'It is a Civility, (said she) due 'from us for the Instances of Generosity we have already 'experienced in him, My Sister, the Lady Steinbock, is 'undoubtedly unwilling to do it, but I shall do my utmost 'Endeavours to obtain her Consent.' Mademoiselle Koningsmark, who had lost all Command over her Passion, was fully overcome by the irresistible Power of Love, made but few and very weak Objections to her Sister's Arguments, and at last consented to depart for Mauritzbourg.

The Countess of Steinbock was highly afflicted, when she saw her Sisters persevere in their fatal Resolution, and finding herself incapable of dissuading them from it, pretended Sickness, to excuse her of the Journey. Before the Elector quitted Dresden, he sent the Lady Koningsmark an extraordinary rich Dress, with a Trimming of the choicest Jewels. His munificent Disposition was not altogether forgetful of the Countesses of Lowenhaupt and Steinbock; the Presents he sent them were very splendid, though far inferior to those designed for their sister, Mademoiselle Koningsmark.

The Countess of Lowenhaupt, being accompanied by the most beautiful Ladies of the Court, dressed as Amazones, departed a little while after the Elector, who diverted them in an extraordinary manner. They had no sooner made their Entrance into the Forest belonging to Mauritzbourg, than they saw a Palace most magnificently built. The Coach stopp'd at this Palace, that they might have Leisure to take a particular View of the Magnificence of this Edifice, and whilst they were viewing it, they saw the Gate open on a sudden, where Diana presented herself, surrounded by her Nymphs. She addressed herself to Mademoiselle Koningsmark, and, alluding to the name of Aurora, invited her, as if she had really been that Goddess, to enter the Palace, there to receive the Homages of the Wooden Deities.

The Ladies stepp'd out of their Chariots, and Diana conducted them into a large Hall, adorned with several Pictures, that represented that Goddess's chief Actions. Tender Endymion and rash Acteon's Death were painted there with all the Art a Workman could be capable of. Diana enjoined her Nymphs to divert Aurora and all her Attendants. Soon afterwards the inlaid Floor open'd, and on a sudden a Table covered with the most delicious Sweetmeats was seen to rise from out of the very Earth. The Ladies placed themselves, and instantly heard the Sound of Fifes, Hautbois, and other musical Instruments. At the same time the God Pan made his Appearance, followed by the Gods of Fields and Woods; these were represented by the Elector and the most graceful Persons of his Court. Diana, whose Part the Lady Beichling acted, invited Pan to sit down by the beautiful Aurora. The God entertained her with the most delightful Discourses, insisted pressingly upon being serviceable to her, endeavoured carefully to please, and convince her of his Passion. They often told each other reciprocally, of the amiable Charms they possessed, of their mutual Affection, and promis'd an endless Continuance of the same.

The Repast being at last ended, they heard the Horns blow and Hounds crying as if some Huntsmen were near. The Ladies ran in great Surprize to the Window, and saw a Stag run by to escape the Pursuits of the Huntsmen; they were desirous of following the Chase, and had no soon expressed their Desire, than they saw some Horses ready, with open Chaises for the Reception of those that were unwilling to mount on Horseback.

THE GRAND SIGNOR

The Stag being at last surrounded by the Huntsmen was obliged to throw himself into a Pond near the Castle of Mauritzbourg; the Hounds pursued him, and the Ladies being arrived at the Waterside found Boats ready for their Reception, that carried them to an Island in the middle of the Pond. They arrived here at the Death of the Stag, and saw the Dogs rewarded immediately.

At the further end of the Island they saw a magnificent Tent built after the Turkish manner. They enter'd it and found, that all the Furniture was no less Turkish, than the structure of the Tent. Whilst they were in Admiration of the Beauty of this Place, they saw twenty-four young Turks richly dress'd, who presented them with all kinds of Refreshments in large Silver Dishes. Few Moments afterwards they saw all the Officers of the Grand Seraglio appear from another Tent; in the midst of these was the Grand Signor, adorned with the most pretious Stones: This was the Elector, who came to join the Ladies, and having thrown a richly embroider'd Handkerchief at Mademoiselle Koningsmark sat down by her upon a Sopha. The Ladies were presented with delicious Cakes, and as soon as they were sat down, several Dancers came in, who by their Leaps, Postures and Turkish Dances diverted them for some time. At last the Company rose, and the Elector handed the Lady Koningsmark into his Boat. The Elector, the Lady Lowenhaupt and the Prince

A SPLENDID APARTMENT

of Furstemberg followed her, the other Ladies took their respective Gentlemen into their Boats. In this manner they diverted themselves for some time upon the Water, entertained with the harmonious Sound of a Concert of Musick. The Company being all landed the Elector stepp'd into an open Chaise with the Lady Koningsmark, surrounded by Janizaries and the great Officers of the Seraglio. The Ladies followed in several Chaises, and thus they arrived at length at the Palace of Mauritzbourg. The Elector conducted Mademoiselle Koningsmark into the Apartment designed for her Use, which was furnished in an uncommon rich manner. The Bed was in particular surprizingly Splendid, whose Furniture was of yellow Damask embroider'd with Silver. It was adorned with Representations of the Amours of Aurora and Tithon in several Compartments. Pictures of Amours supported the Curtains in Festoons, and seem'd to strew Poppies, Roses, and Wind-Flowers upon that incomparably beautiful Bed. 'This is the Place, Madam, (said the gallant Elector) in which you are truly Sovereign, and 'in which a great Lord, as I was, now becomes your 'Slave.'—'Sir (replied Mademoiselle Koningsmark) what-'ever Condition you present yourself in, you shall be 'ever dear to my Eyes.' The Elector kiss'd her Hand, and left her alone to change her Dress, and himself to put on another Habit. Mademoiselle Koningsmark dress'd her-self in that Habit, which the Elector had given her, and

never did her Person seem more beautiful than it did
then. The Elector on the other hand, seemed by his
Apparel, which was enriched with Diamonds and Pearls,
to have taken the Pains of a Person, whose sole Endeavour
is to please. When he was informed that Mademoiselle
Koningsmark was dress'd, he went to her and was
extreamly pleased at her graceful Appearance. He conducted her to the Theatre, where Psyche and all her
Charms were display'd.

The Comedy was no sooner ended, than Supper was
ready, and Mademoiselle Koningsmark when she sate
down to Table found upon her Napkin a Knot of Diamonds, Rubies, Emeralds, and Pearls, by which she
perceived that she was the Queen of the Ball that was to
follow the Supper. She did effectually open it with the
Elector, and the amorous Couple drew upon themselves
the Regard and Admiration of every Spectator; every one
was surprized with Wonder and Delight at the Sight of
them; all the Ladies envied her Happiness in the Enjoyment of so amiable a Lover, as the Elector, and the
Gentlemen wished they were in Possession of a Mistress
equal to Mademoiselle Koningsmark. This great Day
Ended at length to the entire Satisfaction of both the
Lovers, and they unexpectedly disappeared from the
Ball-Room, but no one of the Company seemed to
observe their Absence, since they knew very well, that
they desired to be alone. The Elector enjoy'd the most

alluring Pleasures with Lady Koningsmark, who gave him the most essential Tokens of her Tenderness.

This great Feast was during the space of a Fortnight, succeeded by Games and Diversions of all kinds. Dancing was more particularly practis'd, and Mademoiselle Koningsmark's Appearance was always amazing, for her Person was ever distinguishing among any of the rest.

Whilst nothing but Pleasure was the Employment of the Noble Company of Mauritzbourg, the Lady Steinbock, highly displeased at her Sister's Conduct, resolved to depart from Dresden. She pretended to have received Orders from her Spouse to return into Sweden, but the Electresses easily perceiv'd the real motive of her Departure, and thought her for that Reason more deserving of their Esteem. She writ a Letter to the Elector, in which, without making the least mention of her Sisters, she returned him hearty Thanks for the Civilities she had received from his Hands.

This Prince, not in the least dubious, but that Lady Steinbock's so sudden Departure would cause great Grief in Mademoiselle Koningsmark, concealed it from her, and taking Horse instantly, ran to Dresden, in order, if possible, to dissuade the Countess of Steinbock from the performance of her Resolution; but his Precaution was unnecessary, for he found that she was gone that same Morning, which so mortified him that he forgot to visit the Electresses. These Princesses were informed, that he had been at Dresden, and extreamly grieved at his indifferent Behaviour towards them. The young Electress cried bitterly, and the Mother-Electress protested, that she would no longer be exposed to such Affronts, but retire to the Castle of Lichtenberg, which had been settled upon her as a Dowry. At the same time she gave immediate Orders to prepare her Equipages.

Mademoiselle Koningsmark's Grief at the Lady Steinbock's Departure was excessive; but it was greatly increased, when she heard of the Injury the Elector had done to the two Princesses. She reproached him severely for his rude Deportment, and told him, that the greatest proof she expected of his Love would be a Continuation of all the Regard he had formerly had for the Electress, and of which that Princess's Virtues rendered her so deserving; she even threatened that if he acted otherwise, she would directly retire from his Country; and to alleviate the Electress's Trouble, she desired he would return to Dresden, saying that she would not occasion that Princess of the Pleasure of seeing him. The Electress, informed of these Proceedings, was charmed at them, and renew'd her Esteem for the Lady Koningsmark. This Favourite has certainly always made the most surprizing Returns for that Esteem, she has always used the Electress with all the Respect and Deference imaginable, and was so far from dissuading the Elector from the Sight of that Princess, that she frequently told him, that the Loss his Spouse sustained of his Heart was so great, and that it could not but so sensibly affect her, that it was impossible to him sufficiently to comfort her in her Distress, or to use her in too obliging a manner.

The Electress hearing of Mademoiselle Koningsmark's generous Concern for her, saw the Favour she was in without Jealousy. 'I am pleased (said she sometimes) 'with having a Rival, since she is a Person of great 'Merit.' The Mother-Electress, whose rigorous Virtue always supported in her an Enmity against all kinds of Gallantry, could not disapprove of her Son's Passion for so amiable a Person. The two Electresses saw and entertained her with great Familiarity. The Courtiers had a Respect for her, whose sole Foundation was a great Esteem: Even the Ladies could not think her an Object of Hatred. Her Majesty, Sweetness of Temper, and uncommon Politeness never forsook her; her Favour was not disagreeable to any one, and she prevented the approaching Calamities of the Unfortunate. Her Memory is still held in Veneration by all those that knew her Merits.

The Elector being returned from Mauritzbourg to Dresden order'd a House to be prepared for Mademoiselle Koningsmark; lodg'd her there, and furnish'd it very richly. A little while afterwards he prevailed upon the Canonesses of Quedlinburg, all Princesses or Countesses, to chuse her Abbess of the Chapter. By this Pro-

motion she obtained the Title of Madame. The Elector
supped with her every Evening and gave her splendid
Treats, of which all the Court partook. Strangers came
from all parts of the World to Dresden, and returned in
full Admiration both of the enamour'd Elector and his
amiable Mistress.

In the mean while Madame Koningsmark's Happiness
was lessen'd by the Departure of the Countess of Lowenhaupt, who having for a long time resisted her Husband's
Orders, who desired her Return, was at last obliged to
depart. 'Now behold me in Solitude (said with a tender
'Air, Madame Koningsmark, addressing herself to the
'Elector) for your Sake I renounce all that is most dear to
'me. How unfortunate shall I be, if you forsake me!'—
'No, Madame, (cried the Elector) you need not fear that;
'I am totally yours for all my Life-time. Be assured
'thereof, and that those Perfections, that have long since
'charmed me, and can only be found in you, are sure
'Guards of my Fidelity. In you only can I find that
'excellent and charming Mind, which occasions my
'thinking myself in your Presence the most happy Mortal
'on Earth. Cease therefore to harbour a Suspicion, that
'afflicts and vexes me. In you, my dearest Countess, I
'adore not only the most perfect Beauty; but also that
'virtuous Soul, that exalted Mind, that benevolent Heart;
'and in short, all those great Qualities, that distinguish
'you so advantageously among all the Women, that I

'know, and which I cannot possibly find any-where else.'
—'How amiable are you, my dear Prince, (replied she) and
'how capable are you of removing the Fears of a Heart,
'that is only apprehensive because you are too fond of it!
'Preserve these Sentiments, they only affect my Happi-
'ness, my Joy. Yes, my Dear, for I can no longer give
'you any other Appellation, since Love banishes all
'Constraint, I prefer your Tenderness to your Grandeur
'and Sovereign Power. I find you much greater by your
'Sentiments, than your Rank. You are Master of my
'Person, my Heart and my Life.' Our two Lovers having
entertained each other with numberless more Discourses
of this kind, supped and remained together till the latter
part of the Night.

They made so good use of their Time, that nine
Months afterwards Madame Koningsmark was deliver'd
of a Son, who was the true Picture of his Father, whose
Air, Strength, Behaviour and Manner of thinking he
still possesses. The Birth of the Child rejoiced the
Elector extreamly. He was denominated Mauritz, (Mauri-
tius) in memory of the Victory, that had been gained over
his Mother at Mauritzbourg. He was afterwards honoured
with the Title of Count of Saxony. This is the same
Person, who by his Merit has acquired the Esteem of all
Frenchmen, for whose benefit he serves as Lieutenant-
General in a Regiment of Infantry.

The Elector did not leave his Mistress during the

Time of her Illness; he passed whole Days at the Bolster of her Bed, and as her Illness was at first extream, he incessantly conjured the Physicians to take care of her, and to employ all their Art for the preservation of her Health; but, notwithstanding all the Pains they took, Madame Koningsmark retained an almost continual Sweat, very disagreeable to the Sense of Smelling, and which not even the strongest Scent could exceed. This unfortunate Disease was instantly the Cause of an inexpressible Grief in the two Lovers, but it at last gave the Elector so great a Disgust, that by insensible degrees he avoided his formerly beloved Countess, till having entered into other Engagements, he entirely ceased to live with her as her Lover, but visited her daily, and always testified a very great Esteem for a Person, well deserving of it.

CHAPTER IX

Of the Elector of Saxony's *Behaviour at the Imperial Army in* Hungary, *his Return from thence to the Court of Vienna, his Passion for the* Countess d'Esterle, *her Answer, the Entertainment prepared for him at Court, his Success in his new Amour, an extraordinary Adventure at the Imperial Court by the Fallacies of a Roman Catholic Priest, the Interruption the* Count d'Esterle *gave the enamoured Couple by surprizing them in Bed together, and the Consequence of it, the Reception the Lovers met with from* Madame Koningsmark *at Dresden, the Mother-Electress's Displeasure at her Son's Passion for the* Countess d'Esterle, *and her Retirement to Lichtenberg.*

Few Months after the Birth of the young Prince the Court of Vienna made the Elector an Offer of the Command over the Imperial Army in Hungary. This valiant Prince, who begun to shake off those Chains that confined him to the Company of Madame Koningsmark, and whose Love of the Female Sex after all gave way to that of Glory, almost innate in him, readily accepted of the Emperor's Offer; he departed for the Army and behaved himself in a manner, that perfectly answer'd the great Opinion all Mankind had conceived of his Courage.

When the Campaign was ended, he went to pay his Respects to the Emperor, by whom he was received with all the distinguishing Civilities, due to a Person of his Rank. Vienna was the fatal Place, at which this glorious Conqueror of the Turks was again overcome by the

143

powerful Arms of Love, and the Countess d'Esterle was the fatal Person that occasioned the reiterated Loss of his Liberty. His Heart in full Conformity to his Eyes, caused him to fix them upon her as the most accomplished Person on Earth, and a Miracle of Nature. The first time he saw her was at a Ball given by the King of the Romans, Son of the Emperor. The Sight of so beautiful a Woman had so great an effect upon him, that notwithstanding the Boldness he was frequently blamed for, he seem'd speechless. He undertook to address her, but was in so great a Disorder, that he was at a loss for Words to express himself, all his Discourse was only a Confused number of Words, the Sense of which was unintelligible, nor would she have comprehended it had she had a less knowledge of the Language of the Eyes; for by his she perceived all the effects her Charms had produced in his Heart.

As the Countess d'Esterle did not pretend to any reserved Virtue, and desired nothing more than to hear an Expression of the Sentiments of his Heart, she retired to the Chamfretting of a Window. The Elector followed her thither, and she directly spoke to him of the Grandeur of the Entertainment; but he answered not a Word. She thought hereupon that he was indisposed, and presenting him with some Hungary-Water, 'Sir, (cried she) do you 'understand me?'—'Yes, Madam, (replied he giving a 'doleful Sign) I understand and see you very well, and 'am as sensible, as I ought to be of the Assistance you are

Countess d'Esterle

'desirous of giving me. But Hungary-Water is not
'capable of recovering me. You have other Remedies,
'vouchsafe, I beg of you, to make use of those, and suffer
'me to wait for my Cure from you, who are the only
'Cause of my Indisposition.'—'I am ignorant (answered
'laughing the beautiful Countess) of any Disease, I have
'been able to infect you with, for no contagious Dis-
'temper perplexes me. I am moreover but little expert in
'the Use of Remedies. Was I however but acquainted
'with your Distemper, I should with Pleasure employ
'the little Knowledge, I can boast of, to recover your
'Health, which cannot but be precious to all Europe.'—
'If all Europe neglects me, Madam, (said the Elector) and
'you will but condescend to have a Regard to my Con-
'cerns, I shall esteem myself the happiest of all Mankind.
'Yes, adorable Countess (continued he with a Transport
'that easily discovered his Passion) my Disease is no
'other, than the most lively and most tender Affection I
'have for you. Nothing can cure me of it; unless you
'afford some Comfort to the Pains I undergo. I ask my
'Life of you for no other Reason, but to devote it wholly
'to you, and to adore you as the most deserving Person
'of my Admiration in the Universe.'—'I promised before,
'Sir, (answered the Countess d'Esterle) to employ all the
'Remedies I have any knowledge of, to procure your
'Recovery. I am too exact in the performance of my
'Promises, and too faithful a Subject of his Imperial

K   145

'Majesty, not to return you a Health, which is certainly
'very precious to him. Enjoy therefore your wonted
'Tranquillity, and allow me sufficient time to consider
'upon what will be requisite for me to do.'

The Countess spoke so eagerly that the King of the
Romans, who came to accompany the Elector was at the
distance of some Steps, when she saw him. His sudden
Presence gave her not the least Disorder; for as if she
had been answering the Elector, 'I love Musick (said
'she) and more particularly Singing.' The King of the
Romans was persuaded, that the Subject of their Discourse was no other but this; he intreated the Elector to
go into an Apartment hard by, in which a grand Entertainment was prepar'd for Supper. The Table was in the
form of a Piece of Fortification; the Inside of it was
hollow, in the Form of a Bason of Water, in the middle
of which Zephyrus and Flora, to whom the Gods of
Love presented Flowers. The four Corners of the Room
were adorn'd with artificial Waterfalls of an agreeable
Smell, which gave a charming Prospect, with the Light
of a thousand Wax Candles upon branched Candlesticks
of Crystal. At one end of the Room was a Theatre, whose
Curtain presented Psyche in a Magnificent Palace, which
Cupid had caused to be built for her. Laughing, playing
and Diversions of all kinds surrounded her. Nothing ever
appeared more beautiful than did this young Princess:
She was in short such, as was capable of increasing the

A GRAND ENTERTAINMENT

Flame of Love itself. The King and Queen of the Romans, and the Elector of Saxony being seated, the Curtain was drawn, which discovered a magnificent Stage, representing the Heavens, where all the Gods were assembled. Jupiter presented the Council of the Deities with the Picture of the Elector of Saxony, and desired that a stop might be put to his Life, as Mortal, and he be received among the number of the Gods. The Gods gave an Universal Applause to Jupiter's Proposal, and afterwards by Dancing and Singing shew'd their Joy at the Resolution that had been taken. After Supper, whilst the Tables were removing, the Count approaching towards the Window saw an excellent Firework display'd. After this the Ball was open'd, and this grand Entertainment was not ended till the next Morning, after Sunrising. The Elector would have been exceedingly well satisfy'd with this Feast, had he been capable of finding means of continuing the Discourse he had begun with Madame d'Esterle, but she shunn'd his Addresses; for though she did not pretend to oblige any one to be a long while in pursuit of her, yet would she keep at a sufficient Distance to lay the Person under an Obligation, to whom she surrender'd herself.

Two Days passed in which the Elector could not see his beloved Lady. He met with her at the Apartment of the Queen of the Romans, but could not converse with her, because, as was before observed, she kept at a

Distance from him. At last the King of the Romans happened to come in and propose to the Queen and Elector to play at Cards. Madame d'Esterle was desired to make a Party, and was by Chance placed next to the Elector. The Prince was careful not to lose a moment, but using numberless short and gallant Expressions, in as low a Tone as possibly he could. He was obliged for that purpose to take Snuff, and frequently to make use of his Handkerchief to hide the motion of his Lips when he spoke to her. He did not look at her, being in Fear, that the Count d'Esterle, who, as Chamberlain in Waiting, stood behind the King's Chair of State, should perceive his Passion: but he ceased not however in that manner to tell her that he adored her, that all the Recompence he was desirous of was a Permission to serve her with a Deference due to the Gods, and that his Disinterestedness deserved some kind Return. Tho' she feigned not to understand, yet did she comprehend his Expressions very well. The Elector's Eagerness in speaking to her was such, that he did not at several times regard nor hear the Queen's Words when her Majesty spoke to him. The Countess was charmed with the Elector's Addresses, but made very few Answers, fearful of being observed by the Queen of the Romans and the Count d'Esterle. The few Words however, that she spoke, signified to him, that nothing should be wanting as to her part, if she could soon compleat his Felicity.

'READY TO DIE FOR IMPATIENCE'

The next Morning the Elector, who was desirous of seeing her persevere in her Resolution, writ to his Dear whatever Words his Heart inspired him with, as a Person enamoured to a great degree, and pleased with the Hope of not being despised. As a certain inexpressible Delicacy and Vivacity accompanied all his Thoughts, so were they expressed in Terms so choice, so natural, and so noble, that his Mind was no less enchanting than his Person. He was ready to die for Impatience for the happy Hour in which she would give him Leave to pay her a private Visit; he begg'd this Favour of her, and to render his Intreaties more effectual, enclosed in the Billet a pair of Ear-Rings to the Value of Forty Thousand Florins. The golden Shower had not a more seducing effect upon the Heart of Danaë, than the Ear-Rings had upon that of Madame d'Esterle. All the Arguments, that opposed her Inclination to surrender herself, instantly vanished, and to be deficient in her Acknowledgment to so generous a Prince, was in her Opinion the only Fault she could commit. She answered him in Terms that required no Explanation, and gave him Notice, that she should expect him at Eight o'Clock at Night.

The Elector waited upon her at the expected Hour. He found the Countess lying negligently upon a Couch of Gold Brocade, in an Apartment where nothing was seen but Gold, Paintings, and rich Brocades; it seemed to be the Dwelling-place of the Mother of Cupid. Madame d'Esterle was charming. Her Hair, that was of the most lively Colour, that ever was seen, fell in Buckle upon her shoulders, and was tied up with green Ribbons. Her Dress was of Rosy-Colour mixed with Silver, set off with Flowers that truly imitated natural ones. A rich Lace added to the natural Beauty of her Neck and Breast; her red and white Complexion might be compared to a Parcel of Roses and Lilies joined together. She seemed to be in great Disorder at the Elector's Arrival, either through Fear or Joy; which was no small Addition to those Graces she naturally possessed. The Prince look'd at her with a certain Pleasure, a Description of which I should find as impracticable, as of all that passed between the two happy Lovers. It is certain that the Elector was so well satisfied with his Visit, that when he retired from her, he spent the best part of his time in thinking of her.

In these delightful Thoughts he had employed the greatest part of the Night, and begun to take a Little Rest in the Morning, when he was informed, that the King of the Romans was desirous of his Company in his Apartment. He arose instantly and waited upon the King. But how great was his Surprise, when he saw that Prince, whom he had before left in a perfect state of Health, at present lying in his Bed pale, wasted, and in the posture of a Man, deprived of the right use of his Senses! 'Good God! (cried the Elector) what do I see, and what 'has befel your Majesty?' 'The most cruel of all Adven-

'A GHOST ALL OVER WHITE'

'tures (answered the King of the Romans) I am threaten'd
'with a sudden Death, but what perplexes me most, is,
'that you are to undergo a more terrible Fate.'—'What
'frightful Dream (said the Elector) has disturbed your
'Rest, and what unfortunate Reason have you, Great
'Sir, to foresee a Thing of such Incertainty?'—'Sit down
'a little while (replied the King) my dear Cousin, hear
'me, and you will perhaps after having given Ear to
'my Narrative have as great Reason to be in fear, as
'I at present have.' The Elector being seated, the King
related the Subject of his present Misery. 'I have, (said
'he) had a more frightful Apparition this Night, than per-
'haps ever any Mortal has been sensible of. Two Hours
'after I had begun to take my last Night's Rest, I heard
'my Chamber-door open and some-body enter. Sup-
'posing the Person to be one of the Gentlemen of my
'Bed-Chamber, I mutter'd at their disturbing me in the
'Night. But judge how great my Surprise must have
'been, when I heard a great Noise of Chains. I look'd out
'and saw a Ghost all over white, which in a dreadful
'Tone said: "*Joseph, King of the Romans, I am a Soul, that*
' "*now undergoes the Pains of Purgatory! I am come by Order of*
' "*the Gods to seek for thee, to give thee Notice of the Precipice,*
' "*that is ready for thy Destruction, by reason of thy Alliance*
' "*with the Elector of Saxony. Deprive him of all Pretensions*
' "*to thy Friendship, and do thou renounce his or prepare thy self*
' "*for eternal Damnation.*" Here the Noise of Chains was

'increased, and as the Fright had render'd me speechless,
'the Apparition repeated his Threats, and said: *"Dost thou*
' *"not think fit to answer me, Joseph? Art thou so unfortunate,*
' *"as wilfully to resist God? and is the Friendship of a human*
' *"Creature more dear to thee, than his, to whom thou art beholden*
' *"for every thing? I give thee Leisure to form what Resolution will*
' *"seem best to thee. In three Days I shall return for thy Answer;*
' *"and if thou dost persist in conversing with the Elector of*
' *"Saxony, both thy Ruin and his will be inevitable."* At these
'Words the Ghost disappeared, and left me, I assure
'you, in a strong Uneasiness. I had not sufficient strength
'to cry out, and the first Gentleman of my Bed-Chamber
'found me thus terrified by this uncommon Adventure.
'I am a little more easy, since I have taken a Resolution
'to change the Course of my Life. I hope to receive
'Pardon for my Sins. You, my dear Cousin, are the only
'Person I am in a deep Concern for; wherefore let me
'conjure you to embrace our most holy Religion, and
'with me to Merit everlasting Life.'

The Elector had heard the King of the Romans with
Attention; but could not at last contain himself from
saying: 'Are you positive, Sir, that you was awake, and
'was it not rather a Dream of which your Majesty has
'still retained an Impression?' The King assured him that
he did not sleep, and protested that no part of his
Relation was the effect of a Dream. 'Then I cannot com-
'prehend it, (cried the Elector) for no Person shall be

'capable of persuading me that an Apparition should 'appear in, or carry Chains. I cannot however imagine 'that any Person can be guilty of so much Rashness as to 'impose upon your Majesty in this manner.'—'How could 'they? (answered the King) is there any Probability of 'an Imposition? Who would dare to make use of such a 'Deceit upon me?'—'What can we say, after all (said 'the Elector) you have Priests about you, Sir, that are not 'only able but even fertile in Frauds; their Power at this 'Court is great. They imagine perhaps that when I have 'the Honour of conversing with your Majesty, I make 'Religion the subject of our Discourse, and then expose 'their Impostures. Permit me, Sir, to ask Your Majesty, 'whether your Father-Confessor has not given Rise to 'several Scruples in you upon the Honour you do me of 'your Friendship?' The King owned, that his Confessor had threaten'd him with a Refusal of the Absolution if he continued to converse with the Elector. 'Since I find 'the Case to be so (replied the Elector) we shall soon 'discover the Apparition. I beg, Sir, you would give me 'Leave to undertake the Care of so important a matter. 'I will be responsible for the Event, provided your 'Majesty will promise to continue your usual Goodness 'to me, and let no-body know that I am acquainted with 'the Adventure.' The King promis'd to keep the Secret, and the Elector to be the better assured of his Fidelity staid with him; at Bed-time he went to his own Chamber, was undress'd and went to the King by a private Door.

The third Night the King of the Romans and the Elector heard a Motion of Chains, and a Voice that said: '*Joseph, King of the Romans*—' The Elector would not hear any more, but leap'd out of Bed and seized the pretended Ghost, who was on the other hand in a much greater Fright, than the King of the Romans had before been in, cried '*Jesu Maria!*' and upon his Knees begg'd his Life, and said he was a Priest, but the Elector, deaf to his cries, carried him to the Window, and throwing him down, '*Go (said he) return to the Purgatory from whence you 'came.*' But the pretended Apparition's last Hour seemed not to be come yet, for though he fell from a high Room, yet did he only break one of his Thighs. He was very desirous of concealing his Adventure from the Knowledge of the Common People, but could not resist the Pain; for he cried out for Assistance; the Guard came up to him, and he was known to be Assistant to the King's Father-Confessor. This Prince was greatly displeased at having been thus highly imposed upon; he swore he would one day banish all the Jesuits from his Country; but after he was informed by whose Persuasions the Priests executed this Project, he pardon'd them and forbid any further mention of the Adventure.

Whilst this Affair was transacted at Court the Elector was deprived of the Sight of his dear Countess, and she,

ignorant of thè Cause of his Absence, suspected him
guilty of Infidelity. She was even so impatient, that she
could not wait for an Opportunity of speaking to him,
but writ a Billet in which she desired him to come to her.
The Elector, no less impatient than she, waited upon her.
She was in a rich Deshabille; her Head-dress, though it
seem'd to have been put on with a careless Air, was very
genteel; she carried the Elector's Picture in her Bracelet.
In this Dress she received the Prince. When he enter'd,
the Lady was playing upon a Spinet and singing a doleful
Tune. She no sooner saw him than her Eyes were overwhelmed with Tears; she remained, as it were destitute
of Motion in her Chair. The Elector, surprized to see her
in that Condition, desired to know the Cause of it. 'How
'dare you (said she sighing) desire to know the subject
'of my Grief? does not your Heart check you for being
'the occasion of it? Have I not sufficient Reason to shed
'these Tears, when I consider, that another Person has
'been capable of robbing me of your Tenderness, and
'those Moments you are come to spend here are only
'stolen from her, and which you think you cannot yet
'refuse me.' The Elector sensibly touched with her
Reproaches, threw himself at her Feet, took hold of her
hands and squeez'd them between his, kiss'd them
incessantly, and assured her upon Oath, that he had no
Object of Love but her. 'Do you love me (said she, look-
'ing on him tenderly) and can you leave me three Days

'without giving any Assurance of your Love?' The
Elector related to her the Adventure that happen'd
the King, which Relation, together with the Assurances
he gave her of his Love and Fidelity, appeas'd the
Countess and renewed her former pleasant Humour. As
she was naturally very hot in her Passions, she fell about
his neck, embraced, kissed, and addressed him often with
the Appellation of her Dear and Adorable Prince. The
Elector who was never backward with his Mistresses in
Tokens of Tenderness, gave the Countess most lively
ones. She could not prevail upon herself to let him go,
and though he had promis'd to sup with the King of the
Romans at the House of Mademoiselle Palsi his Mistress,
she obliged him to break his Promise and to sup with
her. The Elector consented to it, provided she would let
him spend the whole Night with her, which the Lady
did not refuse, and he thereupon occupied the Place of
the Count d'Esterle, who by the Advice of the Physicians
had not lain with her for a considerable time.—Our
Lovers had so many agreeable subjects to discourse upon
that Day-light surprized them before they had slept a
Minute, at last they fell asleep, and had not awaked at
Ten o'Clock had not the Count d'Esterle disturbed their
happy Repose. This Nobleman having some business to
consult with his Lady, went to her Bed-Chamber. As the
Chamber-door was shut he opened it softly, and walked
along very slowly, intending to have the Pleasure of

surprizing her; but he was sorry to find the Reverse, for he was himself greatly surprized, when approaching the Bed, he there saw the Elector resting on the Countess's Arms, and his Head leaning upon her Breast. 'O thou 'perfidious Wretch!' (cried he), and instantly waked the two Lovers. The Elector leap'd out of the Bed, took hold of his Sword and so frightened the Count, that he ran away and left the two Lovers in great Confusion at their unexpected hard Fate.—The Countess was in great Despair, not knowing what to do, and very apprehensive of her Spouse's Resentment. The Elector who knew that her Fear was not ill-grounded, began to invent some method to secure the Countess from any Abuse, and could think of none better, than to take her to the House of his Envoy, which the Law of Nations renders a safe and privileged Place. The Countess objected some Difficulties, but the Elector represented to her that their private Familiarity had reached the Knowledge of a Person, that ought to be the most ignorant of it, and that, since the effects of his Resentment would in all probability be dreadful, she ought no longer to hesitate about the matter. She at last consented to it, and having taken a Box, in which were her Jewels, stepp'd into a Hackney-Coach, and the Prince conducted her to the House of his Envoy, and recommended her to him as a Depositum that was extreamly dear to him.—Whilst Madame d'Esterle was absent from her Husband, the unfortunate Gentle-

157

man was in the Emperor's Anti-Chamber; there he expos'd his Shame and published his Despair. His Friends afforded him what Comfort they were capable of, in telling him that he had no reason to be so highly afflicted at so trifling a matter. They quoted Instances from the Fiction of the Poets and both antient and modern History. 'Amphytrio (said they) was in a Rage no ways 'inferior to yours at present, at his Wife Alcmena's per-'fidious Behaviour, but instantly pacified when told that 'Jupiter himself had been his Rival. How many Husbands 'do we read of in the Roman Histories, who willingly gave 'up their Wives to the Emperors? In France Mr. Monte-'span deliver'd his to Lewis XIV; and in England, where 'the Royal Power is more limited, numberless Husbands 'suffered King Charles II to converse with their Wives.' —'All the Arguments you have advanced (replied inno-'cently the Count d'Esterle) are both true and prevailing, 'but Amphytrio submitted to the Pleasure of a God, and 'the Others to that of their Sovereigns'—'Very well, '(answered the Count of Martinitz, who was at that time 'Ambassador from his Imperial Majesty to Rome) that 'you may imitate the Examples of those Husbands we 'mentioned to you, enter into the Elector of Saxony's 'Service; and he may lye with your Wife without your 'being obstructed by any Person on that Account.' The whole Assembly gave a general Applause of this Advice, and the Count d'Esterle was so well pleased with it, that he went directly to Mr. Beichling, and desired his Interest in procuring him some Office under the Elector.

The Prince was in great Surprize when Mr. Beichling delivered the unexpected Message; he thought that it was a Whim of his own, but the Favourite protested, that the Count d'Esterle's Intreaties had induced him to petition his Highness for that Favour. The Elector by a Billet directly acquainted the Countess with it and desired to have her Advice about the matter. She answer'd that she begg'd his Electoral Highness would not take the Count d'Esterle into his Service; but allow him a Pension upon the Conditions she would require of him. The Elector told her that he left the Management of that matter entirely to her Discretion, and that he would allow the Count Twenty Thousand Florins as a Present. Hereupon the Countess obliged her Husband to sign the following Treaty, which she compos'd herself:

I. That he should consent to her Return to her former Apartment.
II. That he should never mention what was passed in her Presence.
III. That he should renounce all the Right of a Husband, and no longer live with her.
IV. That she should be at liberty to set out on what Journey she should judge convenient.
V. That he should come in his Coach to fetch her from the House of Mr. Gerstorff, Envoy of Saxony, and conduct her to his own House.

She would have begun these with an Article, That her Husband should ask her Pardon in the Presence of Mr. Gerstorff and his Lady for daring to surprize her, but Mr. Beichling pitied the poor Count, interceded for him, and prevailed with her to mitigate the Articles by omitting that, but he added, That the Count d'Esterle should acknowledge those children to be his of which his Wife should after that be deliver'd, and that both the Sons and Daughters should have the Name and bear the Arms of Esterle. This Treaty was signed by both Parties, and every Particular of it was rigorously observed. The Elector related the whole Matter to the King of the Romans, who was very much diverted with it, and from that time the Countess d'Esterle passed publickly for the Mistress of the Elector. That Prince, the King of the Romans, Mademoiselle Palsi, and Madame d'Esterle supp'd together frequently by several Turns. At one of these Meetings the King by a promissory Note laid himself under an Obligation, if he had any Daughters, to marry the eldest to the Electoral Prince of Saxony. By virtue of this Note that Prince did obtain the eldest Archdutchess of the Emperor Joseph, to the Prejudice of the Elector of Bavaria, his Rival.

The new Amour of the Elector being known at Dresden, Madame Koningsmark willingly gave up her Place; she instantly thought of a Retreat, but an honourable one, and one that could be expected of none, but a Person of her Prudence and Conduct. The Publick thought she designed to go to her Abbey, or to return into Sweden; but she acted more wisely, for she staid at Dresden to see the Elector and her new Rival make their Appearance. She did not in the least reproach the Lover, and received his Mistress with uncommon Civility. By these means she preserved a Reputation sufficient to retain the Veneration of the Courtiers, who were all extreamly concerned for her, and highly troubled at her Disgrace. She experienced more, than perhaps ever any Mistress did before her: She retained the Friendship of many, and knew no Enemy, whilst she was out of Favour.—Madame d'Esterle had not so excellent a knack at procuring the publick Affection and Esteem. This Favourite was haughty, revengeful; her Sincerity in Friendship equall'd that in Love; Interest had the first place in all her Undertakings; she had a large number of Followers, whom she sacrificed one to the other, but always to her own Profit; her Expences were excessive, and no Mistress prov'd more expensive to Frederick-Augustus.

The Electress gave no sign of a Displeasure at her Arrival, and when Madame Brandstein told her that the Elector desired she would suffer the Countess d'Esterle to visit her, 'The Elector is the Master, (answered she) let 'him bring to me whomsoever he will.' But though this Princess so prudently concealed her Uneasiness, yet did she resolve never to converse with the Elector again, except in a publick manner. Which Resolution she carefully observed, and when the Elector expressed a Desire of performing his nuptial Duties, she always had some pretence to excuse herself.

The Mother-Electress refused absolutely to receive the Countess d'Esterle; she refused it in a manner, that seemed very insolent to that Lady, and as little obliging to the Elector. She then put her former Intention of retiring to Lichtenberg in execution, and took with her the young Prince her Grandson, who lately succeeded his Father, and educated him with a Care, that testified an extream Tenderness.

CHAPTER X

Augustus is chosen King of Poland, and Crowned at Cracow, his Constancy to the Countess d'Esterle, *her Infidelity, and Banishment from Warsaw, she cheats the King of his Jewels, he is enamoured with* Fatima *a young Turkish Lady, the event of this Amour. The King is again enamoured with the* Princess Lubomirski, *he succeeds in this Amour, and being afterwards tired with her, entered into Engagements with the* Lady Hoyhm, *who is divorced from her Husband, the King is opposed by the Cardinal-Primate, and the King of Sweden advances with an Army towards Poland.*

THE Heart of Frederick-Augustus was not sufficiently employed in Amorous Intrigues, to neglect the Care of Glory—John Sobiesky King of Poland's Decease gave the Elector of Saxony Hopes of succeeding him. His Competitors were indeed great and renowned Men, but equalled by him in Merit, and exceeded in Riches and Power. He did not want for Men that favoured his Party in Poland, and among the rest Brebendorfsky Governor of Culm, who had married the Daughter of Count Fleming Field-Marshall in the Service of the Elector of Brandenburg, and formerly Field-Marshall in Saxony, promoted his Interest. The Elector sent the Chevalier Fleming, Cousin-German to that Palatine's Lady, to him.—Whilst Fleming was making all necessary Preparations for his Embassy, the Elector changed his Religion privately in the Presence of the Prince of Sax-Zeitz,

163

Bishop of Javarin. It is well known what passed in Poland at that Election of a King; that the Cardinal Radziowsky chose the Prince of Conti, and the Bishop of Cujavia proclaimed Frederick-Augustus Elector of Saxony, who at last was chose to the Prejudice of his Rival.

This Prince having received the Diploma of his Election departed for Cracow, where he was crown'd with Royal Splendor. The Countess d'Esterle accompanied him thither, and her Lover's Coronation was a kind of Triumph for her. She saw the Ceremony in a Gallery that was built on purpose for her, and made her Appearance there, shining all over with Jewels. It was observed that when the King drew nearer to the Offertory, he looked at his Mistress, as if he was desirous of saying, that She was the Person to whom he offer'd the Incense and his Heart. The greatest part of the Polanders, being extreamly superstitious were highly displeas'd at it, and dubious of their new King's Sincerity in regard to his Religion.

The Ceremony of the Coronation being ended, the King and his Mistress went to Cracow, where the new Sovereign received the Homages of the Palatinates. The Nobility eager to please him, honour'd him even in his Mistress. Madame d'Esterle became so proud of the Deference she was used with, that she was unmindful of any Person, except those, that had obtained her Favour.

ADVANCES ON THE ROAD TO FORTUNE

Of this number was the Chevalier Fleming. This
Gentleman made his future Prosperity his only Aim:
and though the Prince had declared him Marshal of the
Field in his Army to the Prejudice of Officers superior
to him in Age and Experience, yet did he endeavour
to procure more Employments. His Cousin Madame
Brebentau, advis'd him to engage himself with the
Countess d'Esterle and if possible to gain her tender
Affection. Mr. Fleming represented to her, that to
deprive his King of his Mistress's Heart would shew a
want of Fidelity and Acknowledgment to his great
Benefactor; she objected that those, that always strictly
regard Decency, could never make any great Advances
in the Road to Fortune, that she should never be accessary
to his betraying his King; but that she could not look
upon him, as guilty of a criminal Action, if he partook
with him in the Favours of a Mistress, who was more
beloved, than esteemed, for whom the King would not
long retain an equal Passion, and whom he would one
day see with Indifference in Another's Arms. Mr. Fleming, who was by nature of an easy Disposition and
quickly to be persuaded, followed his Cousin's Advice,
made his Addresses to Madame d'Esterle, and met with
a favourable Reception. She undertook to make his
Fortune, and the King, in regard to her Recommendation,
made him Lieutenant-General, Minister of State to the
Privy-Council, and chief Master of the Horse over all

Lithuania. Mr. Fleming adapted himself in every respect to the King's Temper, and his Majesty accustomed himself on the other hand so much to his Favourite's submissive and complaisant Deportment, that he could scarce live without him. Mr. Fleming behaved himself with so much Caution, that the King never suspected him to be his Rival; and had Madame d'Esterle been as prudent as he, she would in all probability have retained the King's Favour, who admired in his Mistresses that haughty Carriage, and has always given the Preference before those, that had an outward shew of Modesty, to Women of that Character. Madame d'Esterle looking upon the King's Favour, as an Inheritance of which she had acquired an everlasting Possession, acted so very rashly, that the King at last discovered her Infidelity; but as his great and passionate Love would not suffer him to rid himself of her at once, he resolved to dissemble with her, till at last he surprized her with the Prince Wiesnowisky. He was in a very great Rage, when he saw her, but did not in the least reproach his vile and abusive Mistress, but sent her a Message by Mr. Fitztuhm, by which he desired her to go from the Palace within two Hours, from Warsaw within twenty-four, and to quit the Kingdom without Delay.

She obey'd; and was no sooner gone, than her Enemies, who were innumerable, insinuated to the King, that he should have obliged her to return some of the Diamonds,

A CLEVER IMPOSTURE

which he had given her, since such a Punishment would have affected her more sensibly than her Disgrace. The King, not recovered of his first furious Rage sent a Messenger after her. She was overtaken at the distance of two Days' Journey from Warsaw. A Gentleman of the King's Life-Guard, demanded in his Majesty's Name, her Box of Jewels. She told him, that she was ready to deliver up the Jewels, but as she would not be subject to his Majesty's Suspicions, in case any of those Diamonds, he gave her, should prove deficient, she desired the liberty of locking the Box, and enclosing the Key in a Letter she designed to write to the King. The Gentleman believing he had got the right Box, because he had that, which had been described to him, and one, whose Lock could not be seen, made no Opposition to the deceitful Countess, and thus she sealed the Box and Key, left them in the Hands of the Gentleman of the Life-Guard and continued her Journey with great Expedition. She arrived at Breslau, at the same time, when the Gentleman arrived at Warsaw. He delivered the Box to the King, who having open'd it found only a Heap of Cut-Paper; for Madame d'Esterle foresaw the Event, and had entrusted an Italian Musician with her Jewels, who went in Haste through Dantzig while she took the Tour of Silesia. The King, seeing the Imposture, could not help laughing at it, and was no longer displeased at the Countess d'Esterle.

FATIMA

His Majesty was now destitute of a declared Mistress:
but as Idleness was hateful to him, he diverted himself
with those trifling and accidental Amours, which might
properly be only called by the astronomical term of
Ignis fatuus; but in which he found so great a Pleasure
that he was tempted to make frequent use of them. The
first, he fixed his Eye upon, was a Young Turkish Lady,
who had been taken Captive at Buda, when the Imperial-
ists made themselves Masters of that Place. She was at
that time but six Years of Age, and together with her
Liberty lost both her Parents, who have since then never
been heard of. Mr. Schoning[1] Lieutenant-General in
the Service of the Elector of Brandenburg, to whose
Share she happened to fall, took her to Berlin and
baptized her; but she kept her name of Fatima. Mademoiselle Fleming having a great value for young
Fatima asked Mr. Schoning to give her to their Family,
which he willingly granted. When she was married to
the Palatine Brebentau, Fatima followed her into Poland.
As the Beauties of her Mind equalled those of her Body,
Madame Brebentau used her with great Tenderness,
and introduced her into all Companies. At her House
the King had the pleasure of first seeing Fatima. Though
he thought her Beauty great, at the time of his Amour
with Madame d'Esterle, yet was his Engagement with

---

[1] He died Field-Marshall in the Saxon Service, after having enjoyed
the same Place under the Elector of Brandenburg.

that Lady so inviolable, that he looked at the other with
Indifference, and could scarce prevail upon himself to
speak to her. But the Countess d'Esterle was no sooner
banished from his Heart, than he sought for an Opportunity of making his Addresses to Fatima, which he
procured, and had a long conversation with her one day,
when he was so charmed with her excellent Genius, that
from that Moment he became enamoured with her. He
then went daily to Madame Brebentau. All the Court
resorted thither, and the most beautiful Ladies endeavoured to please him. But his Eyes were only fixed upon
Fatima: he could not be satisfied without dropping now
and then a gallant Expression, which was only understood by her. Fatima answered him with Modesty and
Politeness. She avoided the Passion of loving for a long
while; but what Slave can be capable of resisting the
pursuits of an amiable, magnificent, and generous King?
That Prince gave her so lively Assurances of a lasting
Tenderness, and made so seducing Promises to her,
that the young and innocent Fatima was at last overcome.
—It is not known how she could possibly escape Madame
Brebentau's vigilant Care, but most certain, that she did;
the Change of her Shape discovered her Intrigue, and
Madame Brebentau perceived instantly; she was so
incensed against the poor Girl, that she would have
banished her from her House: but the King, informed of
her Proceedings, begg'd she would take care of the

Young Lady, and look upon her as a Depositum, which he had a greater regard for, than even his Life. Madame Brebentau very desirous of obliging the King, kept Fatima, who was some Months afterwards delivered of a Son, who by reason of his extraordinary Beauty the King acknowledged as his, and whom he has since thought fit to educate as such, and to give him the Title of Count Rotofski.—The King who could never be long attach'd to one Mistress, and was chiefly pleased with married Women, and those who discovered a nice Capacity for intriguing, shewed an early Disgust to Fatima. She was too soft, too modest to suit his Taste. However as he esteemed her, he thought a speedy Settlement would render her happy, and gave her in Marriage to one Spiegel, Lieutenant-Colonel in his Troops. Fatima willingly promised that Officer her Fidelity, with whom she has led so happy a Life, that a Person most given to Detraction has been obliged to respect her. The King had not with Fatima totally forsaken Love; but another Beauty of a more eminent Rank took possession of his Heart. This was the Princess Lubomirski, Wife of the Great Chamberlain of the Crown, and Niece of the Cardinal Radziowsky, Primate of the Kingdom. It was a common and received Opinion in Poland, that the King pretended a Passion for this Lady to procure her Favour, and to make use of the great Influence she had upon her Uncle's Mind, who did ever oppose him. But

SPLENDID DIVERSIONS

if a political View induced Frederick-Augustus to court
the Princess Lubomirski, it is certain that that Lady's
uncommon Merit, render'd the amorous King at last
in Reality her Adorer.—He attacked the Heart of Madame
Lubomirski according to all the formal Rules and
Ceremonies of Courtship; and she on the other hand
encountered him as a true Heroine, pretending neither
to understand his Sighs, nor tender Looks. When his
Majesty addressed her, she answered respectfully, but
at the same time like a Princess of a free Kingdom. This
increased the Royal Passion. The Princess loved Diversions, and a profuse Method of living, and herein to
indulge her Inclination no Expence was thought too
great: the French Comedians and Musicians were sent
for from Dresden. Their daily Diversions were Plays,
Balls, Feasts, Hunting, Games, Entertainments upon
the Vistula, and other Pleasures of equal Splendor; never
had Warsaw made so bright an Appearance.

One day, as they were running at the Ring, after the
King, whose Dexterity was superior to any other, had
won the Prize; he ordered some young Horses, which
he had lately sent for from Turkey, to be brought to
him. Tho' these Horses had had no Instructions yet would
he mount them, and order'd others to be mounted by
the first Lords of the Court. The King and Mr. Fitztuhm
happened to mount the most unruly ones: they were
wont to hit their Heads together, but the King pull'd

AN ACCIDENT

his briskly back, and rid so violently against a post of the Riding-House, that the Blow made the Horse throw him. The Spectators ran directly to his Assistance and thought he was much wounded. Madame Lubomirski thought him more hurt than any of the rest. The Concern she had for him, gave her a Trouble and an Apprehension which she could not conceal. She drew nearer to him, and observing some Drops of Blood was so terrified, that she swooned away in the Arms of the Countess Tobianski her Cousin. When the King was recover'd and had lifted up his Head the first Object, that struck his Sight, was his dear Princess Lubomirski. The Condition he saw her in, revived him; he rose and ran to her Succour. She happened at the same time to open her eyes and in a languishing Tone to say to her Cousin, *Is the King dead?* She saw the same Moment that Prince beholding her in a manner, that signified sufficiently, how sensible he was of her Condition. She was so rejoiced at the bad state of Health, and the Presence of her Husband, to whom such Behaviour seemed undoubtedly indecent, she cried out, 'Great Sir! do you live? do I again enjoy the Happiness 'of seeing you, has God returned you at my humble 'Intreaties!'—'Yes, Madame, (answered the King) but I 'beseech you to believe that I am more grateful for the 'Tokens of Compassion you have expressed, than even 'for my Life itself.' The Great Chamberlain's Presence hindered her from saying any more.

'THE HAPPIEST DAY OF ALL MY LIFE'

Madame Lubomirski retired from the Riding-House to the Princess Constantine Sobiesky, who had invited the King to a Ball that Evening. His Mind was wholly employed upon what was past, and notwithstanding the late unfortunate Adventure, he went thither in a splendid Dress, and made the Appearance of a Man insensible of the Accident, that had happened but a little before: He even appeared with more Gaiety than usual, and his Joy at what he had that day seen gave him an Air which was no small addition to his other endearing bodily Perfections. All the Assembly was amazed at his Entry, and every-body congratulated his happy Deliverance, except Madame Lubomirski. The King after having given the Ladies a polite Salutation, and passed some Moments in discoursing with the Princess Sobiesky, went to Madame Lubomirski, whom he addressed in a low Tone, 'Madame, '(said he) this Day I may justly call the happiest of all 'my Life.'—'I think, (replied the Princess, who would not 'give him time to express himself) that your Majesty may 'add it to the number of your most fortunate Days, since 'you have escaped so great and imminent a Danger.'— 'The Danger (answer'd the King) is but trifling in 'competition of the Benefit it has procured me. I only 'recollect the Danger I was in, to call to mind the Con- 'dition I saw you in. But, Madame, is that, which was 'then the only Cause of my Felicity to cease already, and 'will you repent of having given me Tokens of your

173

PRINCESS LUBOMIRSKI'S BILLET

'Affection at that time?'—'For God's Sake, Sir, (replied 'Madame Lubomirski) be contented with what you have 'seen, and exact not of me the Confession of a Thing, 'too well known to you, and which I am in vain desirous 'of hiding. Consider the Presence of my Husband, and 'that I must not explain my Sentiments before him.' The King could scarce contain the Transport of Joy this Answer caused in him; however that he might not expose his Mistress, notwithstanding his Royal Authority, he obey'd and retired from her.—He opened the Ball with the Princess Sobieski, and had no sooner danced once, than he fell very ill, and obliged to be carried away; when he arrived at his Palace, he was let Blood, and found himself much better. The Physicians imputed this Accident to his Fall and Refusal of Bleeding immediately after the Misfortune, as they had advised him (but he was far from consenting to it) apprehensive of being deprived of the Sight of his Mistress at the Ball. His Disease was however soon cur'd, and what contributed chiefly to his speedy Recovery was a Billet deliver'd to him by his first Physician in the name of Madame Lubomirski. It was expressed in the following Terms:

'What Uneasiness hath not your Majesty given me in 'one Day! Be assured, Sir, that this last has been the most 'miserable Night I ever had in my Life, and the Danger 'I thought you to be in, has almost broke my Heart. I 'have just now been informed, that you are better. May

'you be speedily capable of witnessing the Joy that
'Report has occasioned in me! Yet I still tremble, O!
'if I lose my King—my Lover—what Advantage will
'a temporal Life afford me?'

The King perused this Billet frequently and with
Great Care; he read it to Mr. Fitztuhm, whose Interest
begun to be more prevalent, than that of the Chancellor
Beichling. This Favourite was not sparing in his Praises
of the Stile. 'She wishes (cried the King) that I could be
'Witness of the Joy the Recovery of my Health has
'caused in her. Wherefore, dear Fitztuhm, I ought to go
'to her, I ought to make her Witness of the Joy her
'Kindnesses have caused in me, such a Mistress deserves,
'that I should hazard my Health for her Sake.'—'The
'Princess Lubomirski deserves all the Favours you can
'confer on her (replied Mr. Fitztuhm) but I am persuaded
'your Majesty will offend her, if you expose your Health
'to see her. Let me manage the Affair, Sir, I hope to be
'capable of inducing her to come hither; that will be
'more advantageous both for her and you.'—'O! dear
'Fitztuhm (cried the King) if you procure me that Happi-
'ness you shall ask nothing of me, but what I shall give
'you, and you may expect the best Tokens I am capable
'of shewing my Acknowledgment'. Mr. Fitztuhm thanked
the King for his excessive Goodness, and begg'd he would
write an Answer to Madame Lubomirski, and to make
him the Bearer of it. The King writ the following Billet:

'Pardon me, dear Princess, for all the Uneasiness I
'give you. But what do I say! I should have been sorry
'had I not given you any; I should still have remain'd
'ignorant of your Sentiments for me. You should cer-
'tainly see me at your Feet, to return you Thanks for
'your obliging Behaviour to me, did not my Physicians,
'and Fitztuhm himself confine me to my Chamber. I am
'ever sensible, that it is impossible for me to live without
'you. Whatever they do I am resolved to escape their
'vigilant care to enjoy the Happiness of your Conversa-
'tion. If my Life is in Danger, I will at least lose it, for
'which I shall have a most plausible Reason.'

Mr. Fitztuhm found a large Assembly of Gentlemen
and Ladies in Madame Lubomirski's Apartment; but
told her nevertheless, that he desired to confer with her
about some private Affair. She went into a Closet, and
he followed her, where he delivered the Billet, and told
her, that the King would die, if she did not come to visit
him. 'How, or what can I do? (said she) I cannot go to
'see the King, without subjecting myself to my Husband's
'Resentment, and the Censure of the whole Court.'—
'Every Affair may be managed by some method or other,
'madame, (answered Mr. Fitztuhm) and provided you
'will follow the Rule I shall propose, everybody except
'the King, you and I shall be ignorant of this Visit.'—
'Speak, then, (replied the Princess) What must I do?'—
'Retire into a Convent under a Pretence of a devout

A WELL-LAID PROJECT

'Disposition (said Mr. Fitztuhm) for Retreats of this 'kind are very customary at the present Season of the 'Year, this being the first week in Lent. When you are in 'the Convent, you are to leave it at Ten o'Clock at Night; 'to step into a Coach, which I shall take care to prepare 'for your Reception, you are to step out of this Coach 'at the Door of my Lodgings, and I shall conduct you to 'a private Stair-case, only made use of by me, and from 'thence to the Royal Apartment.'—The Princess found the Project extreamly well laid and promised to follow him the next day. She then left Mr. Fitztuhm and returned to her Company. Her Husband, who observed her Absence asked where she had been; she told him instantly, that she had been in conference with Mr. Fitztuhm, and consulted with him about Matters which the King desired her to communicate to the Cardinal-Primate. The Prince believed that no other Affair had detained her, and she afterwards began to discourse about the Devotions of the Lent-Season. 'As for me (said she) I 'shall not make use of any corporal Austerities, because 'they will be inconsistent with my Health; but shall 'mortify myself by seeing less Company. In order thereto 'I intend to pass four Days in each Week in a solitary 'manner in a Convent.' This Religious Zeal was admired by every one, and Mr. Lubomirski was the first Person, who gave his Approbation of it.

The Princess executed her Resolution the next Morning,

and at Ten o'Clock at Night she followed Mr. Fitztuhm's
Directions in every respect, and arrived at his Majesty's
Bed-Chamber; who waited for her with an Impatience,
which no Pen can possibly describe. Mr. Fitztuhm being
retired, Madame Lubomirski sate down upon the Bed.
She was in a negligent Dress, but as amiable as she had
ever appeared before. The two Lovers were together
for some time without speaking a Word to each other.
The Princess looked at the King with a languishing Air,
which sufficiently told him, that her Heart was entirely
devoted to him. The King was so transported, that after
having returned her Thanks for the Favour she did him,
he kiss'd her Hands for a quarter of an Hour, telling her
incessantly, that he was the Happiest Man on Earth, and
look'd upon himself as the greatest Monarch in the
World in the Enjoyment of her Love. 'I think myself
'no less happy (answered she) in the possession of the
'Heart of so great a King, and so accomplished a Man.
'Let us therefore love each other always, dear Prince;
'be not unfaithful to me: May Heaven punish me, if ever
'I love any other Person but you!' They proceeded at
that time no further than tender Expressions; the King
indeed was desirous of a further Enjoyment; but
Madame Lubomirski to whom his Majesty's Health was
very dear, suffered him not to run the Hazard of it again.
The King insisted upon her Promise to return in the same
manner the next Day. It was near Four o'clock in the

A DIVORCE

Morning when she retired. When she was arrived at the Convent, she endeavoured to preserve the Character of a pious Woman by attending at the Morning-Prayers and Masses, after which she took the Repose her Body was in great need of.

She returned to the Palace the two next Days, and the King was no sooner able to go out, than he began to visit her in the Convent. With these delightful Meetings the two Lovers passed the whole Lent Season, but could not do so after Easter. The King however continued to visit Madame Lubomirski, and her Husband had Intelligence of the Matter, he mentioned it to his Wife, who answered him in a very arrogant manner. The Prince not a little dissatisfied with his Wife's Conduct, happened to drop some words, that were highly offensive to the King, whereupon he was forbid to appear at Court, this obliged him to resolve to retire to his own Estate, and desired his Wife to follow him thither, which she presumptuously refused; he summoned her after this Refusal to appear before the Pope's Nuncio, and there demanded a Dissolution of his Marriage-Bonds, and as she consented to it, the King, who was glad to meddle in this Affair, obtained for them a Divorce from his Holiness, and to this Effect, that Either Party could marry again. As no other Obstacle hindered the two Lovers from doing what they pleased, the King departed for Saxony. Madam Lubomirski followed him soon afterwards, accompanied by her two Sisters, one of which was married to Mr. Vopofski, a Polish Gentleman. The other was unmarried, but soon afterwards entered into a conjugal Life with Mr. Glasnap, an Officer in the Life-Guards, a Gentleman of eminent Birth, and no less eminent Merit, but without a Fortune which he designed to procure by this Alliance, but was deceived in his Expectations, and saw himself at last reduced as well as Mr. Vopofski to dissolve his Marriage since which time he has married another Woman.

The King desirous of appearing in as magnificent a manner as possible in his own Country, shewed his Mistress the Chief Towns of Saxony. When he was arrived at Wittenberg he left her to go and see the Queen, who had resided some time since at the Castle of Pretsch at the distance of two or three Leagues from that Town. Tho' he was to leave her but for the Space of two Days, yet were both Parties unwilling to be separated. The Mistress sigh'd and wept. 'How! (said she) will you leave 'me? shall I live two Days without seeing you? and will 'you spend all that Time with the Queen? whom, not-'withstanding the Respect I owe her, I cannot look upon 'any otherways than as my Enemy, since she cannot but 'hate me, who deprive her of the most perfect Heart in 'the Universe. O! what should I do, if she was on the 'other hand to deprive me of it? even the Idea of that 'Misery gives me a mortal Uneasiness, judge then, dear

'Prince, what a Condition I shall be in, if you forsake me.
'I own, that I should rather see you return to the Arms of
'the Queen, than in those of any other Rival: but in
'short whatever way I lose you, Death only can procure
'me Comfort.' The King touch'd with these Words
embraced his Mistress, and begg'd her not to be afflicted
about a Thing, that could not possibly happen. 'How
'can I be unfaithful to you? (said he) where shall I find
'so accomplished a Person as you, and one that can love
'like you? No, my Dear, you need not be apprehensive
'of any thing. Your Accomplishments will for ever secure
'my Fidelity.' This Discourse revived Madame Lubomirski; but she intreated the King nevertheless to delay
his intended Journey three Days longer. This Prince,
incapable of making her a Refusal, consented to it, and
that Interval of Time was employed in Diversions,
Balls and Feasts, in which the King's Politeness and
Grandeur were ever conspicuous.—At one of these
Entertainments the King presented his Mistress with a
little Box of a precious Stone full of Jewels of all kinds,
and in the midst of them the Emperor's Diploma,
declaring her Princess of the Empire by the name of
Teschen. 'How much am I obliged to you, Sir, (said she)
'and what Tokens can I give of my Acknowledgement?'
—'The only one I desire, (replied the King) is an endless
'Continuation of your present Love. The Rank, by which
'his Imperial Majesty is pleased to distinguish you, is

'far inferior to your Deserts, what reason then, have you
'to be grateful to me? I wish a Crown was at my Disposal,
'with what Pleasure should I see you wear it.' In this
manner did they divert themselves with such pleasant
amorous Discourses, till they thought proper to retire
and meet again in private. The Night would have seem'd
to be of too tedious a length, had the Lovers been in
separate Apartments, wherefore they agreed to pass it
together.

The next Morning his Majesty departed for Pretsch,
where he met with a submissible and obliging Reception
from the Queen's Hands; but her Heart had received too
bitter a Wound by the long Course of his unlawful
Amours, to give him any sensible Tokens of Love, and
tho' the King address'd her in all the affectionate Terms,
natural to a Husband, that respected her Virtues and
unparallel'd Merit, yet was she resolved to continue that
cold and indifferent Behaviour, which she had long since
accustomed herself to.

The King was too impatient for the Sight of his
Mistress, to stay any longer than one Night at Pretsch,
he set out the next morning, and met her in a Wood
between Wittenberg and Pretsch. She was dressed in a
Riding-Apparel, the Body of which was yellow, and
the Petticoat blue embroidered with Silver, those Colours
were at that time in Fashion in Saxony. Her Hat was
adorned with a blue and white Feather. This Dress gave

the Princess so enchanting an Air, that no other could have set off her Charms more advantageously. The King hastened to her as soon as he saw that she was coming, and when he had approached her, he stepped out of his Chariot, she offer'd to answer this Civility by dismounting, but her tender Lover would not suffer her, he kiss'd her Hand with Eagerness, and she complimented him in an endearing manner on his Return. His Majesty having asked for a Horse, mounted, and proposed a Hunting-Match to his Mistress, and as he had the day before given Orders for the Preparation of this Match, the Hounds were ready. The King was in fear lest any unfortunate Accident should happen to this new Huntress, intreated her to keep at his Side, and he would not forsake her. After having given her the Pleasure of seeing the Stag, that was hunted, run by her, he retired with her to the most hidden part of the Wood, to take a small Refreshment with her. The Gentlemen and Ladies of the Court soon perceived their Retirement, but would not interrupt their quiet Fruition of the solitary Pleasures. The Event has sufficiently manifested, that this was in reality the occasion of an Agreeable Conversation between the King and his Mistress; for since that time she was perplexed with Pains in her Stomach, and frequent Vomits, which raised a Suspicion that the King and she had not made a trifling use of their time. She was in due time deliver'd of a Son, who is at present distinguished by the Title of Prince of Teschen, and resembles his Mother's Lover in every respect.

The day after this Hunting-Match the King and his Mistress set out for Leipzig, which was at that time, by reason of the Fair, frequented by a large number of Persons of Distinction. The Queen went thither to assist her Consort in receiving the King of Prussia, who was come to visit them. Madame Teschen saluted the two Queens at the Redoubt, and the King himself presented her to those two Princesses, who gave her a very different Reception. The Queen of Poland received her with an Indifference, not agreeable to her Rival, and asked her how long she had been in Saxony. 'I am come 'hither with the King, Madame, (answer'd the Favourite) 'and hope soon to return from hence with him again.' The Queen was so mortified at this answer, that her Eyes were filled with Tears. She pretended Sickness to excuse her Retirement.

The Queen of Prussia on the contrary was extreamly obliging in her Deportment to Madame Teschen, but as that Prince was only diverted at the Expense of another Person, she invited the King to sup with her in private, pretending that the Noise and Grandeur a Court is perplexed with, was very inconvenient to her. 'But if 'you please (said she to the King) I'll name those Persons, 'that I design to invite, which number your Mistress is to 'be excluded from. I long to see you once without her,

The Princess of Teschen

Pastel by Rosalba Carriera

'and to have the sole possession of you. I know that she
'occupies all Your Thoughts; but shall chuse Persons,
'whose Conversation will be capable of diverting you
'from her; and if they do not, I shall rather have you
'think of, than always speak to your Mistress.' The King
promised an entire Compliance with all her Desires, and
permitted the Queen to invite whatever Persons should
seem most agreeable to her.

She invited the Ladies, Koningsmark, Hauchwitz
and Esterle, the three disgraced Mistresses of the King,
whom Chance and some particular Affairs had occasioned
to meet at Leipzig. The Queen of Prussia was attended
by both the Princesses of Hohenzollern and Henrietta
Princess of Anhalt-Dessau. The young Princess of
Hohenzollern could boast of a most beautiful Person;
but her tender Years gave her too innocent an Air to suit
the Taste of Frederick-Augustus. The Princess of Dessau
was not altogether so beautiful in her Person, but was
possessed of that *Je-ne-scai-quoi*, which does equally
please and affect; her Shape, Graces, Behaviour and
entertaining Discourse could not be exceeded; and the
King could not but give her the Preference before the
Princess of Hohenzollern, whose Mother was so mortified, that her Daughter did not gain the Conquest over
the King, (as she expected) that she mutter'd at her
Daughter all the Evening, whose Eyes were constantly
filled with Tears.

COLD AND DISAGREEABLE ANSWERS

Madame d'Esterle, to whom his Majesty had granted a Pardon for her Treachery and Deceit, endeavoured to gain the Superiority by forced and artificial Charms, and seemed not to have lost all Hope of recalling the King to her Arms. Madame Hauchwitz sate in a pensive and doleful posture; in short, no one behaved in a more indifferent manner than Madame Koningsmark, and with that Lady her Prussian Majesty was pleased to divert herself in observing and reflecting upon the various effects the King's Presence produced in that Assembly.

In the meanwhile the King conversed for a considerable time with the Princess of Dessau, whose Charms had so great an effect upon his Heart, that she may truly be said to have been the first occasion of Madame Teschen's Disgrace. But that Princess answered all his tender Expressions in very cold and disagreeable terms. 'Your Majesty (said she) is incapable of promoting me to 'the Royal Dignity, and was it in your power, you would 'perhaps think me unworthy of so great a Promotion, 'but let me persuade you that I think my Birth too 'eminent to be your Mistress.'

At Supper-time Madame Koningsmark observed to the Queen, that Madame Teschen's Presence would be no small addition to the Pleasure of the Entertainment, and the Queen pretended to be sorry for not having invited her, which occasioned the other Lady to say that it was not too late for the Pleasure of her Company, that they need only open a Ball after Supper and admit all the Masques. 'Be assured, Madame, (continued she) 'that the Princess of Teschen will not fail to come.' The Queen gave a ready Approbation of the Expedient, and offered a Dance to the King; after whose Consent the Musicians were called in; and her Prussian Majesty ordered one of the Servants in waiting, without the King's Knowledge, to acquaint the Masques that they might be admitted. The Noble Company rose from Table and the King opened the Ball with the Queen of Prussia. After having danced, his Majesty placed himself by the Princess of Anhalt, whose reserved Behaviour had not discouraged him from making his Addresses to her. He spoke to her in so lively and eager a manner that he did not perceive three masqued Ladies, approaching near enough to hear whatever Words were spoke. One of these Masques listened for some time and then broke out in these Words to the Princess of Anhalt; 'O! Princess, the King made use of the same Expression 'to me but this morning, believe him not, I conjure you.' —'Alas! (answered the amazed King) it is the Princess 'of Teschen!'—'Fear not, masqued Lady, (replied the 'Princess of Dessau) the King has a Fluency of Speech, but 'all Princesses do not resemble you.' She then rose up, and the King was doing the same, when Madame Teschen stopped him, saying, 'You shun me, notwithstanding

187

THE KING DESPERATELY VEXED

'all your Promises this morning, never to love any other 'Person.' The King, apprehensive of undergoing the Censure of her Prussian Majesty, was desperately vexed at this Accident. 'For God's Sake, Madame, (said he) let 'us not be the Jest of all the Strangers here present, for 'we are taken Notice of. Go to your own House, I shall 'follow to reassure you, that you shall ever be the sole 'Object of my Love.' Madame Teschen well satisfied with the King's Answer, departed, and the King would have followed her, had not the Queen of Prussia, who designed to divert herself at the Expence of that Favourite, as soon as she saw him going, proposed to join in a Country-Dance with him, which, as he consented to, she occasioned to last very long; after these Dances she discoursed with him upon several Subjects, jested about his amorous and inconstant disposition, and, as if she had not seen Madame Teschen, told him, that she was heartily sorry for not having invited that Lady to Supper, 'Perhaps, (said she) 'the Poor Lady is at this very Instant mortally uneasy, 'and your Majesty ought to let her know, that I hindered 'you from going to ask her Pardon, for the Preference 'you have this Evening given the young Princess of 'Dessau to her in Beauty.' The Railleries disordered the King very much, he endeavoured to answer her, but all his Words testified his Confusion; and the more Disorder he discover'd the more the Queen perplex'd him. 'My Inconstancy, Madame, (answered he at last)

'doth in some measure deserve a free Pardon. If I might
'boast of a Spouse, permit me to say a Mistress, equal to
'your Majesty, you may be assured, I would not occasion
'my Enemies to censure me for being too fickle.'—'If
'your Majesty is inclined to wheedle me (replied the
'Queen of Prussia) I shall directly send for the Princess
'of Teschen; it will however be in vain, for Day-Light
'appears, and the Masques are all retired. Come hither,
'Princess (cried she to the Princess of Anhalt) the King
'mistakes me for you.' With these and other Discourses
of this kind she detained the King till Seven o'Clock the
next Morning.

He then went to Madame Teschen whom he found in
a deplorable condition. She was sitting in a flood of Tears,
her Sisters sate by and comforted her, but she gave no
ear to their words, and found no other Comfort but in
her Despair. The King was so transported at this sight
that he asked her Pardon in the most submissive terms,
and kissed her Hands for a considerable time. She cast a
tender look upon him and said; 'How great will be my
'Misery, Sir, if you refuse me your Pity!' The King made
all the Excuses he could, complained of the Queen of
Prussia, whom he accused of being the occasion of all
that had happen'd, and added to these Excuses, that all
he said to the Princess of Dessau was designed for an
Amusement. As we are most apt to believe what we
wish for, Madame Teschen gave ready Credit to the

King's Words. The two Lovers were happily reconciled and parted at last in a very amicable manner.

In the mean while the King was in reality pleased with the Princess of Dessau's great Merit, and greatly afflicted at her Departure. The Queen of Prussia perceived his Melancholy, and the cause of it, and told him with that pleasant Air, natural to her, that she advised him to quit that pensive posture. 'Believe me (said she) you shall 'accompany me to Orangenbaum, where I design to 'remain some days with the Princess-Dowager of Anhalt-'Dessau. You will be more at liberty there; a Wife and 'three or four Mistresses, to whose Humour you are 'here obliged to adapt yourself, cannot be but very 'troublesome.' The King consented to the Proposal, and that the Princess of Teschen might not oppose his Design, he pretended that State-Affairs, obliged him to have a private Conference with the King of Prussia. He begg'd she would go and wait for him at Dresden, he would there return to her in few Days. This Separation grieved Madame Teschen mortally; but the King represented to her in so persuasive a manner, that it was absolutely necessary for the Interest of his Kingdom, and swore so often that he would return to her with a faithful Heart, that she at last consented to it.

The King then set out on this small Journey, and arrived some Hours afterwards at Orangenbaum. The Princess Henrietta, displeased at seeing him there, gave

him a very cold Reception. She related to her Mother all
the King's Words, and begg'd her permission to keep
her Chamber under pretence of Sickness. 'No, (answered
'that Princess) dear Daughter, it will directly be suspected
'not to be a real Indisposition. And I have moreover
'too good an Opinion of you to be persuaded, that you
'can by no other means, than shunning your Lover,
'secure yourself from answering to a Passion, which can
'only offend you.'

The Princess Henrietta saw herself obliged to submit
to her Mother's commands, but always kept at such a
distance from the King, that he could not make any private
Addresses to her, though he was during the space of
four Days in constant search after means, whereby to
gain his end. At last he departed from thence for Dresden
on the same day, that the Queen of Prussia set out for
Berlin. His Return caused an inexpressible Joy in the
Princess of Teschen, who notwithstanding the King's
solemn Protestation, was dubious whether she should
see him again. The first Days were wholly employed upon
Endearments on both sides. But as she saw several
Coquets striving to deprive her of the King's Heart, and
knowing his inconstant mind, she began to be uneasy,
and Dresden at last proved quite insupportable to her,
for she foresaw, that she should lose her Lover, if he
made any stay there: this induced her to persuade him
to return into Poland, whither the War, undertaken

against Sweden, and carried on with little Success, seemed beside to require his Presence.

The King's Affairs in Poland, and the Campaign in Livonia, separated him frequently from his Mistress. These Absences were very advantageous to the Favourite-Lady; they were not a sufficient length to occasion him to forget her; but long enough to create a Desire in the King to see her again, and to meet her, as if lately enamoured with her. Madame Teschen enjoyed his Favour in the mean time for some Years without any interruption; this time she spent in procuring Riches sufficient to maintain her usual Grandeur in her Disgrace. The King's ill Success in his War obliged him to fetch a fresh Recruit of Soldiers from Saxony, leaving his Mistress at Warsaw. This Departure did not occasion so many Tears, she was accustomed to his Absence, and that Vivacity, which is the true Delight of a real and ardent Passion, subsisted no longer. The King upon his Arrival at Dresden was resolved to drive away all Melancholy from his Heart, and to that purpose frequented Places where Debauchery was practised to a great degree. At one of these Conversations, which consisted at that time only of Men, they happened to discourse about their Mistresses. Every one boasted of his, and related Wonders of her. Mr. Hoyhm, Minister of State, of the Privy-Council, who was present there told them, that he had no Mistress, but that his Happiness

consisted in a Wife, whom he loved as a Mistress, and
who was much more charming than any that had yet
been described. As Wine had deprived him of the free
use of his Senses, he delivered so exact a Description of
his Wife, that not the most able Painter could have better
set off her Beauties. The King, not ignorant that Jealousy
occasioned him to confine her to the Country, told him
that he could not possibly believe his Assertion, that
his Discourse was like that of a Man married but three
Months before, and still charmed with his Wife's Accomplishments, and that if Madame Hoyhm's Beauty and
bodily Perfections did but in the least answer his Description of her, she would have been much more noted than
she was. The Prince of Furstemberg maintained the King's
Argument, and added, that he would lay a Wager of a
Thousand Ducats, that if Madame Hoyhm was to make
her Appearance at Court she would not be found so
beautiful, as he had persuaded them to believe. Mr.
Hoyhm laid the Wager, and the King offer'd to decide
it; the Gentleman was instantly obliged to write to his
Wife, and ordered her to come directly to Dresden, a
Servant was at the same time dispatch'd with the Letter;
and that Mr. Hoyhm, might not be capable of altering his
Mind, they forced him to drink so much, that he could
scarce speak, act, or think. He was in a great Surprize
at his Wife's Presence the next Morning at Dresden,
repented of having sent for her, and would have sent her

back the same Hour, had he not been apprehensive of the Censure of the whole Court for his great Jealousy.

The Queen of Poland was at that time at Dresden, and Madame Hoyhm was presented to her Majesty. The King and those who laid the Wager were at the Queen's Apartment, and found themselves obliged to acknowledge, that Mr. Hoyhm had even been sparing in his praises of the Lady's Beauty. The King condemned the Prince of Furstemberg to pay the Thousand Ducats. 'I find '(answered the Prince in Jest) that we must pay dear for 'your Majesty's Diversion.' The King, extreamly fond of the Prince, desired him to pay the lost Sum, and to go and receive Ten Thousand Ducats of his Treasurer. The Prince kiss'd his Majesty's Hand, and thank'd him, he paid the Debt, and received the Sum he had been presented with.

Before I proceed any further in this History, I think it not improper to delineate as exactly, as possibly I can, the incomparable Beauty of this Lady, and relate some Particulars concerning her. The remarkable Distinction she was honoured with at the Saxon Court, requires an Account of her Person and Character.

Her Face was of a charming length, her Nose, by reason of its fine shape the chief Ornament of her adorable Face, her Mouth was beautifully small, her Teeth incomparably fine, her Eyes black, agreeably large, bright and alluring, all her Features were most delicate; the Beauty of her Face, when laughing, was unparallell'd and capable of captivating the most insensible Heart. Her Hair was black, her Breasts could not but raise any Person's Admiration, her Neck, Hands and Arms were extreamly graceful; her natural Complexion was seldom seen, but the Paint was commonly red and white. Her shape could not be conceived to be the performance of Nature, and a majestic Air added to the great perfection she had acquired in Dancing.

Such was the Person of this young Lady, but her Character was not equal to the other accomplishments she had just Reason to boast of. She was lively and pleasant in her Repartees, but discover'd little solid Sense, and less Sincerity. She was of an inconstant Disposition; complaisant to those, who used her with the Deference she claimed as due to herself, and very arrogant in her Deportment to those who resisted her; selfish and nevertheless liberal; grateful to her Benefactors, unappeaseable in Wrath, absolute in her Commands, and not always desirous of Things conformable to the strict Rules of Justice. Nevertheless no Prejudice against her was able to defend an amorous Person's Heart from being imprisoned by her Charms. Sometimes her Behaviour was charming, and at other times as unpleasant; she would condescend to act the meanest part for Riches and Honour. She was no sooner the King's Mistress, than she endeavoured to secure that Prince from a dangerous Solitude and Tranquillity. She cast off all her unpleasant Deportment, lest it should displease those who were enamoured with her; and constantly preserved Victims to sacrifice to the King's Jealousy; a Jealousy, which she was capable of giving rise to, supporting and refraining according as she thought most proper. Her greatest Art consisted in concealing her Aim at Glory; her Interest was always hid under the cover of the King's. She pretended to love Feasts and publick Shows, the better to amuse her Royal Lover. That Prince intended by distributing Favours to acquire a larger number of Creatures, but those Favours served only to establish the Power of his Mistress, who, notwithstanding the great Discernment of Frederick-Augustus, was the sole Judge of the Merit of those Persons, who received any. Thus did the Subject, who was distinguished by some new Dignity, or heap'd with the Sovereign's Bounty, attribute his Happiness only to Madame Hoyhm. Notwithstanding the Designs formed for her Destruction, notwithstanding the Hatred of the Ministers, did she support herself in his Favour during the space of nine Years; and may be said to have seen Poland and Saxony prostrate at her Feet during that time.

Madame de Hoyhm could, besides her other Qualifications, boast of an eminent Birth; she was born in the Duchy of Holstein, and had followed the Princess of Holstein-Ploen to Wolfenbuttel, when that Princess was

given in Marriage to the hereditary Prince of Brunswick-
Wolfenbuttel; this was the Court at which Mr. Hoyhm's
Marriage was celebrated. This Gentleman was for a long
time in search after a Wife; he was unwilling, tho'
himself a Native of Saxony, to marry a Saxon Lady; he
thought them too much inclined to Coquetry and too
expensive; was desirous of a beautiful, prudent Wife,
and one noted for Œconomy. One of his Friends, who
was just returned from the Court of Wolfenbuttel,
acquainted him that all those excellent Qualities were to
be met with in Mademoiselle Brouchstorff, Maid of
Honour to the Princess hereditary of Wolfenbuttel. Mr.
Hoyhm believed his Friend and departed for Brunswick,
under pretence of seeing the Fair, but in effect to see
Mademoiselle Brouchstorff. He found her such as she
had been described to him, and directly thought of being
joined to her in Marriage. As he was a Person of Quality,
possessed of great Riches, and distinguished by an
eminent Rank at the Court of Saxony, he met with a
favourable Reception, and the Matrimonial Engagements
were soon afterwards enter'd into. When the Celebration
of the Marriage-Ceremony was ended, he conducted his
Wife to one of his Seats in Saxony, where he intended
to leave her till the King returned into Poland. But as
his Destiny was inevitable, he happened, as I before
mentioned, to be guilty of Indiscretion in making
mention of her before the King, and was obliged to send

for her to Court, where she had soon the Happiness of seeing herself the Distributor of Royal Favours, and Promoter of the Fortune of private Persons.

The King at the first sight of her was charmed with her Beauty. He found in her a gay Disposition, which he desired to see in a Mistress. No further Endeavours were requisite to render him amorous. His Passion for Madame Teschen opposed for some time his Sentiments in regard to the new Rival. 'This will only be a little 'turn of Gallantry (said he to himself) I shall forget 'Madame Hoyhm when she's out of my sight.' His Conquest seemed very easy to him, but when he made mention of Love to that Lady, he found her not so pliable as he expected. Never was the Acquisition of a Mistress more expensive to him, he was obliged, as it happen'd, to take Pains, Assiduity, and spend large Sums of Money upon his Conquest; but this Resistance only increased the Desire of a Victory over her. When Madame Hoyhm thought herself sure of the King's Heart, she became more easy and compliant, and at last surrendered hers upon Conditions, whereby she obtain'd an absolute Command over the Heart of Frederick-Augustus. This Prince laid himself under an Obligation, for ever to forsake Madame Teschen, to dissolve the Bonds by which Mr. Hoyhm and his Spouse were joined together; he obliged himself by a promissory Note, writ and subscribed by himself, at the Queen's Decease to honour her with the Royal Dignity, and to acknowledge those Children, that might be born before or after, to be legitimate Princes of Saxony. To these Articles she added an annual Pension of an Hundred Thousand Rix dollars.

Upon these Conditions Madame Hoyhm accepted the Title of his Majesty's Mistress; and lest her Husband should have any reason to accuse her of ungrateful and treacherous Behaviour, went herself to inform him of the Resolution she had taken to leave him. In order thereto she went into his Bed-Chamber one Morning, and finding him there, 'I am come, Sir, (said she) to return 'you my hearty Thanks for the Favours and kind Tokens 'of Affection, you have hitherto honoured me with, 'which give me leave to assure you shall never escape 'my Memory; but I am also come to tell you, that, since 'that mutual Sympathy, which only causes and promotes 'the Happiness of a Marriage-Life, was never the con-'comitant of our Love, I design to be separated from 'you. The King is enamour'd with me, Sir, and I cannot 'conceal from you my Resolution of answering the 'Honour he thereby confers on me. I am however not 'desirous of giving you occasion to complain of me, and 'therefore propose to your Consideration a Divorce, 'which as it will render us independent of each other, 'will also secure your future Reputation. I think, Sir, it 'will most become you readily to accept of this Proposal,

INDIGNATION, RAGE, AND DESPAIR

'which if you do, be assured of my future Friendship, and
'Readiness at all times to contribute, as far as I am able,
'to your Prosperity. If on the other hand you give me the
'least Uneasiness, you shall not only be incapable of
'forcing me to change my Resolution, but will also
'oblige me to forget the Obligations you have laid me
'under, that I may the better remember the Opposition
'I meet with to my Desires from your Hands.'

The Surprise Mr. Hoyhm was in at this unexpected
Compliment can neither be described nor conceived.
He was ready to break into Reproaches and Expostulations, but his Wife interrupted him instantly. 'I know,
'Sir, all you can tell me, wherefore you may spare the
'pains of opposing a Resolution, which nothing shall
'change. Acquaint me therefore, if you please, with
'your Intention, and give me a positive Answer, that
'I may know what measures to make use of.'

Mr. Hoyhm, finding himself so strangely abused by
a Wife, whom he adored, and was upon the point of
losing in so extraordinary a manner, felt in his Heart all
the Motions, Indignation, Rage and Despair could raise.
He walk'd up and down his Room in a great Passion,
lifted up his Eyes and Hands and seem'd almost render'd
senseless by Grief. Madame Hoyhm waited in the meanwhile quietly for his Answer. When she found she could
not perswade him to speak. 'I see, Sir, (continued she)
'you at present want Resolution, and require time to

'consider what you are to do. I beg you will recollect
'in the mean while, that the Establishment or Subversion
'of your future Welfare depends entirely upon yourself.'
Upon this she retired without waiting for any further
Answer.

The unfortunate Husband remained in a Condition,
whose Misery cannot be expressed. He was in the
greatest pain imaginable, rose up, sate down, and thought
his Misery so great, that all further Assistance would be
useless. His Mind, little accustomed to yield, was not so
greatly disordered in having the King for his Rival, as
his Lady's supposed Passion for that Monarch. 'O,
'perfidious Wretch! (cried he) why did you marry me?
'why did you testify any Tenderness for me? Alas! have
'you promised me your Fidelity with no other Design,
'than to deceive and render me the most unhappy Man
'on Earth!'

Mr. Fitztuhm found him in this perturbation of Mind,
when he brought a Message from his Majesty to the
distressed Gentleman. He told him, that the King
desired he would resign all further Pretensions or Claims
to Madame Hoyhm in consenting to their immediate
Divorce. He assured him that the King would retaliate
his Complaisance in that respect; but if he resolved to
oppose an Affair, which he could not obstruct, and
persisted therein, the King would remember his Dis-
obedience, till he felt the effects of his Royal Resentment.

THE MARRIAGE DISSOLVED

Mr. Hoyhm seeing himself obliged to comply with the King's Demands, consented to what was exacted of him, and all the Favour he desired in return was a Permission from his Majesty to absent himself for some time from Court, which the King readily granted.

Fitztuhm had no sooner carried the Answer to the King, than that Prince ran hastily to his Mistress to inform her of the delightful News. 'I am then (said she) 'entirely devoted to your Majesty; may my prosperous 'Days be of an endless duration.' After this she returned her Thanks to Mr. Fitztuhm, promising never to forget the Service he had done her. She presented him with a Gold Snuff-Box enrich'd and adorned with Jewels, and desir'd he would accept of that as a slight Token of her Acknowledgment. The King desired to see this Box, opened it, and finding his Mistress's Picture in it, 'No, 'Fitztuhm, (said he) this is too beautiful, and no other 'Person but myself shall ever have this Picture. Let me 'keep it, and be satisfied with Twenty Thousand Rix 'dollars which I give thee.'

The Convocation of Dresden being in due time assembled, Mr. Hoyhm and Spouse appeared there by Proxy, desiring the Dissolution of their Marriage. Their Inducements for this Petition seemed just and reasonable to the Assembly of Divines, who declared their Marriage dissolved, permitting both Parties to marry again. The

MADAME COSEL'S PALACE

King confirmed the Sentence, which was the same day posted upon all the Church-Doors.

Madame Hoyhm changed her Husband's Name and took the denomination of Madame Cosel. As her Ambition was very great, she desired to be distinguished by some Title; and the King procured her by several Intreaties with the Emperor that of Countess of the Empire. By this Honour she obtained a very large Court, and the Envy of most Ladies of the greatest Distinction.

As by the Divorce the King found himself at liberty to act according to the Dictates of his Passion, he resolved to satisfy and publish it. He lodged Madame Cosel in the Neighbourhood of his Palace, and built a covered Gallery by which he might visit her whenever he pleased without any Person's knowledge. Some time afterwards he built a Palace for her, in which were several Apartments only to be made use of at the several Seasons. Two were appropriated for Summer, lined with Marble; and two others wainscotted, inlaid, adorned with the finest China-ware and Brocade-Hangings, were intended for the Winter; he paid Two Thousand Rix dollars for the Furniture of this Room; and those who saw it fancied themselves in an enchanted place. The Dishes and Plates were all Silver-gilt, the Vessels and Tables enriched with Crystal; the Beds of Brocade, and finely embroidered. In short, all the Furniture shewed so exquisite and uncommon a Taste in the Buyer, that every thing in the Palace might serve for a Model to others.

Madame Cosel now saw her Favour established, and the better to secure it she thought proper to remove those from the King's Person, whom she suspected to oppose her Interest. The Chancellor Beichling was the first Victim sacrificed to her irresistible Ambition of reigning.

He had made too liberal an use of his Tongue in speaking of her, and represented to the King, that the Sums expended for her Sake might be better employed. This was sufficient to prove him guilty. She accused him of great Misdemeanours and Embezzlement of the publick Treasure. The King order'd him to be arrested and carried to Koningstein, seizing besides upon his Goods and Estates which were very considerable. By this publick Action did Madame Cosel establish her Authority, and let all the World know, that nothing would be more dangerous than to offend her.

After the Chancellor's Disgrace Mr. Fitztuhm was the only Favourite, or rather the only Confidant of the King's Amours. This Favourite was of a large Size, had a fine Shape, and an amiable Aspect; his Deportment was in every respect such, as became a Person of Quality; he was compliant, supple, affable, and truly honest. He respected the King as his Master, and loved him as his Friend. The Prince of Furstemberg and the Field-Marshall Count

THE PREACHERS' PRIVILEGE

Fleming were looked upon as Favourites, but all those whom their private affairs or Favour at Court induced to approach the King, could scarce gain Admittance, without being very submissive to Madame Cosel. She governed so absolutely, that she might be said to have been Mistress both of the King and State.

Whilst all the Court was cringing to her, a Lutheran Priest boldly reproached her in the Pulpit; he compared her to Bathsheba; and lest the Auditors should mistake the Person, he described her in so nice a manner, that her Picture drawn by the most expert Painter could not have represented her in a better Light. She heard of it, was extreamly enraged, made bitter Complaints to the King, and desired a severe Punishment might be speedily inflicted on the Preacher for his Indiscretion. But the King, who was always a professed Enemy to Violence, could not himself deny the Justice of the Comparison, was not so complaisant to satisfy her; he told her, Preachers have one Hour every Sunday and Holiday, during which time they may speak whatever their thoughts suggest to them; that he could not deprive them of that Privilege, but if any one was to be wanting in his Respect to her out of those Hours, be would punish them according to their Deserts.

The King was in the mean while called into Poland, and begg'd of Madame Cosel to remain at Dresden; but she was too timorous of losing him, to let him go without her. She answered, nothing but Death should separate them; and he was obliged to take her with him.

Madame Teschen was informed, that the King was on his return to Warsaw, accompanied by Madame Cosel, and at that News directly quitted Warsaw, and retired to the Seat of the Cardinal-Primate her Uncle fully resolved to foment that Prelate's Hatred against Frederick-Augustus. But this eager Desire of Revenge was cooled as soon as she received a Letter from her former Lover. In this Letter he made a pleasant Mention of their former mutual Love.

MADAME,

Is it possible that Hatred should so immediately succeed an ardent Passion? As for me, I do still, and shall always retain the great Esteem and friendly Regard I have hitherto had for you; such I mean as is capable of forming the strictest Alliance; my Happiness consists in the sight of yours, and am at all times ready to contribute whatever may conduce to your Satisfaction. Can you harbour any other Sentiments of me? You, whose natural Benevolence is not unknown to me, who has loved me, and in whom I never once discovered any other than generous Thoughts? Will you oppose me in Favour of a King utterly unknown to you, and ignorant of the Nature of the Adoration of the Fair Sex? I cannot believe it, Madame; all the Ladies in Poland will, I'm persuaded, promote my Interest in Opposition to you, and blame you for preferring a Savage-King to a Prince, who has always admired you. Support therefore, I beg of you, my Interest with the Cardinal-Primate your Uncle: Persuade him not to break the Oath he has sworn to be faithful to me, to remain favourable to my Party, that we obtain a Glorious Peace for the Benefit of a Nation, of whom you are so worthy an Ornament, and of a King, whose Troubles cannot occasion the Oblivion of his former passionate Love for you.

The King sent this Letter by a Gentleman to Madame Teschen. She could not peruse it without bursting into Tears. She forgot the King's Infidelity, and could think of nothing but having loved him. In her answer to him, she concealed not from him, her Intention in retiring to her Uncle's Seat was chiefly to prejudice him: 'But, Sir, 'I am sensible, that it is not wholly in my Power to 'hate you. I shall convince Your Majesty, that I am not 'in the least, unworthy of the Confidence you honour me 'with; and shall not be sparing in my Intreaties to my 'Uncle to conform to your Request.'

She did effectually all, that a discreet Woman was capable of doing to support her Uncle in the King's Interest; but the Cardinal had before resolved to dethrone that Prince. He had for this purpose a Meeting with the King of Sweden, and Madame Teschen could never divert him from that pernicious Design. She gave the King Notice of it, who finding no Refuge, except in his own Courage, guarded himself with a patient Constancy, and sent for his Army from Saxony to encounter the King of Sweden, who advanced in great Haste towards Warsaw.

THE DESIGN OF THE BOOK

Here I shall, perhaps, be expected to make a short Digression, and relate the Particulars of the War; but, as the Design of this Book is not to mention his military Atchievements, but to entertain the Reader with his Amorous Adventures; and as those may be read in other Histories,[1] I shall closely follow my first Intention and proceed with the other amours of this Great and Gallant Prince.

[1] See the *History of Poland under the Reign of Augustus,* lately published in two volumes, octavo.

CHAPTER XI

Of the King's Intrigue with Henrietta *a French Merchant's Daughter, an Accident occasioned by this Amour*, Madame Cosel's *Suspicions. The Swedes invade Poland, and hasten to Warsaw. King Augustus's Conduct, he flies into Saxony*, Madame Cosel *is delivered of a Daughter, and* Henrietta *is likewise delivered of a Daughter.* Madam Cosel *is enamoured with another Gentleman, the King is informed of it, and reproaches his Mistress. The King of Sweden advances towards Saxony with the new King of Poland.* Augustus *submits to the Conquerors, and retires to Flanders to make a Campaigne under* Prince Eugene, *his Behaviour in the Army, his Return through Brussels, and Amour there with a French Comedian; she follows the King to Dresden, his Intrigue with her there.* King Frederick IV of Denmark *visits* Augustus, *and meets with a splendid Reception. The two Kings visit* King Frederick, King of Prussia. Charles XII, King of Sweden, *is conquered by the Russians*, Augustus's *Re-accession to the Throne of Poland, His Amour with* Madame Denhoff, Madame Cosel's *Disgrace after her third Delivery.* Madame Denhoff's *Disgrace, and the King's new Amour with* Madame Dieskau, *and after that with* Mademoiselle Osterhausen. *The* Prince-Royal of Poland *is married to the* Arch-Dutchess of the Empire, *and returns to Dresden, where Grand Entertainments are prepared for him. The King renounces to his new Mistress all further Amours; marries his Daughter by* Henrietta, *and continues the usual Gallantry of his Court to the end of his Life.*

KING AUGUSTUS was now perplexed with State-Affairs, but could nevertheless not subdue his amorous Inclinations; Madame Cosel was the principal Object of his

Passion, but he sometimes disappointed her, to visit another Beauty of an inferior Rank.

There lived at this time in Warsaw a Wine-Merchant, Native of France, nam'd Duval, who had a Daughter possessed of great Beauty, whose name was Henrietta. The brightest young Persons of the Court made their Addresses to her, and no Coquet in Warsaw had so large a number of Adorers; she received all their Addresses with equal Behaviour, and no-body could distinguish which was the Favourite Lover. This young Lady was the common subject of Conversation with those, who were called the Gallants of the Court. A Company of these made mention of her one day at his Majesty's Levee. The King overheard them, and asked who was the fair Subject of their Discourse? Mr. Rantzau, Aid de Camp to the King, answered, That the Person of whom they were speaking, was the Daughter of a French Merchant, and certainly the most lovely Creature in the Kingdom. The King made no Reply, but was no sooner dress'd, than he ordered Rantzau to follow him into his Apartment, where he enquired in a more particular manner after Henrietta, and desired he would conduct him to her. This Visit was appointed for the next Night. The King told Rantzau he would disguise himself, and desired not to be known by Henrietta, or any Person whatever. The new Confident was forbid to mention this nocturnal Intrigue to Madame Cosel, and he promised to keep it secret, but begg'd the King would also promise not to expose him to the Resentment of the revengeful Mistress. The Monarch told him his Fears were groundless, and ordered him to be in the Anti-Chamber in the Dusk of the Evening. He then went to Madame Cosel, and told her, his Presence had been desired in a private Conference the next Night with Count Tobianski, Nephew to the Cardinal-Primate, but that Lord being known by every one, he dared not see him in the Palace, therefore they had determined to meet in a private House, where they were both to be in Disguise. 'I intend to take Rantzau 'with me (said he) and have the more Reason to trust 'to his Fidelity, because he is related to, and recom- 'mended by you.' The King expressed himself in so sincere a manner seemingly, that he soon deceived his cunning and penetrating Mistress. 'Though my Cousin 'is to have the Honour of going with you, Sir, (replied 'she) yet shall I be very uneasy. A thousand unforeseen 'Accidents may happen to you; Warsaw is inhabited by 'innumerable Traitors, who are by Oath resolved upon 'your Destruction, one Person happening to know you 'may put an End to your Days.'

The King answered her in Jest, that he should think those Fears pardonable in any other Person, but would not excuse them in her. 'Alas! Sir, (replied she fixing her 'Eyes tenderly upon him) have we not the liberty of 'being intrepid or fearful of a Danger approaching the

HENRIETTA EASILY DECEIVED

'Object of our Love?' The King made endearing Answers to those Tokens of Tenderness; but was very much disordered at a whimsical desire of Madame Cosel to accompany him in his nocturnal Journey. 'Suffer me, 'Sir, (said she) to follow and guard you; if any one 'dares to make any Attempt upon your Person, Rantzau 'and I may defend you; for before you shall be offended, 'I will lose my life.' The King was touch'd with all the Tokens of Love he received from his Mistress, repented of having undertaken to deceive her, and was tempted to acknowledge the Truth, but thought such an Acknowledgment would only afflict her, he judg'd it most proper to conceal it; begg'd she would not follow him, telling her, he would rather disengage the Conference, than expose her to the Hazard of so fatal an Adventure. Madame Cosel submitted to his Desire, she not having yet acquired that Absolute Power, which she has since been seen to make use of.

The impatiently expected Night at last approached, the King disguised himself as well as possible, took Mr. Rantzau with him and went on foot to Duval's House. They desired a private Room, and sometime afterwards Mr. Rantzau, one of their best Customers, sent for the young Henrietta, and presented the King to her, as if he had been an Officer and Friend of his; the young Person, who had only seen the King go by, and could not expect a Visit from him, was easily deceived.

THE KING IN A TRANSPORT

In the mean while they conversed together for some time, the King entertained her with his usual pleasant Discourses, and she look'd at him more attentively. 'The more I look at you (said she) the more I find you 'resemble the King.'—'I own (replied he) several Persons 'have told me I had the Honour of resembling his 'Majesty, but I would rather equal him in Power than 'Shape, that I might be capable of raising your Fortune.'— 'Interest, (said she) is not the sole guide of my Actions; 'and was I so happy as to be beloved by him, I should 'think myself more fortunate by reason of the good 'Character I daily hear of him, than because he would 'make my Fortune.'—'O! Mademoiselle (cried the King) 'if those be your Sentiments, let me beseech you to love 'me in Favour of the Resemblance I bear to his Majesty.'— 'You have, indeed (replied she) those Graces which the 'King is distinguished by; but I doubt whether you can 'boast of so tender a Heart, as his is said to be, which 'can only charm me.'—'Yes, Mademoiselle (replied the 'Prince in a Transport which deprived him of all Com- 'mand over his Passion) I can boast of that tender Heart, 'and all the Qualities of that Prince, in short, I am the 'King.' He then cast off a great Coat and Periwig, which hid his dark-brown Hair, and shewed her the Star of the Order of the Elephant fixed to his Coat. Young Henrietta was at the sight of this in great Disorder, fearful of not having behaved herself with due Respect in the King's Presence, but he soon removed her Fears, by asking her Pardon for surprising her in that manner: but told her he had been informed of her Charms, and was desirous of seeing, whether they did in reality correspond with the Report he had frequently heard of them; but found her Beauty far exceeded the Description given of her, and he could not enjoy the same Liberty when he departed from her, which he could boast of before he saw her. Henrietta fixed her Eyes upon him, answering with great Respect, but so disordered, scarce knowing what she said. The King took advantage of her Confusion, making an Offer of his Heart, which Henrietta had not the power of refusing. In this excessive Joy he forgot Madame Cosel was sitting up for him, and he spending the Night in jesting and diverting himself with Henrietta, who being by degrees more familiar, made use of her natural Gaiety. She sung, and plaid; the King would have persuaded her to let him proceed further, but her Virtue opposed any Criminal Action, and the Monarch was obliged to conform to her Will. They parted at length, promising faithfully to meet again the next Night.

Daylight appeared when the King returned to his Palace, where he found Madame Cosel at the Fire-side. As his Mind was wholly employed upon the beautiful Henrietta, he asked her with much Indifference, why she was not in Bed before? 'I waited (answered she in a dole-

'ful Tone) and have been very uneasy for you, Sir.'—
'You must accustom yourself to bear my Absence more
'patiently (replied the King) when I am at the Head of an
'Army, I see no probability of your following me thither.'
—'Why not? (answered she) I shall follow you everywhere,
'when I am near you no Fear shall cast me down. But
'what has happened to you? (continued she) you seem
'troubled.'—'Nothing troubles me (answered the King)
'except not finding you in Bed.' The Coldness with which
he spoke gave Madame Cosel Reason to suspect an
Intrigue; but she thought proper to conceal her Suspicions, till the event proved them to be just. She went
into Bed, and the King, repenting of having caused any
Uneasiness in her, would not leave her. They testified a
most lively Tenderness for each other, which nevertheless did not remove Madame Cosel's Doubts.

The King rose early to hold a Council, and she made
use of his Absence in enquiring of Mr. Rantzau where
he had been with the King. This Confident shewed no
Disorder at her Question, telling her, they had been in
Conference with the Count Tobianski. 'I believe your
'words (said she) but take care not to deceive me, for if
'you do, you shall assuredly have good reason to repent
'of it.'

Mr. Rantzau acquainted the King with his Conversation with Madame Cosel. 'I protest (said that Prince)
'your Cousin perplexes me very much. I love her: yet she

'is a desperate woman, capable of undertaking any thing.
'But Henrietta does never the less please me. What
'can I do?'—'You may engage yourself, Sir, (answered
'Mr. Rantzau) with the Person who pleases you most,
'and no longer think of the other.' The King made no
Reply, but went to his Mistress, whose Eyes he found
full of Tears; 'What troubles you, Madame, (said he)
'and what occasions the Affliction I see you in?'—'Alas!
'Sir, (answered she) I don't know what Reply to make,
'but my Heart tells me you are unfaithful.' The King
did his utmost endeavour by endearing Speeches and
Assurances to hearten her, he conjured her not to load
him with groundless Suspicions. And to divert her mind
from those perplexing Thoughts, he discoursed with her
about the State of his Affairs, telling her, he should be
obliged to have another private Conference with Count
Tobianski. 'I readily consent to it, Sir, (answered she)
'but fear Count Tobianski is not the Person you confer
'with!' The King, highly displeas'd with this repeated
Affront, told her Suspicions and Reproaches were very
disagreeable to him.

In the mean while the Night was coming on, which
he impatiently waited for to see Henrietta, he went, and
was pleased to find her less reserved, than she was the
Night before; She had consulted her Mother, whom she
acquainted with what had passed between the King and
her, and who had instructed her how to behave herself;

Henriette Duval

these Instructions had adapted her much more to the King's Humour, and removed the Doubts she was before perplexed with. The King triumphed over her Shame; but she shed numberless Tears, and no Virginity was ever lost with more Sighs and Regrets. The two Lovers assured each other frequently of their mutual Love, and the Assurances of both Parties were made in a very different manner.

The night was almost past before the King retired. Before he left his dear Henrietta he begg'd her Consent to keep their amour secret. He promis'd to visit her frequently, and agreed, that she should visit him in a Man's Dress, and Mr. Rantzau should conduct her to him.

When the King was going home with his Confident, he met with an Adventure, which almost discover'd this whole Intrigue. A Gentleman of the Life-Guard was desperately in Love with Henrietta, intending to be marry'd to her. He had been two days out of her Company, when told by a Servant, Henrietta had spent the two last Nights with Mr. Rantzau and another Officer. This rais'd a furious Jealousy in the Gentleman; he resolved to take away the Person's Life, who durst deprive him of his Mistress, and that his success might be infallible, he took with him his Brother, a Gentleman of the Life-Guard like him, both waiting for Mr. Rantzau at some distance from Duval's House. They no sooner saw him,

than they cried out, desiring him to draw his Sword;
but Mr. Rantzau in fear of discovering the King, thinking
the Persons who threaten'd him were perhaps mistaken,
he having no Quarrel with any-body, told them his name,
and if he was really the Person they intended to fight
with, he was ready to give them Satisfaction; but desired
they would allow him half an Hour to go and return an
Answer to a Message his Majesty had charged him with.
'By no means (cried the other) you shall not escape me;
'be ready for your own Destruction. You have deprived
'me of my Mistress, and I will in return occasion the
'loss of your Life or mine.' The King suffer'd them to
fight, whilst the other Person remained a Spectator like
him; but when he saw him run to his Comrade's Assistance to kill Rantzau, he ran to the latter's Succour with
Sword in hand, and assaulting the second Life-Guard-
man, gave him so violent a Blow that he dropp'd his
Sword. Whilst he was taking it up again, a Coach passed
attended by Servants with Flambeaus. The disarmed
Soldier knew the King, called out to his Brother to
desist, throwing himself at the King's Feet; 'Sir, (said
'he) I have deserved Death, and should be too happy,
'was I to receive it from your hands. I desire no Favour,
'because I acknowledge my Crime is unpardonable.'—
'You are mistaken (replied the King) with me all Faults
'are pardonable, provided they were not perpetrated with
'an evil Design. I excuse that which you have just now

'committed, being persuaded you did not intend to 'offend me, but enjoin you both, to make some Excuse 'to Rantzau for having assaulted him, and use him for 'the future with the Respect due to him from your hands.' He gave them a slight Reproof for offending a Person they were not acquainted with, desired they would be more considerate for the future, and forbid them under the Penalty of incurring his Displeasure, to make any further mention of this Adventure, or to let any-body know they met him. The next morning the two Soldiers thought their Ruin inevitable, applied to Mr. Rantzau, and after asking his Pardon for their late Offence, begg'd he would obtain leave for them to depart, not being able to believe, after committing so great a Fault, they could ever hope for Promotion. Mr. Rantzau deliver'd the Message to the King, who sent for them both immediately. 'I have assured you (said he) of my Pardon, and 'sent for you to-day to reproach you for the little Regard 'you have to my Words. I desire you not to go out of my 'Service. Behave yourselves like Gentlemen of Honour, 'and be assured I shall endeavour to advance your 'Fortune'. Hereupon they were admitted to kiss his hand, and after they were gone, the King sent to each a Present of an hundred Ducats.

In the mean while Madame Cosel easily perceived the Ardency of the King's Passion to be much diminish'd. She doubted not but some Mistress caus'd an Alteration in his Heart, but whatever pains she gave herself could not discover the Person. After many useless Enquiries she was informed by one of the King's Valets de Chambre, that the King passed many Hours with a young Man, who by his great Beauty, and the mysterious method by which he was introduced to the King, gave him reason to think the Person might perhaps be a disguis'd Woman. This Information cleared at once innumerable Doubts, which tormented her, but her Condition was not much better. As she was naturally very arrogant, she could scarce prevail upon herself patiently to put up with it; but she had not yet been at variance with the King, and thought it would look more prudent in her not to exclaim against him, if he could not be convinced, than to ruin herself by a Resentment. She was thus meditating on what would be most proper for her to do, when the King surprized her in a deep Thought. As she sate in a melancholy posture, he told her she seem'd distressed, and he had for some time always found her bright Eyes drowned in Tears. She answered him by this passage in a Tragedy;

> What reason have I not to cry?
> My senseless Lover bids me die.

The King blush'd at these Words, and looking with a tender Air; 'What is it you mean (said he) by Reproaches, 'I so little deserve?' She soon expressed herself in a lively and sorrowful manner. The King surprized to find her so well acquainted with his Intrigue, assured her in a seeming sincere manner, no greater Falsehood was ever invented. He told her the pretended Woman, mentioned to her, was Nephew to Brebendofski, Governor of Culm, that that Nobleman had sent him to give Notice of the measures taken by the Polish Rebels; that he had indeed detained him for some time in his Chamber, but no longer than was requisite for an Answer to the Governor; since that time he had never seen the young gentleman, and if the Person had been a disguis'd Woman to whom he had been amorously inclined, it would not have been impracticable to find her again; but to all outward appearance the Persons who reported these Falsities to her, intended to supply her with Arms for her own Destruction, since he hated nothing more than Expostulations and Broils. The Countess vexed to see him persevere so stedfastly in the Denial of his Infidelity, was highly enraged. 'I believe you (said she) but be now assured by 'me, I am resolved not to undergo the Fate of your other 'Mistresses. I have for your Sake quitted a Husband, lost 'my Reputation, and done all this, because you promis'd 'me upon Oath an everlasting Fidelity. I will not suffer 'your Abuses, except your Life pays for them; I am 'resolved to break your Head with a Pistol, and then to 'make use of it upon myself, as a Punishment for my 'Folly in loving you.'

THE 'MAGNANIMOUS PRINCE'

However insolent this Rage of the Countess was, the King pitied her; endeavoured to appease her Anger, and did not leave her till very late. He was considering of the means by which he might extirpate this Mistress's Jealousy, when an unexpected Courier brought him Advice the Swedes were advancing in great haste towards Warsaw. Other Cares employed his Mind at this time, and he found no other way left, than to take to his Flight, the Polanders being so imprudent as to prefer the Yoke Charles XII was going to impose on them to the pleasant and happy Reign of Frederick-Augustus, forsook him; and those few who remained loyal to their King were incapable of keeping him upon the Throne, and even unwilling to consent to his sending for his Army from Saxony to his Assistance. This magnanimous Prince found only Refuge in himself; he acted as the most refined Politician, when he endeavoured to stop the Progress of his Enemy, retired to Cracaw, there assembled a Body of Soldiers, and sent for the Saxons; and when he saw himself able to compare his Forces to those of the implacable Charles, he marched on to encounter him, resolved to hazard all, and leave it to the decision of a Battle. But before he placed himself at the Head of his Army he sent Madame Cosel back into Saxony. This Departure was very tender on both sides, and nevertheless exempt of any Weakness. Madame Cosel conjured the King to consent to her Stay near his Person. 'I will

'cloath myself in a Man's Dress (said she) and fight by
'your Side. My Blood and Life are but of a very small
'Value; and I am ready to sacrifice either for your Sake.'
—'No, Madame, (replied the King) your Days are too
'precious to me, preserve them. Desire me not to place
'all that is most dear to me, you and my Crown, at the
'Hazard of a Battle. Depart for Dresden; that I may be
'more certain of your Safety, I shall then fight more
'vigorously; and as the Pleasure of seeing you again will
'be the first Prize I shall gain by the Victory, I dare
'promise myself to enjoy it.' The Countess not daring to
insist on her Demand any longer, consented to depart;
but as those Suspicions, which were first founded at
Warsaw, were still inherent in her Mind, she made use
of those tender moments which preceded her Departure
in asking the King whether she had any just Cause for
those Doubts. The King, who no longer thought of
Henrietta, whom he had left at Warsaw, confessed the
whole Adventure. Madame Cosel seemed not in the least
displeas'd, but her Heart was very much vexed at it, and
she fully resolved to sacrifice Rantzau to her Vengeance.

At length she departed for Dresden, where she may be
truly said to have had a greater Command than the
Prince of Furstemberg, who was in the mean while
Stadtholder or Vice-King of Saxony. The King continued
his March towards Charles the Twelfth's Army. These
two Monarchs met in the Plain of Clissau. The Battle

begun, and both exerted an extraordinary Valour, but Charles at last prevailed by the Number of his Troops, and carried a compleat Victory. Frederick-Augustus retired to Cracaw, but the Conqueror pursued him, and he flew from that Place to Lublin, where he assisted at a Diet, which, however, came to no particular Resolution. He retired at last to Saxony. When he arrived at Dresden, he found Madame Cosel in Labour; but this did not hinder him from running to her. His Presence afforded her comfort, and some moments afterwards she was delivered of a Daughter. Madame Cosel had undergone so much pain, and was so weak, that she could not speak to the King, but squeezed his Hand, and looked at him tenderly. The King was so touched with her Misery, that his Eyes were drowned in Tears. Her Pain being a little lessened, she made use of all the most tender Expressions her Fancy could inspire her with. The King asked her whether his Defeat did not occasion her Love to cease. 'I shall love you (cried she with more Force 'than her Condition would admit) if I even see you in 'Chains.'

During the forty Days in which she kept her Bed, the King passed his time at her Bed-side, and took all possible care to please her. One day, as they were discoursing together, Mr. Bose, Minister and Secretary of State, brought the King Word that he had receiv'd a certain Message with a Letter, which came from Warsaw, and

Countess Cosel as Venus

Engraving by Vallée

which he presented to the King. The King when he opened the Letter, blush'd, and was in great Disorder. Madame Cosel desired to know the Subject of it, and to see it herself, but he refused to shew it to her. This rais'd Madame Cosel's Curiosity, she leap'd out of Bed, and pull'd it by force out of his hand. She shewed the King and Mr. Bose on that Occasion what no modest Woman would have shewn her Husband without many Perswasions. She found that the Letter came from Henrietta, who acquainted the King that she was delivered of a Daughter, and desired to know his Pleasure concerning the Child. 'Let her drown it, (cried Madame Cosel) and 'would to God it was in my power to drown the Mother 'too!' The King laugh'd heartily at this impertinent Sally, but Madame Cosel considered of the matter seriously, and told him, that if he made any Answer to that Creature, or acknowledged the Child of which she said she was deliver'd, she would instantly take Post, and go to Warsaw to strangle both the Mother and Child. The King to prevent any Disturbance, promis'd to think no more of either Henrietta or her Infant Daughter. This Child, however, which was at that time so abus'd, has been since acknowledged by the King; she has been to the King dearer than any of his other Children, and he has honoured her with the Title of Countess of Orzelska, and married her to a younger Prince of the House of Holstein-Beck.

THE COUNT OF LECHERENNE

This Mistress was in the mean while, notwithstanding her great Jealousy, thought by several Gentlemen a proper Object of Adoration, and their Offers were very agreeable to her. She did indeed receive them only as Victims to sacrifice to the King and her own Interest. One of these Lovers was the Count of Lecherenne, a Nobleman of Savoy, whose Necessity induced him to come with his Brother, a Knight of the Order of Malta, to Dresden, in search after a Lady of Fortune. The two Brothers directly made their Addresses to Madame Cosel; this they thought would be the most proper means to accomplish their Point, for she had the chief Disposal of Honours and Royal Favours. She admitted them as Gentlemen of the King's Bed-Chamber. Whilst she was alone at Dresden, these Gentlemen insinuated themselves into her Favour; but the Count was preferr'd to the Knight: he had a fine Shape, and made a graceful Appearance; as he was a Man of exquisite parts, was witty, complaisant, had a nice Taste, and was never perplexed with any Doubts. The particular Kindness Madame Cosel testified for him, was wrongly censured by her Enemies. As they could do her no greater Prejudice, than set the King and her at Variance, they did their utmost endeavour to perswade him, that the Love he testified for her was too great for the little return he received from her hands. This was certainly no very easy Undertaking, but they took so essential a method

to carry their Point, that, except any of 'em were overheard by the King, their Design could not be discovered,
nor the Project be in the least suspected. The better to
succeed in the Plot they represented to the King, that
Madame Cosel had shewed but little Deference to his
Majesty in certain Assemblies, and seemed to give this
Report in so disinterested a manner, that the King,
notwithstanding his great Subtilty in Affairs of this
kind, could scarce help being deceived by their seeming
sincerity.

All these Words, however, made but a slight impression
upon the King's Mind, till Madame Cosel's Enemies,
at the Head of which was the Prince of Furstemberg,
mentioned the Count of Lecherenne, as the Rival he
should be in fear of. Hereupon he went to his Mistress, to
expostulate with her about the matter. He found her in
her Closet looking considerately upon a Picture, wherein
was represented the Ceremony of his Coronation. 'How!
'Madame (said he in a disdainful manner) do you still
'condescend to look upon my Picture? or is it some other
'Object, which you regard so stedfastly upon that Table?'
—'How can a Person, Sir, (said she) so graceful as your-
'self, have any Reason to think, that Spectators can fix their
'Eyes upon any other Object but yourself; and if you are
'even enamoured with the most fickle Woman on Earth,
'your shining Merit should keep you from all jealous
'Thoughts.'—'Hitherto (replied the King) I thought I

'had no Grounds for suspicion; but find myself highly
'mistaken, and those Persons who judge only by outward
'Appearances are most apt to be deceived.' By these
words Madame Cosel soon perceived the King's Jealousy,
at which she felt a secret Joy, it proving sufficiently that
he loved her. In the mean while, pretending to be offended
at his Discourse; 'I cannot imagine the meaning of
'those intricate Terms, Sir, (said she) and till you express
'yourself in a more intelligible manner, you cannot
'expect me to say anything for my own Justification.'—
'You will, perhaps, find it a more difficult matter to justify
'yourself, (replied the King in a serious manner which
'began to perplex Madame Cosel) than I shall to convince
'you of Things which you wished undoubtedly not to
'reach my knowledge.' She made no further Answer to
these Words, than her former Tokens of Tenderness;
put into practice whatever a most passionate Love could
inspire her with, and the Tears, which accompanied all
these Transports, appeased the Anger of her incens'd
Lover. She no sooner saw him a little pacified, than she
begg'd he would tell her what had occasioned these
Reproaches which she had just before heard; she swore
to own the plain Truth; and added to this, that if she
did even think herself criminal, she reposed so great a
Confidence in him, and was perswaded that his Love to
her was so great, as to pardon any Folly she had been
guilty of. The King told her all he heard to her Prejudice,

and she did not deny that the Count of Lecherenne had made amorous Addresses to her; but would not own that she had ever given ear to them. She told him, that he should have been banished her Presence, but that she was excessively uneasy during his Absence, and therefore thought a little Conversation with the Count would not be criminal; and that she had only admitted him to her Company, after having forbid him ever to mention Love again. The King comforted her, and promis'd for the future not to regard the slanderous Reports of envious Persons; he protested that no ridiculous and ill-grounded Fear should ever induce him to lose the Affection he had sworn ever to retain for her; and desired she would be perswaded of that by his own Word and Promise.— 'O! Sir, (said she) if your Majesty suffers Detractions of 'that kind so nearly to approach your Throne, I have 'reason to fear that your Person will in a little time 'be injured by them, and they will offend that, which 'I esteem most sacred.'—'Be no longer perplexed about it '(replied the King) I shall myself regulate those matters.' She still insisted upon being told who was the Person that first rais'd this Report; but the King refus'd. 'Let 'it suffice (said he) that I look upon them as evil Reports, 'which I shall never believe.' He then left her fully convinced of her Innocence, and greatly prejudiced against those who injured her by asserting these Falsities, and more especially against Lecherenne, for occasioning them to speak evil of his Mistress, whom he ordered instantly to quit his Service, and directly afterwards to leave Dresden.

This unfortunate Gentleman was desirous before his Departure to see Madame Cosel, and in order thereto attended at her Door, but she sent him Word, she could not admit those whom the King banished from his Presence. To let him know, however, that she saw him depart with much Regret, she sent him a Ring, which the King had some time before presented her with, with this Ring the Count left Dresden. Few days after this the King seeing her dress herself, observed that she had not the Ring and demanded the reason of it. She seemed surprized at the Loss, and asked her Servants, whether they had seen the Ring, who unfortunately, or for want of better Instructions answered, that they had not seen it within the four or five last days. This being exactly the time of Count Lecherenne's Departure, the King doubted not of her having given him the Ring at their last Farewell. This Thought revived his Jealousy, and enraged him in an uncommon manner, he reproached her severely, and the Countess heard him with Patience, which had she been innocent, she would have resented.

Whilst these trifling Affairs were transacting at Court, Charles XII who had caus'd Stanislaus Leczinski, Palatine of Posnania to be crowned at Warsaw, advanced towards Saxony with the new King, the shining Trophy of all his Victories. The King having no Army to oppose him, was forced to sign the Treaty of Peace, such as that implacable Prince was pleased to prescribe. This did not, however, prevent the King of Sweden's March further into Saxony, where he raised immense Contributions. Whoever is conversant in the History of those Times, cannot be ignorant, that That Prince left Saxony with the Design of dethroning the then Czar; and that he was himself the most remarkable Instance of the Inconstancy of Fortune, and Instability of humane Grandeur.

Frederick-Augustus retain'd his usual Magnanimity during the whole course of his Adversities. He was never heard to bemoan his unhappy Fate, nor to complain of the Ingratitude of the Polanders. Madame Cosel, daily apprehensive of his being troubled with some private Uneasinesses, did her utmost Endeavour to remove all the Troubles of his Mind; she prepared every day some new Entertainment for his Diversion. The King loved Pleasures, but was not wholly given over to them. War and Hopes of Glory were his chief Delight; and as the state of his Affairs would not supply him with a sufficient Number of Forces to carry on a War against the Usurper of his Crown, he went into Flanders to search after Renown in the Army of the Allies. He made his Appearance there *incognito*, and made use of the Equipage belonging to Prince Eugene of Savoy. All the Men of various Nations of which this great Army was compos'd admired his great Experience in the Art of War, and undaunted Courage. He expos'd his Life several times with so little Precaution, that Prince Eugene and the Duke of Marlborough took the liberty of remonstrating the Danger to him. He answered them laughing, That Warriors ought to be Calvanists, and sincerely believe Predestination.

This Great Monarch, after having acquired an entire knowledge of the Nature of an Attack, and foreseeing that the Siege of Lisle would perhaps be extended to a great length of Time, even after the French would have ceas'd making fresh Attempts to raise the Siege, resolved to return into Saxony. He passed through Brussels, and to avoid all tedious Ceremonies assumed the Name of Count of Torgau, and arrived at that Town just before the Gates were shut. He went the same Evening to the Opera; there he saw a Dancer named Duparc, who was possessed of great Beauty and extraordinary Graces, and deserved incontestably the Preference to any Dancer out of France at that time. The King was pleased with her, and desired her Company at the House of Vernus a celebrated Cook, who kept a very great Ordinary. She readily accepted of the Invitation, and Duparc appeared with three other Comedians at the Entertainment. The King was by the Name of Count of Torgau accompanied by Mrs. Fitztuhm, Bauditz, and the Count of

Angélique Duparc

SHE WISHES TO GO TO DRESDEN

W—— who had joined in their Conversation. When they were at Table Duparc, who was extreamly beautiful, but more particularly with a Glass in her hand, wholly captivated the King's Heart. He entertained her with pleasant Discourses, and charmed the Coquet, whose Discernment was certainly great. But as her Prejudice in Favour of the French Nation was so great, she could not imagine any but a Frenchman to be given so much to Gallantry, she could not be perswaded the Count of Torgau was a German. 'You are a Native of France '(said she) your Gallantry, Air and Politeness witness it.'— 'No, really, (answered the King) I am an honest Saxon, 'whose Words correspond with his Thoughts, and give 'everything its true Appellation.'—'Are you a Saxon? '(replied Duparc) then I beg you would describe your 'King to me; I have heard that he is really an incompar- 'able Prince.' She added, that within the two last Years she had teazed an old Aunt of hers who belong'd to a Company of French Comedians at Dresden, to procure her a Place in the King's Service; but that all the Answer she could receive, was, that no Place was vacant for her. The King replied, that her Aunt surely did not take much Pains, or was not very desirous of seeing her there, else it would be no difficult matter to get her the Place of chief Dancer; That if she did still intend to go to Dresden, he would procure her Admission and some advantageous Post. Duparc accepted the Offer, and the King told her, if she pleas'd she might go the next day, and offered her a Place in his Coach; but she thank'd him under pretence that some Affairs detained her at Brussels, promis'd however to follow him thither in a Month's time. The King, to engage her to the performance of her Promise, gave her a Purse of a Thousand Ducats to defray the Expense of her Journey. He desired to exact some pleasant Acknowledgment of her; but she, quite contrary to the Custom of Persons of that kind, told him in a merry Air, that he possessed not only the gallant Disposition, but also the Vivacity of a Frenchman; but that, though her Virginity was lost, yet did she not love to be wholly taken up with Amours; that her Heart must first be captivated before she gave any essential Tokens of her Love: but before she entered into any amorous Engagement she would first be acquainted with the Character of the Person to whom she discover'd her Heart. The King oppos'd her Sentiments, but in vain; and his Passion for her became more violent. He conjured her not to delay her Journey to Dresden, which she promis'd, and at his Departure he adorned her Finger with a Ring of great Value.

The King quitted Brussels the next Morning, and arrived in few days at Dresden. He there found Madame Cosel a second time in Child-bed, and his Family increased by another Daughter. His Mistress made grievous Complaints of the Prince of Furstemberg, Stadholder, and the Field-Marshall Count Fleming, whom she accus'd of having behaved very disrespectfully to her; these Noblemen, having received Instructions from the King, had indeed refus'd to obey Madame Cosel's Orders, such as she thought herself entitled to give them. The King, who was never fond of private Broils, occasioned by Envy or Malice, and always desirous of a happy Union between his Mistress and Ministers, reconciled them; but this Reconciliation did not remove their great Desire to injure each other as much as possible, for which they neglected no Opportunity.

The King enjoyed a happy Peace with Madame Cosel, a Peace not interrupted by any Jealousy, till Duparc came to disturb their Felicity. She arrived at Dresden whilst the King was at Mauritzburg; and enquired every-where for the Count of Torgau, but could no-where be informed how to meet with him. Her Aunt conducted her to Mr. Murdacho, Chamberlain and Director of the King's Diversions, who gave her a Reception very different from that, which Persons of her Function commonly met with at his hands; he told her, that the King had given him Orders to admit her to the Number of the Dancers belonging to the Court, to provide her handsome Apartments, and to furnish them as would be found necessary and agreeable to her Pleasure, and that his Majesty desired she would begin to dance at the Opera of Elida, which the Comedians were to repeat to represent her at the King's Return. Duparc was surprized with Wonder and Delight at so Gracious a Reception; she testified her Acknowledgment to Mr. Murdacho, and asked by what singular Fortune she was honoured with the King's Acquaintance? He answered, that he had good reason to think she was obliged to the Count of Torgau for the King's unexpected Munificence. She could get no better Information, and retired with her Aunt, who was no less astonished than her Niece at what had happened. They could not imagine who was this Count of Torgau, and dared not to name the King tho' he was suspected to be the Person; The Aunt was in fear lest she should flatter her Niece too much, was she to speak of it; and the Niece was fearful of being deceived in her Expectation, and having the Aspersion of a Vain Person. 'But if it was 'the King, (said she to herself) why should he conceal 'his Name? Why should he be unwilling to acquaint me 'with his Dignity? What could be his Intention in sending 'for, and receiving me in this manner?' In this Perplexity did she remain till the Day on which the King made his Appearance at the Theatre, saying to herself, It is the King undoubtedly, and perhaps a Moment afterwards, It cannot be.

The same Morning an extraordinary Present was brought her of a Box cover'd with Crimson-Velvet and Gold-Lace, and was told, that it came from the Count of Torgau. The Bearers of this Box would not inform her of any further Particulars, notwithstanding her diligent Enquiries, they remained as it were speechless, and returned her no other Answer but by intelligible Signs. When she open'd her Box she found in it two Rich Suits of Cloaths, one for the Stage, and the other to wear in Town; to these were added all the Things requisite to dress her from Head to Foot, not even the Slippers were wanting. The Pockets were full of Toys of a great Value, among which was a small Pocket-Book enriched with Gold. She open'd it, and found upon the first Leaf the Count's Excuses for not having paid her any Visit yet; He begg'd her acceptance of the Cloaths he sent her, as Fore-runners of the Kindnesses he should distinguish her by; and finished the Letter, by telling her, he intended to pay his Respects to her at Supper the same Evening. Duparc was overjoy'd, when informed of the true Condition of her Lover.

She dressed herself with all the Care of a Person, intending to gain a great Conquest, and at last appeared upon the Stage more like a Queen than a Dancer, so bright was her Appearance. All her Companions were in Admiration of her, and could not comprehend from whence she received so magnificent a Dress.

They waited some time for the King, who at last appeared with Madame Cosel. The young and amiable Duparc was extreamly impatient to see him, and for that purpose plac'd herself in a Wing directly opposite to the Monarch's Seat. But how can I describe her Joy on finding her Lover was the King himself! Psyche could not be more pleas'd, when told that the God of Love had rais'd her to the fatal Rock. The King seeing her swoon away, called to Beltour a Comedian to run to her Assistance, and reach'd to her from his Seat a little Flask of Carmelite's Water. Madame Cosel was highly displeas'd at the King's great Civilities to a Stranger; and reproached him for it. 'It seems, Sir, (said she with 'a disdainful Air) that you are very profuse of your 'Kindnesses, in conferring them on a Creature utterly 'unknown to you, and undoubtedly little deserving your 'Regard.' The King offended at her Insolence, answered with Indifference, that he might justly be blamed for being munificent to a great degree, and to Persons who abus'd his Liberality; but that he hoped for better Tokens of Gratitude from the hands of Duparc. Madame Cosel exasperated at his Reply, told him, that none but Vagabonds were the Objects of his Love. The King unwilling to let all the Court be Witnesses of their Differences, rose up, and went to the Queen's Apartment, who was discoursing with her Brother the Margrave of Brandenburg-Bareith. Madame Cosel scarce capable of putting up with the Affront, and unable to conceal her Wrath, feigned an Indisposition, and left the Theatre. The King was not so complaisant as to follow her, nor did he send any Messenger to enquire after her Health; which made her Uneasiness insupportable. The King having been some time with the Queen, called Mr. Murdacho, and whisper'd to him, that he had ordered his Servants to carry the Supper to his House, and had invited Duparc, with three other Actresses, whose Names he mentioned.

The Comedy was no sooner finished, than the King went immediately to Mr. Murdacho's. His beloved Duparc made her Appearance there in the Apparel which the pretended Count of Torgau had sent for her Use in the Town. The King ran to meet her, when he saw her coming; but she kneel'd down and thank'd him for his excessive Goodness. The King rais'd and embraced her, and told her that she was not to lye at his Feet; and that he should not even suffer that Deference, if he had not conceived those tender Sentiments for her, which render all conditions equal. This Preamble was succeeded by many Demonstrations of Joy and Tenderness. Duparc could not yet recover from her Astonishment; she thought herself in a Dream, to see a King her Lover, and moreover a polite, generous, amiable King, a King who testified a Regard for her, due to none but a Princess.

They were not so merry at Supper as could have been expected. The King and his new Mistress spoke in a very low Voice to each other; and after the Dyssart they went together into a Room hard by. The other Ladies were put to a stand, and, tho' well accustomed to act the parts of Queens and Princesses, could not find Expressions suitable to the Presence and Company of a real King. But they were in much better Humour, when Duparc returned with the King, and told them, that his Majesty intended to present each of them with a new Suit of Cloaths; to which the King added an hundred Pistoles to each.

Since that time Duparc was the King's private Mistress, for Madame Cosel remained Reigning-Mistress all this while, the King being unable to surmount the great Ascendant she had gained over him. She was nevertheless inform'd of the King's frequent Visits to Duparc, but did not either look upon her, as a formidable Rival, or was in fear of offending the King by too outrageous Jealousies, and only gave him slight Reproofs for it. 'You invent Chimeras (answered the King) for Arms to 'resist me with; for, what reason have you after all to 'complain? do you find me less fond, less liberal, and 'not so free-hearted to you as usual? How can you think 'I am enamour'd with Duparc? Can't I see or speak to a 'woman without being enamour'd with her? I conceal 'nothing from you. Was my former Love in the least 'diminish'd I should instantly forsake you for mistrusting 'me in this manner.' Madame Cosel was greatly pleas'd with the Trouble the King took to justify himself; she

answered, jesting: 'I know that I tire you with my
'Reproaches; but I know also that I cannot have too
'watchful an Eye upon your Gallantries, and that you
'are never in want of means whereby to deceive me and
'thirty other Mistresses as suspicious as I am.' By these
trifling Reproaches and · Justifications the King and
Madame Cosel supported their mutual Love, which
would else have been subverted or remain'd in a languishing State.

About this time Frederick IV, King of Denmark,
whom an earnest Desire to see Italy once more, which
had afforded him Abundance of Diversion in his Youth,
had induced to quit his Kingdom, returned from his
Journey. Before he went to his own Metropolis, he
resolved to visit the King of Poland, and her Royal
Highness, Mother to the latter, and Aunt to the former.
The Danish Monarch met with a splendid Reception,
and all the other Ceremonies usual on the like Occasion.
The King sent the Princes of the Blood, the Prince of
Furstemberg, the Counts of Fleming and Pflug, and
several Noblemen and others to meet the Royal Guest.
He went himself two Miles from Dresden to meet the
King of Denmark, with whom he made a grand Entry into
the Town. The Queen and Prince-Royal of Poland waited
upon and received them at the Bottom of the Stair-Case,
and after they had testified their Pleasure in seeing him,
they placed him between them. The King of Poland

walk'd by himself. The Guest was conducted into the
Hall, where the Queen presented to him the Ladies of the
greatest Quality at Court. Madame Cosel was not present
there, the King being unwilling so far to mortify the
Queen, as to oblige her to present that Lady to the King
of Denmark, nor did he think proper to present her
publickly to that Prince. The King of Denmark, after
having for some time conversed with the Queen and
Prince-Royal of Poland, went with his Majesty to the
Apartment intended for his Use, and from thence the
two Monarchs went to Madame Cosel. They remained
with her till they were called to Supper, which was
certainly very splendid, and where none of those grand
Ceremonies commonly used on the like Occasions were
omitted. The King of Denmark sate between the King
and Queen. When he drank the first time twenty-four
Pieces of Cannon were fired, and the Supper was accompanied by a fine Consort of Musick. Among the Ladies,
that surrounded the Table, appeared Madame Cosel
shining with Jewels of all kinds. The King of Denmark
was unwilling to see her stand, and desired his Majesty
to permit her to sit down: A Chair was directly reach'd
her, which displeased all the other Ladies, and kept them
in a disagreeable Humour all Night.

The following Days were spent in Entertainments
and Feasts, and the forty Days of his Danish Majesty's
Stay at Dresden were all signalized by some new Diver-

sion, whose wondrous Magnificence both surprised and delighted them. Madame Cosel was the principal Object of these Feasts; every one, even the two Monarchs, honoured her by wearing her Coat of Arms every-where. No King's Mistress was ever distinguished by more splendid Honours.

The two Kings went to Lichtenberg to visit his Royal Highness. From thence they departed for Pretsch, where they were magnificently treated by the Queen. They departed from this Palace for Potzdam, to pay a Visit to Frederick I King of Prussia, who by the Reception he gave them, deservedly maintained the Sir-Name of Magnificent, which he had before acquired. Both Monarchs were equally gallant in respect to the Ladies of the Prussian Court; and tho' his Danish Majesty could not boast of so fine an Aspect as Frederick-Augustus, yet was he equally fond of the Fair Sex, and seldom without a Mistress. The Prussian Court was adorned with a vast number of beautiful Ladies, but they had not that gallant Disposition innate to those of Saxony, and appeared very disagreeable to the two Kings. The Countess of Wartenberg, Wife of the Great Chamberlain, and Prime Minister to his Prussian Majesty, thought her Charms sufficient to enslave the King of Poland; and for that purpose made bold and indecent Addresses to him; but as no Beauty could be found in her Person, her Complexion excepted, and as her Conversation savour'd too much of the meanness of her Extraction,[1] the King could not be pleased with her. He knew that Lord Rabbi,[2] the British Ambassador was her Lover; for which Reason, when Fitztuhm took notice of the Countess's incessant Endeavours to please him, he answered that Favourite, that whatever Pains she took, she should not be able to set him at Variance with the Maritime Powers. The Countess was in Despair, when answered so coldly by the King; as she was the most vain and most prejudiced in her own Favour, of all other Women, she was almost certain, that she should not fail of her Conquest, and that the King's amorous Heart could not escape her victorious Charms. She was in constant and careful search after Opportunities of speaking to him in private, and he avoided them as carefully. Fortune was at last inclined to favour the Countess. The King of Poland's Chief Design in visiting the Prussian Court was to persuade Frederick I to send him some Assistance towards his Re-accession to the Throne of Poland; Those Times happen'd luckily to be favourable to his Design. Charles XII of Sweden was involved in great Troubles in Muscovy, and conquered by the Czar, without any extraordinary means. The King of Denmark had promis'd to invade Sweden, and if he could but perswade the King of Prussia to declare himself in his Interest, the Recovery of his Crown

---

[1] She was Daughter to a Waterman of Emmerick.
[2] At present Earl of St——d.

was not impracticable. But the Prussian Ministers seem'd
little inclined, or rather averse to interpose in the civil
Broils of other Nations; the King knew, that by gaining
Count Wartenberg's Interest, who was absolute Regent
of his Master, he could not fail of that of his Prussian
Majesty; and as he was not ignorant of that Minister's
vast Fondness for his Wife, he thought it most proper
to obtain her Favour first. In order thereto he was obliged
to visit her, which he could scarce prevail upon himself
to do; but the Necessity of his Affairs required it. He
sent Mr. Fitztuhm to acquaint her, that he should pay
her a Visit that Afternoon; and as he desired to consult
with her about Affairs of Importance, he desired she
would be alone. The Countess took particular Care not
to displease him by inviting others. He found her on a
Couch, lying as tho' she had been indispos'd. All the
Light they had in the Room penetrated thro' Silk-
Curtains of a Crimson-Colour, which were drawn before
the Windows. Her Deshabille was of Green Silk enriched
with Silver; and she had under pretence of the Heat of
the Weather, laid open her Arms and Breasts, which were
really very beautiful. She directly made Excuses to the
King, for receiving him upon a Couch; and told him,
that the Honour of hearing his Commands was the only
Cause of her rising that Day, since she was perplexed
with a violent Head-Ache. The King told her, that he
was very sorry his Visit should put her to any Incon-

venience, that he would not abuse the Regard she testified for him, but tell her in few Words the Occasion of his coming there. He then informed her of his Intentions, and desired she would perswade her Husband to induce the King of Prussia to second his Views. The Countess promis'd to do whatever he desired, and accompanied her Answer with so many Protestations of Tenderness, that, tho' Frederick-Augustus was never scrupulous in Affairs of this kind, yet was he highly displeas'd at them. The Situation of his Affairs obliged him however to have some Regard to her amorous Expressions, answered her in his usual polite manner, being always reserved, when she endeavoured to draw him into an Amour. The Countess absolutely resolved to reap some Benefit of that Conversation, fell upon his Neck, and pressing him in her Arms, pull'd him upon the Bed with her. His Majesty, instead of being in the least enamoured with her, despised her, and was at a loss how to disengage himself from this Adventure, when Lord Rabbi the Britannick Ambassador happened fortunately to come and deliver him from his Trouble. Tho' the Countess had given strict Orders to her Servants not to admit any-body whilst his Polish Majesty was with her; yet did they little think that a Person of such Distinction as that Ambassador, who had never been refus'd Admittance before, was not excepted from such an Order; wherefore they not only admitted, but forgot to tell him, that the King was in Conference with the Countess. The Ambassador perceiving the King in Madame Wartenberg's Arms, in Respect to his Majesty, was about to retire, but the King called out to him: 'Come, come, my Lord, (cried 'he) Your Company will not be disagreeable here.' But no Person could come at a more unfortunate Time, than the Ambassador did then for the Countess. It was certainly a very pleasant Diversion to see the Confusion these Two were in. The King could not forbear diverting himself with Railleries upon the Adventure, and afterwards left them alone, since which time he carefully avoided a private Conversation with Madame Wartenberg; at which she was so displeased, that for complete Satisfaction to her Resentment, she induced her Husband to dissuade Frederick I from entering into an Alliance with that Prince.

The Danish and Polish Monarchs stayed eighteen Days at Potzdam and Berlin, after which the former returned to Copenhagen, and the latter to Dresden. Frederick-Augustus was in few Days after his Return informed of the final and total Defeat of Charles XII near Pultowa, and finding that none of his Enemies were in a Condition to oppose him, he resolved to attempt his Re-accession to the Throne of Poland. The Princess of Teschen and Madame Brebentau proved of important Service to him on this Occasion, by the number of Polish Lords, whom they gained over to his Interest. Before

247

his Majesty went to Poland, he had a Conference with
Frederick I King of Prussia at Leipsig, and another with
Peter the Great Czar of Muscovy at Marienburg. After
having received (a second time) the Homages of the
Polish Grandees, he returned to Dresden, where Madame
Cosel and Duparc had remained. He found the Countess
at a wide Variance with all his Ministers, but more
particularly with the Prince of Furstemberg, and the
Field-Marshall Count Fleming. This latter was naturally
of so haughty a Disposition, that he endeavour'd to make
everybody subject to him; and tho' he did not exact it of
Madame Cosel, yet he could not comply with her Commands, tho' that imperious Favourite required him.
His Majesty endeavoured to reconcile them once more;
he obliged them to speak to one another in a friendly
manner; but all his kind Offices proved entirely ineffectual, the Mistress and Favourite-Ministers proceeded to
bitter Invectives even before his Majesty; and whatever
Arguments he made use of to reconcile them, they parted
fully resolved to bear a perpetual Hatred and Malice to
one another.

Since that time they have formed continual Plots for
each other's Destruction. The Prince of Furstemberg,
tho' formerly an Enemy to Count Fleming, assisted his
Endeavours to effect the Countess's Ruin. They were
thus disposed when the King went to Warsaw. As
Madame Cosel was big with Child she remained at

Marie, Countess of Denhoff

THE COUNTESS OF DENHOFF

Dresden, and Count Fleming departed with the King. This shewed little Policy in Madame Cosel to consent to let him follow the King, and was certainly a Fault most conducive of any to her own Perdition. This Nobleman consulted with his Cousin upon the Means whereby they might occasion in the King an Oblivion of his Mistress. The result of their Conference was that they must procure another for him: and after having consider'd all the Ladies they knew, they made choice of the Countess of Denhoff, Daughter of the Great Marshall Bielinski. 'She is sufficiently amiable (said Madame 'Brebentau) to be capable of pleasing, but her mind is 'not so exalted as to be able to rule.' but the whole Plot consisted in rendering the King amorous, and overcoming the Scruples they feared to meet with in Madame Denhoff. This latter Difficulty seem'd to be of little Importance. Madame Brebentau undertook to remove all her Doubts, and render her as compliable as the Affair would require. 'If she opposes me (said she) I will perswade her Mother 'the Great Marshaless, my intimate Friend, to perswade 'her to Reason, who foreseeing the deplorable Situation 'their Affairs will be in after the Great-Marshall's Decease, 'will be extreamly pleased to find that Opportunity of 'restoring the former Prosperity of their Family.' But to render the King amorous seemed their utmost Difficulty; for tho' he was naturally fickle and gallant, yet every woman would not suit his Fancy; a brisk and lively

Disposition could only captivate him, and this was the chief Quality Madame Denhoff was deficient in, who with a dull, heavy Air affected the Modesty of a Virgin, which was directly opposite to the Character the King required of his Mistresses. Madame Brebentau and Count Fleming were sensible that she would not suit their Monarch's Fancy, but knew no Lady at Court more proper to propose to him, and hoped to succeed in their Design, provided they could obtain the Interest of Mr. Fitztuhm, whom the King had appointed Count of the Empire, whilst he himself was Vicar of it, since the Death of the Emperor Joseph. They mentioned the Matter to him. Mr. Fitztuhm answered, That he should not oppose their Intention, but could not second it; that he was resolved to continue his former Conduct, that is, neither to propose, nor deprive that Prince of any Mistress, and should also respect those, to whom he was pleased to give his Heart.

This Refusal did not dishearten Madame Brebentau; she mentioned Madame Denhoff to the King, as the most accomplished Lady in the Kingdom; this excited in his Majesty a Desire of seeing her. She was at her Husband's Seat in the Country, and a Courier was dispatch'd to call her to Warsaw, where she arriv'd soon afterwards. The two Ladies Bielinski and Brebentau told her the reason of her being sent for so suddenly, and what she must do in order to get the love of her Sovereign; and after having settled all necessary Matters, they gave the King the next day an Opportunity of seeing her. This was at an Entertainment which Madame Brebentau gave the King. The Countess made her Appearance at the appointed Time, accompanied by her Mother and the Starostine Cherinska her Sister. Madame Brebentau presented her to the King, who received her in that graceful manner which was natural to him, and attracted the most insensible Hearts; he discoursed gallantly with her for some time, but his Heart could not yet be affected by her Beauty. A Ball was given after Supper, which the King opened with Madame Denhoff; he liked not her Dancing; and she did not in general answer the advantageous Description Madame Brebentau had given of her.

The King, when alone with Mr. Fitztuhm, 'I am to be 'forced to love (said he) but till they find a better than 'Madame Denhoff, I doubt whether I shall be unfaithful 'to Madame Cosel.'—'I fear not (said he) Your Majesty's 'forgetting her; you may love Madame Denhoff at 'Warsaw, and Madame Cosel at Dresden; which is what 'I take the liberty of advising you to do. For, as your 'Majesty has two Courts, one in Saxony, and the other at 'Warsaw, you ought to be a compleat Monarch, and in 'Justice, keep a Mistress at each Court. This will conduce 'undoubtedly to the Satisfaction of both Nations. At 'present the Polanders except against your keeping a 'Saxon Mistress. If you forsake her, to be enamoured

'with a Polish Lady, the Saxons will find equal Reason
'to complain: whereas by being amorous six Months in
'Poland, and the other six Months in Saxony, both
'Nations will be satisfied.'—'You divert yourself at my
'Expense (replied the King) because your Mistress never
'disturbs you, but if, like me, you was to receive by
'every Post a Letter, in which you are accused of Treachery
'or Inconstancy; and on the other hand, be here per-
'plexed by Persons, whose only Design is to render me
'unfaithful, it would certainly cause a great Uneasiness
'in you.'—'No, indeed (replied Mr. Fitztuhm) I should
'follow my own Inclination, and not regard the Trouble
'they endeavoured to give me.'

In the mean while Madame Bielinski persisted in her
Resolution of rendering the King amorous of her
Daughter, and invited him to Supper. At this Entertainment the Company was more choice and less numerous
than at Madame Brebentau's; the Ladies sung after
Supper; and the Starostine Cherinska and the Countess of
Denhoff exerted their Voices; They sung the Scene of
Atys and Sangaritis. Madame Denhoff, who sung the Part
of Sangaritis, look'd incessantly upon the King, and
addressed to him all the languishing Looks and tender
Expressions belonging to her Part. Her Endeavours
did not prove ineffectual, for the King was affected, and
begun to divert her with his usual gallant Discourses,
which she answered only by her tender and languishing

A NEW AMOUR

Looks. Her Mother and Sister spoke for her, and the King might consequently be said truly to have courted three Persons at once. As he was very much diverted at Madame Bielinski's, he frequented it constantly; and at last on purpose to visit Madame Denhoff, and by the slow Addresses she made to him, his Heart was enslaved. Whilst he was entering into this new Amour, Madame Cosel was deliver'd of a Son at Dresden. She was no sooner informed of the Change she was threatened with than she was resolved to depart for Warsaw, intending to retain the King's Affections, either by Tears or Arms. But the Prince of Furstemberg, acquainted with her Departure, dispatch'd a Messenger to the Count Fleming, to give him Notice of it, and desire him to be careful that he was not deceived by his own Intrigue. This Letter surprized those of Madame Denhoff's Party extreamly. They met at Madame Brebentau's, because she was constantly indisposed, and kept her Bed. No Dyet was ever managed with more Unanimity; all the Members of that illustrious Assembly determined that they must endeavour to prevent Madame Cosel's Arrival at Warsaw, and that in order thereto Madame Denhoff must persuade the King to give Orders for her Return to Saxony. As their Danger was imminent, Madame Denhoff undertook the same Evening to prevail upon the King to comply with her Request. At the time when the King was accustomed to come, she laid down upon her Bed, with her

Head leaning upon one Hand, and holding a Handkerchief in the other; she look'd stedfastly before her, as a Person greatly perplexed. The King, sorry to find her in this Condition, desired pressingly to be acquainted with the Cause of her Distress. The Countess cover'd her Face with her Handkerchief, and pretended the Tears she shed hindered her from speaking. The King moved to Pity, squeezed her Hands, kiss'd them, and conjured her to declare the Cause of her Grief. 'Alas! 'Sir (replied at length Madame Denhoff) I am threaten'd 'to lose my Life. This I should esteem as a Trifle, could I 'carry your Affections along with me; but alas! the loss 'of my Life is to be accompanied with that of your Heart, 'which I am speedily to be deprived of. Madame Cosel 'is on her Journey hither; perhaps now arrived, and you 'are only come to give me Notice to make way for that 'happy Rival.'—'I! Madame (replied the King) can I tell 'you any such thing! do you think me capable of it, and 'can you imagine that I shall ever be induced to forsake 'you? No, Madame, I am tied to you, by indissoluble 'Chains; your agreeable Disposition, that evenness of 'Temper, and those incomparable Charms only appropri'ated and to be met with in you, may assure you, that 'Madame Cosel shall never be able to do you any Preju'dice.'—'O! dear Prince, (answered the Countess) I wish 'your Thoughts corresponded with your Words, and 'your Love for me was as sincere, as I can truly say mine

'is for you! For I declare before you, that I should be
'willing and ready to die; but to leave so great a Happi-
'ness, as I enjoy in your Affection, is utterly impossible
'to me; and be assured, that I shall sooner lose my Life,
'than those pleasing Hopes you have occasioned in me.
'Love me therefore, which if you cease to do, the loss
'of your Heart will render my Life burdensome to me.'
—'What an enormous Crime should I be guilty of (replied
'the King) if after what I have heard from your dear
'Mouth, I should be devoted to any other besides you!'
—'Alas! how pleasing are these Hopes which you give
'me (said she) but I cannot be satisfied; my Rival
'approaches, you will see, and suffer her to resume the
'Dominion she has so long enjoyed over your Heart.'
—'How unjust and even industrious are you (replied the
'King) to torment yourself after this manner. Tell me,
'for God's Sake, what you require me to do, and what
'will conduce to your present and future Ease. Suffer
'your Rival to come, that she may see your Triumph, and
'openly undergo her own Defeat.'—'No, Sir (answered
'she) Madame Cosel is coming, I must leave Warsaw;
'I am too fearful of some Violences she will commit.'

When she had done speaking, Madame Bielinski, who
had listened all the while, came in, as if she had been
ignorant of the King's Presence with her Daughter.
'Come hither, Madame, (said he) come, and assist me in
'removing from your Daughter's Heart those Fears

'wherewith she perplexes me.'—'What reason (answered
'she) has my Daughter to suspect? If she doubts of your
'Fidelity, Sir, your Majesty may look upon that as a
'Token of her excessive Fondness.' The King related
to her the Apprehensions Madame Denhoff seemed to
be troubled with. 'I cannot, Sir, (replied Madame
'Bielinski) in the least blame my Daughter for harbouring
'Suspicions of that kind; and even your Majesty ought
'to be in fear of Madame Cosel, after the Threats she has
'dared to pronounce in your Presence.'—'With all my
'Heart (answered the King) Madame Denhoff and you
'shall be satisfied; I am going instantly to give Orders
'for Madame Cosel's Return to Dresden.'—'O! dear
'Daughter (cried Madame Bielinski) how happy are you
'in the Love of so accomplished, so amiable a Prince!
'But, Sir, (continued she, addressing herself to the King)
'since your Majesty is ready to promote my Daughter's
'Ease, permit me to say, that a Person in whom you can
'well confide must be sent against Madame Cosel, who,
'being naturally so very imperious, will undoubtedly
'refuse to obey your Orders.' The King gave her Leave
to send whom she thought most proper. Madame
Bielinski thanked him for his great kindness, and proposed Montargon, a French Gentleman, who came into
Poland with the Abbot of Polignac,[1] and who, by being
truly attached to the Great Marshall's Family, had

[1] Afterwards Cardinal.

obtained the Place of Gentleman of his Majesty's Bed-Chamber. Montargon was sent for, and the King gave him proper Orders. 'But, Sir, (said that Gentleman) if 'Madame Cosel refuses to obey, what must I do?' The King remained pensive some moments, and resolved upon sending as an Assistant with him La Haye, Lieutenant-Colonel in the Life-Guards, to whom he gave Orders to take Six Soldiers with him, which he thought would surely suffice to bring Madame Cosel to Reason. Madame Bielinski, and her Daughter the Countess of Denhoff were inexpressibly joyful at what they heard; they tired the King with Praises and Thanks. The Lover and his new Mistress pleased themselves with tender Expressions, and reciprocal Assurances of an everlasting Affection. The King having sent for La Haye, gave him the same Orders which Montargon received before, enjoining both to be very expeditious.

The two Ambassadors prepared themselves with all possible Expedition, in order to set out on their Embassy. They met Madame Cosel at a small Town called Widawa in Poland on the Borders of Silesia. They pretended to be arrived there by Chance, desiring to pay their due Respects to the Countess, who received them with great Civility, desiring their Company at Dinner. When Dinner was over, Mr. Montargon, chief Ambassador begun to discourse about the matter in hand. He spoke as by his own Authority, and as a Friend who was willing to give

R   257

her some good Advice. But Madame Cosel, not then
dispos'd to give Ear to his Counsel, answered him in a
very arrogant manner, threatening to make him repent
of his audacious Deportment. He then spoke in the King's
Name, but she refused to obey, saying, the King had
hearken'd to the Advice of his Enemies, and would not
be angry with her for disobeying those Orders. Montargon being naturally of a mild Disposition, and his Actions
all very gentle, told her with a disdainful Sneer, he
begg'd she would not force him to proceed to violent
means. 'How! (said she) will you be so rash to proceed
'so far?' He replied, the King's Orders required her
immediate Return to Dresden, and if she could not be
perswaded to comply by fair means, she must be forced
by rough usage. At these Words Madame Cosel was
enraged, calling Montargon a petty Notary's Clerk,[1]
and taking up a Pistol (for she never travelled without
Arms) threatened to kill him. Montargon seeing her
Sex must be indulged, for the little Regard she had to
the Law of Nations in abusing his Person, retired, and
left his Assistant La Haye to manage the affair, who
spoke in the King's Name, and by his soft Expressions
insinuated himself into the Countess's Favour, whose
Disgrace he pretended to bemoan; persuading her the
Situation of her Affairs then required her Return to
Dresden; that the King would shortly be there, that

[1] He was Son to a Notary of the Village called Chaillot near Paris.

there was no probability of the Countess following him
thither, and then she would perhaps find it an easy matter
to regain his Love, and triumph over her Enemies.
Madame Cosel found she could follow no better Advice,
agreed to return to Dresden. Montargon dispatch'd a
Courier with this agreeable Account to Madame Bielinski.
He afterwards followed Madame Cosel with La Haye
and the other Guards, and arrived always at the Inns as
soon as she left them. They accompanied her in this
manner within one Day's Journey from Breslau, and
then returned to Warsaw to receive the Thanks of the
new Favourite.

The Countess of Denhoff had one more trouble, the
Removal of which would complete her Happiness; this
was her Husband, who being informed of her Conduct,
desired by Letter, she would come to his Country-Seat
without Delay. This was directly contrary to the Countess's
Intention, as well as to that of Madame Bielinski. They
suffer'd the Count to complain for some time, till they
were tired with his Reproaches, then Madame Bielinski
undertook to bring him to Reason. She went to his
Country-Seat, owning without any Evasions the Reason
of Madame Denhoff's Detention at Warsaw. 'If you are
'displeased, Sir (said she) at your Wife becoming the
'King's Mistress, you must consent to a Divorce. The
'Nuncio Grimani[1] is so intimately acquainted with me,

[1] He died in the Year 1734, a Cardinal-Legate of Poland.

259

'that I don't doubt of obtaining his Holiness's Consent!'
The Count of Denhoff accepted of the Offer willingly
without Hesitation. Madame Bielinski returned to
Warsaw, spoke to the Nuncio, the Divorce was solicited
at Rome, and Clement XI granted it.

The new Favourite lost her Father at the Beginning
of her Prosperity. This Nobleman, the most magnificent
and most amiable Person Poland ever produced, left
the Affairs of his Family in great Disorder; but the
Countess of Denhoff restored their former Wealth in a
little time. She induced the King to confer the Effects of
his Munificence on her Mother, Brother and Sister;
these Presents might justly be called a Shower of Gold,
and Bielinski's Family became soon afterwards possessed
of more Wealth than it could ever boast of before.
Madame Denhoff was perhaps, of all the King's other
Mistresses, she, whom he loved best; but may be mani-
festly proved to have been the most expensive, and who
found herself richest of any, when in Disgrace. It was
chiefly owing to the Industry of her prudent Mother,
who knowing very well no Regard would ever be had
to Lovers' Oaths, provided for herself and Family against
the Sunshine of Prosperity forsook her; She demanded
incessantly what she pleased with so much Confidence,
that she never met with a Refusal, or was ever thought
exorbitant in her Requests.

The Grief of Bielinski's Family was soon allay'd; the

MADAME COSEL TO LEAVE DRESDEN

Great Marshall's Funeral Obsequies were scarce yet
solemnised, when his Widow, Daughters and Sons
visited Balls, Races and other Diversions, which the
King prepared to comfort his Mistress. But these Entertainments seemed too trifling to Frederick-Augustus
at the Beginning of a passionate Love; he could procure
more grand and magnificent Feasts at Dresden, and
invited Madame Denhoff to go thither, and be Witness
of the Truth of what he said. She did not refuse her
Consent to this Journey, but was in fear of Madame
Cosel's Presence. She inform'd the King with her
Apprehensions, and begg'd Madame Cosel might be
forced to depart from Dresden. The King sent Orders
to the Prince of Furstemberg for that purpose; but she
refused to obey them, saying, If his Majesty thought her
guilty of any Misdemeanour, he could summon her
before the Judges, and proceed to the Rigour of the Law
with her; but as she deserved no Blame for anything else,
than having been too firmly attach'd to the King, she
hoped he would grant her the Favour of enjoying an
easy Tranquility in her own House. The Prince of
Furstemberg, satisfied in seeing her humbled, would not
insult her in Disgrace, but left her at home. The King,
thro' his new Mistress's Intreaties, sent Mr. Tienen,
Aid de Camp, to Madame Cosel, ordering her instantly
to leave Dresden. She was perplexed and in great Despair,
telling Mr. Tienen whatever she thought would affect

MADAME DENHOFF AT DRESDEN

him, and her mournful Expressions mov'd the young
Officer to Pity, who proceeded to no more Rigour with
her. She gave him as a Token of her Acknowledgment
a fine Diamond-Ring to the value of four Thousand
Dollars, and sent him back to the King with a very submissive Letter, which she wrote to persuade him to
suffer her to remain in her House. Mr. Tienen met the
King at the Distance of a day's Journey from Dresden.
His Majesty was highly enraged with his Aid de Camp,
sending him back to the Prince of Furstemberg, and the
Great-Marshall Baron of Lowendahl to enjoin them to
send Madame Cosel from Dresden either by fair or
violent means. The Great-Marshall having acquainted
her with the King's Resolution, she at length complied,
and retired to Pilnitz the day before the King's Arrival.

Madame Denhoff was informed of this Retreat by a
Courier sent to her on purpose. She then proceeded on
her Journey, accompanied by Madame Bielinski her
Mother, the Starostina Cherinska her Sister, Madame
Brebentau, and several other Ladies, the Choice of
which the King had left to her Discretion. She arrived
at Dresden in Triumph, convoyed by Mr. Chatira,
Lieutenant-Colonel, and six Cadets of the Life-Guards.
She was lodg'd in the House of the Prince of Furstem-
berg; the King's Officers attended her whilst she staid
in Saxony, and Mr. Chatira directed her domestic Affairs.
The King commanded him to guard the Countess all

Night for her better Safety, she being still in fear of
Madame Cosel. Her Fear would indeed have vanish'd,
had not the Field-Marshall Count Fleming endeavoured
to revive it in her, intending to enrage her more vehemently against the Countess of Cosel, whose Disgrace had
not yet satisfied his revengeful Mind. 'Pilnitz (said he to
'Madame Denhoff) is only three Leagues distant from
'hence. Your Rival may be here in two or three Hours;
'the King may happen to see and be again enamour'd with
'her. Believe me, let her be imprison'd, then you may be
'secure from any fatal Event which may happen.' Madame
Denhoff, more generous than the implacable Count
Fleming, answered, she could not prevail upon herself
thus to abuse a Lady of Quality, who had never injured
her.

Count Fleming, who had gone too far to desist at
once, was resolved that Madame Cosel's Ruin should be
for ever, persuaded the King to send a Messenger to
her and demand the Promise of Marriage he had formerly
given her. He foresaw in her present Rage she would
refuse to return it; not doubting but so great a Provoca-
tion would induce the King to arrest her. The Event did
luckily answer his Expectations. The Countess of Cosel
refused to return the Billet, and as she did not doubt but
her Refusal would give her Enemies a good Pretence for
arresting her, she left Pilnitz secretly, and went to
Berlin. But this Place was not so safe a Refuge for her

as she expected. The King of Prussia having acquainted
her by an Officer her Stay in that Town highly displeased
him, she retired to Halle. Her Enemies would not suffer
her there neither, they intended to deprive her of her
Liberty, and perhaps of her Riches likewise; they accused
her before her former Lover of speaking disrespectfully
of him, and fomenting a Conspiracy against his Majesty's
Person. The King, who was continually more exasperated,
wrote to the King of Prussia, desiring him to deliver her
up. The King of Prussia gave Orders instantly to
Ducharmoi, Lieutenant in the Prince of Anhalt-Dessau's
Regiment, to secure her, and conduct her with a Detachment of Soldiers to the Frontiers of Saxony, and there
to deliver her up to an Officer who would come from the
King of Poland to fetch her. 'O barbarous Injustice!'
cried the Countess of Cosel, when they told her she was a
Prisoner. She fell presently afterwards into a raving Fit,
and when she saw the Detachment of Saxon Soldiers
come to receive her, she begg'd of Ducharmoi to accept
of her fine Snuff-Box and Gold Watch, which she
constantly wore; but when he modestly refused them,
she pressed them more upon him, saying: 'Take them,
'Sir, I beseech you to take them; I would choose rather
'to see you reap some Advantage from these Trifles,
'than those unworthy Saxons, whose Slave I'm now going
'to be.' She gave some money to the Prussian Soldiers
under whose Guard she had been; but spoke not one

Mademoiselle Dieskau

IN RETIREMENT

Word to the Saxons, who received and conducted her to Leipzig, from whence she was carried to Pilnitz, and from thence to —— a Seat belonging to the Count of Friese,[1] her Son-in-Law. Here the Countess enjoyed her Liberty again, but in great Retirement. Her Enemies, not able to find any real Pretences for asperging her Character in a publick manner, insinuated, she was going privately into Holland there to change her Religion, and turn Jew. The Artifice was not very cunning, but the Vulgar easily gave Credit to it; and the common People, more superstitious in Saxony than any other part of the World, prayed for a Blessing upon those, who had prevented so shameful an Action. Madame Cosel lived however to see the Death of all her Persecutors, and survived her Rival's Favour.

A Description of the Entertainments the King gave to Madame Denhoff, and the Ladies her Attendants, would require a particular Volume. That Prince was certainly fruitful in ingenious Inventions conducive to the Splendor of his Court. Madame Denhoff was however only present at these Feasts *incognito*; she was commonly masqued, and never appear'd openly, or with her Face uncover'd before the Queen. This Singularity raised her a great many Enemies, and the more because she obliged the King to shut himself up with her; so that he was scarce ever seen in publick. This induced Mr. Kiau to

[1] This Nobleman was married to Madame Cosel's Daughter.

265

say, they ought to pray in all Churches for the Deliverance of their King imprison'd by the Polanders.

The King however was soon tired with that sort of Life. All the Courtiers were surprized he could be pleased with it so long. To be a little free from Slavery he went to Leipzig-Fair. Here he was enamoured with Mademoiselle Dieskau, a young Lady of Quality, who was, her mind excepted, the most accomplished Creature Nature ever formed. Her Shape and Actions were Majestick, her Features incomparably regular, nothing could equal her white and lovely Complexion; her blue Eyes were beautifully large, and expressed her natural Inclinations to Love, neither could she govern that Passion; her Hair was of the finest light-colour that was ever beheld; her Neck was of a dazzling Whiteness, and the sight of her Hands completed the Idea of a Composition of all that was most perfect under the Sun. But, how beautiful soever Mademoiselle Dieskau really was, she could be called no better than a Lump of Snow, no Vivacity could be found in her, she made no other Answers than Yes and No. The King was charmed with the great Beauty of her Person, he spoke to her at the Redoubt, but was in Despair when he found so little Life in her. 'If Mademoiselle Dieskau's Mind was equal 'in Charms to her Body, (said he to Mr. Fitztuhm) I fancy 'she would settle my Heart for all my Life-time.'—'God 'forbid that! Sir, (answered Mr. Fitztuhm) we should

266

'then be soon threatened with the Loss of your Majesty.
—'These are your usual Railleries (replied the King) but
'my Comfort is, you are as inconstant as I.'—'If I might
'be excused the Liberty (replied the Count) of calling
'your Majesty to an Account, I should find it a very easy
'matter to prove you have had ten Mistresses, whereas
'I have only my sixth now. This is certainly conformable
'to the right Rules of Amours, for we find in all Romances,
'Gentlemen distanced their Servants by far. But faithfully
'to discharge my Trust, I ought to take care of Mademoi-
'selle Dieskau and cultivate her Mind, that she may be
'capable of making worthy Returns for all your Majesty's
'Kindnesses.'—'No (replied the King) I shall ease you
'of that Trouble. You may become amorous of her, and
'Madame Lowendahl, whom I esteem, will be displeased
'with me for having contributed to her the Loss of your
'Heart.' In the mean while the King did not profess open
Love to Mademoiselle Dieskau, her Hour was not yet
come; but her beautiful Person made a speedy Impression
upon his Heart, and removed Madame Denhoff from
thence by slow degrees, who, nevertheless, supported
herself in his Favour for some longer time, more by the
Artifices of Madame Bielinski, than her own Charms.

The King returned with Madame Denhoff to Warsaw,
but staid a very little time in Poland. After having held
the Diet, which broke up without coming to any Deter-
mination, he returned into Saxony, pretending, that

MADAME DENHOFF'S GRIEF

Affairs of great Importance recalled him to that Electorate. His last moments with Madame Denhoff were employed in tender Expressions, he promising soon to return to her with a faithful Heart. I cannot determine whether she gave Credit to his Words, but she pretended at least to believe them. She told him, if he gave any Rival the Preference to her, she should undoubtedly die of Grief, but that, if she survived so great a Misfortune, she should pass the Remainder of her sorrowful Life in a Convent. The King accustomed to Proposals of this kind, took these for Flams, and was not at all Concerned about them. He swore however, that Death only should separate him from her. They supped at Madame Bielinski's, and after Supper the King intended to depart, when Tears were shed, and Cries heard. Madame Denhoff fell down upon a Couch as if she had been dead; her Mother sigh'd and groan'd; the Starostine Cherinska, whose Voice was naturally very harsh, cried in a manner very offensive to all Ears; the Count Bielinski, who had been lately made Starost, seemed highly afflicted; and all the other Ladies, particular Friends and Relations to the Family, with a truly cordial Affection. The King, and the Counts of Fitztuhm and Friese seemed only insensible of Grief and were employed in comforting the Afflicted. The King was near the dying Fair, he sprinkled Water in her Face, gave her some Elixirs to drink, kissed her Hands, called her his Heart, his Angel, and conjured her to live. She opened her Eyes at last, fixing them tenderly upon him, and in a manner which expressed the Trouble his Departure gave him. The King conjured her to resume her former Vigour. 'If I am dear to you, (said 'he) think of living, for your Death will be soon followed 'by mine.' She at length recover'd her Senses. Our two Lovers repeated the Sentiments of their Hearts several Times, assuring each other of their mutual Affection, and an endless Duration of it. When the King gave Orders for his Departure, Madame Denhoff cried out telling him, that her Death would be inevitable, and by these Cries and feigned Tears detain'd him very late. He at length appeased her, and having recommended her to the Care of her Mother, and all the Ladies, he stepp'd into his Chariot, and departed; afterwards consulting Reason, the Company left off immoderate Sorrow, wiped their Eyes, were comforted, and went to Bed to take their Rest.

The King arrived at Dresden, where all the Court was in Expectation of him, and after having reposed himself some days, he left that Place to be present at the opening of the Fair of Leipsig, where the Queen waited for him. At this Princess's Apartment he had once more an Opportunity of seeing Mademoiselle Dieskau. She appeared more beautiful than even Venus herself. The King could not defend his Heart from the powerful Attacks of her bright Charms; he declared his.

Passion to her, but could receive no other Return than a Blush and her Eyes fixed wistfully upon him. The King was sufficiently mortified in finding so little Vivacity in so beautiful a Person; but to comfort himself, he said, 'Her tender Years occasion it, which, together with a 'private and retired Education, renders her thus timorous; 'she will undoubtedly improve herself, by learning to 'speak, and behave with more Liveliness, when she has 'seen more of the World.' Some days passed after this, in which the King could not yet tell whether his Sentiments were agreeable to his Beloved. His Impatience would not permit him to stay, wherefore he applied to the Mother of the Young Lady, acquainting her with his passionate Love for her Daughter, and desiring her to be favourable in employing her good Offices for him. Madame Dieskau thought herself greatly honoured by the Confidence the King placed in her, and her Daughter very happy in being loved by so great a Monarch. She promis'd to persuade her to be as obliging as his Majesty could wish. But, as she was an Enemy to tedious Ceremonies, and naturally very bold, she demanded a considerable Sum for her Daughter's Virginity, which was readily granted, and paid soon afterwards.

Mademoiselle Dieskau's Simplicity and Obedience to her Mother induced her to give consent to perform the Engagements she had enter'd into for her. On the day appointed for the Feast she was dress'd in a Deshabille of Silver, and crowned with Flowers like a married Woman, when conducted to the Altar. The King was charmed with her beautiful Appearance, and could not help looking stedfastly; but as she did not in Opposition to his constant Looks hide her Charms, he had Time and Opportunity to contemplate all the Perfections of Nature.

In the mean while however strong this Passion was, Mademoiselle Dieskau was soon obliged to give way to Mademoiselle Osterhausen, who was not in the least inferior to her, either in Beauty or Birth, and vastly superior to her in the Knowledge of the World. She had no Parents, was at her own liberty of acting, and possessed vast Wealth; she appear'd frequently at Court, and it may be said she always made a bright Appearance there. Her fine Shape was incomparable, and her Mind so refined, that her Conversation was both pleasant and improving. She enjoy'd, besides these excellent Qualities, a Sweetness of Temper, an Air of Modesty, and a Deportment extremely engaging; she was ready to serve, benevolent and generous; a Lover of Grandeur and expensive Pleasures; she deliver'd her Expressions in such a manner, that occasioned those to whom she spoke, to believe she desired their Heart. The King saw her at the Queen's Apartment at first, and was directly enamoured with her.

The first Account she received of her approaching

JOYFUL INFORMATION

Felicity was brought to her by Madame Watzdorff, who perceived the Monarch's Passion by his Enquiry after her in an Assembly of Ladies of the first Rank of Mademoiselle Osterhausen's particular Merit, by the Delight he took in hearing Commendations of her, and by his protesting so beautiful and divine a Person was worthy of the most tender Affection; and that he was not surprized that every-body sigh'd for her.

No Person was ever sensible of greater Transports of Joy than Mademoiselle Osterhausen felt when she heard of the King's Passion for her. She remained silent near a quarter of an Hour, not being able to return any Answer to Madame Watzdorff, who brought her this joyful Information; she was greatly surprized at her Silence, which she took as a Token of Indifference or Insensibility. 'How (cried she) Mademoiselle, does the 'King love you, and are you insensible of his Affection?' —'Oh! (replied Mademoiselle Osterhausen fetching a 'deep Sigh from the bottom of her Heart) I am sensible, 'and more than you imagine. But I fear you flatter me 'with vain Hopes; I fear my Merit is not sufficient to 'preserve the good Fortune I am going to enjoy.' She then begg'd of Madame Watzdorff to tell her every Word the King spoke, and advise her what would be most requisite for her to do at this critical Juncture of entering into Happiness. She did not refuse her Advice, and Mademoiselle Osterhausen practis'd it so well, that in

Mademoiselle Osterhausen

few days she was assured of the Possession of the King's Heart; who to convince her the better, that no other Person could justly boast of being an Object of his Love besides herself, he married Mademoiselle Dieskau to Mr. Loos, Marshall to the Count, and since chief Master of the Horse. I shall not here relate the passionate Dialogues between the King and Mademoiselle Osterhausen in the beginning of their Amour; it would be a very difficult matter to find Terms whereby to express their mutual ravishing Enjoyments: they were never better but when alone, every day producing some fresh proof of a tender Love.

The King acted at first with great Caution in regard to Mademoiselle's Osterhausen's Reputation; but it proved at length difficult to the Mistress's Ambition and the Lover's great Passion for a long time to conceal a Secret of this nature. The Courtiers easily perceived it, and her sole Aim was being respected like a Favourite. She reaped all the Benefits of it, but her uncommon Generosity kept her from pecuniary Advantages. Satisfied with being beloved by her Sovereign, she was contented with moderate Presents, never demanding any for herself; and the King, by Age, being more frugal, gave her but little, in comparison to the immense Sums he enriched others with.

Whilst the Flames of the King's Love were sparkling in his Heart at the Saxon Court, the Count Fleming

concluded the Treaty of Marriage at Vienna between the
Prince-Royal, only Son of Frederick-Augustus, and
the Archdutchess Maria-Josephina, eldest Daughter of
the late Emperor Joseph. The Electoral Prince of Bavaria,
at present Elector, was his Rival, but the Emperor gave
the Preference to the Prince of Saxony, by Virtue of a
Contract the deceased Emperor his Brother had formerly
made with the King of Poland. The Electoral Princess
was received with such extraordinary Grandeur at
Dresden, I may truly say, all the Ceremonies were wonder-
ful, no King however magnificent could boast of Inventions equal to those of Frederick-Augustus; for he was
himself the sole Contriver of all the Feasts, which were
innumerable, and so diversified, not in the least resembling each other; the Expences amounting to four
thousand Dollars. Mademoiselle Osterhausen made a
bright Appearance, and partook of all the Diversions at
Court; these Feasts however abated the King's Love by
degrees. He found himself employed several months in
ordering these extraordinary Rejoicings, which deprived
him of the Company of his Mistress. She reproached
him for his Coldness, but he answered, he could not
entrust any Person besides himself with the management
of these publick Solemnities; his only Design was to
procure Amusements worthy herself, that she was the
chief Cause, and should be the chief Ornament of them.
Mademoiselle Osterhausen was satisfied with his Reasons;

she was afraid the King would engage in some other Amour, but did not believe he could cease loving her, and renounce all others.

This was nevertheless the Event; the King's mind wholly employed upon the direction of the intended publick Grandeur, the Arrival of the Archdutchess, and sensible of the Obligation he was under to promote the Honour of his Court, then visited by Numbers of foreign Nobility, accustomed himself by degrees to live without a Mistress. He paid no more Visits to Madame Oster-hausen, except when he discharged her; at which she was in great Despair, and applied to him for Redress by writing several Billets; but the King excused himself, and promis'd to see her the next day, and to acquaint her with the Obstacles that hindered him from visiting her. He assured her she was always dear to him, and intreated her not to be uneasy at his Absence. He continued to act in this manner, whilst the whole Town was taken up with Rejoicings occasioned by the Princess-Royal's Arrival. He afterwards left Dresden without taking Leave of Mademoiselle Osterhausen, at which she was incon-solable, but Time, the Remedy of all Evil, at last allay'd her Grief.

She went as usual to visit the Princess-Royal; but met with such a cold Reception, that it sensibly mortified her; but her Vanity would not suffer her yet to leave the Court; perhaps she flattered herself with the pleasing

Hopes of regaining the Heart of her Sovereign at his Return thither. Her next Endeavour was to insinuate herself into the Princess-Royal's Favour; and as she hoped to obtain her End by turning Roman-Catholic, she abjured Lutheranism in the Chapel belonging to the Palace. The Princess-Royal congratulated her on her Conversion, but told her, that to be distinguished by the Name of a Roman-Catholick was not sufficient, but it was likewise requisite that both her Faith and Actions should demonstrate her to be such; and if she would convince her of her real Conversion, she must retire to some Convent for a Year or two, and there be wholly employed in following the Precepts of the Religion she had so lately embraced. Mademoiselle Osterhausen not expecting the Princess to make such a Proposal to her was put to a Stand; but Necessity obliged her to be virtuous. She answered the Princess, that it was her Intention, and she hoped her Royal Highness would condescend to name a convenient Place for her Retirement. The Princess proposed Prague to her, and she faithfully promised her to go thither.

She did, in pursuance of her Promise, set out for that Place in few days afterwards, and was particularly recommended to the Countess of Collsbradt, Daughter of the Countess of Hiresau, Lady of Honour to the Princess-Royal. All the Nobility of Prague received her with particular Tokens of Respect. She was look'd upon as another Magdalen; all the Corporations came in several Bodies to pay their compliments, and congratulate her upon her Conversion. She resided there for several months before she could prevail upon herself to go into a Convent, and at length took an Apartment among the Urseline Nuns in the new Part of the Town; but she only lay there, and spent the Days in publick Pleasures.

She had led this penitent Life for the space of three months, when a Polish Nobleman demanded her in Marriage. This was Mr. Stanislafski, Chamberlain of the King of Poland, who not being possessed of very great Wealth, proposed to gain immense Riches by marrying Mademoiselle Osterhausen. She suffer'd him not to sigh for her long; the Pleasure of returning to Dresden, and appearing again at Court, hindered her from enquiring whether or no Mr. Stanislafski's Rank was suitable to hers. The Marriage-Ceremony was celebrated at the House of Madame Collsbradt, and the new-married Couple departed in few days for Dresden; where I must leave them, and return to the King in Poland.

This Monarch lived there free from all Passion; paternal Fondness succeeded his amorous Inclinations. He gave a particular token of that to the Daughter of Henrietta, whom Fatima's Son had discovered to him to be his Daughter. This young Lord, whom the King created Count of Rotofski, when he acknowledg'd him to be his Son, was moved to Compassion at the obscure

277

HENRIETTA'S DAUGHTER

Condition of Henrietta's Daughter. He had taken her into his House, expecting an Opportunity of shewing her to the King, which happened soon after. His Majesty, after he had reviewed his Regiment, walked up and down in the Palace-Garden, and said, he was extreamly well satisfied with the Behaviour of his Soldiers at the Review. The Count of Rotofski informed him that he had a Young Lady at his House, more expert at the Military Evolutions than the most experienced Soldier. The King demanded to see her, and she came in a Man's Dress, the Livery of one of the Grenadiers of the Life-Guard. The King was at the sight of her moved to Compassion; her Features assured him that she was his Daughter. He embraced her, called her his Child, and created her Countess of Orzelska. Some days after this he promised her large Pensions, and presented her with a fine Palace, whose Furniture was very splendid. When she was thus provided for, the King passed his Evenings at her Palace; the whole Court resorted thither, and she enjoyed the Honours due to a lawful Daughter. The King conducted her into Saxony, where the shining Grandeur of his Court dazzled before her Eyes. Several Ladies strove to gain the Royal Heart, but their endeavours proved ineffectual; paternal Love had smother'd in him all unlawful Affection. The King being wholly employed upon settling a Daughter so dear to him, he Married her to the Prince of Holstein-Beck. The marriage was celebrated with a Grandeur truly Royal; the Festivals and Rejoicings were innumerable, equall'd each other in magnificent Gallantry; and the Court of Frederick-Augustus was until the Death of that Great Monarch the brightest Court in Europe.

A CHARACTER SKETCH OF AUGUSTUS THE STRONG

By JAKOB HEINRICH VON FLEMING

Translated by RAGLAN SOMERSET

THE King is a ruler, whose genial and good-natured address, captivates the hearts of all who come to know him. If, instead of trusting too much to his strong constitution, he would but live a more temperate life, he would certainly reach a great age. There is joined in him both a capricious disposition and a lively power of perception. His fancy paints the hues of future delights too brightly, while it exaggerates what is disagreable. His keen understanding prevents him from communicating his cares to others, since he deems it useless to seek in them that consolation which he has failed to find in himself. He is persuaded that no man whom he would win to his interest, can withstand him and has often put this to the proof; thereby he has become the dupe of those rogues whom at times he fails to distinguish from honest men, thus affrighting the latter and encouraging the former in their villainies.

His boundless mistrust seems ill to accord with his keen understanding, since in general the possessor of such is free from suspicion. Ambition and a lust for pleasure are his chief qualities, though the latter has the supremacy.   Often his ambition is curbed by his lust for pleasure, never the latter by his ambition. His knowledge is comprehensive and the extent of his information, by which in his youth he set little store, now gives him satisfaction. Owing to his defective bringing up, he has learnt little of the history of the world and repeatedly mistakes the idealism of the historian for historical truth, so that his judgement is often extravagant. He is generous and openhanded: none the less many have thought him avaricious and even his Ministers have believed that if they could but procure him money, their own fortunes would be established. In this they would have been right, if avarice had been his master passion, for then he would have striven to conserve his resources. But he needs money in order to give the rein to his generosity, to gratify his wishes and satisfy his lust for pleasure, and thus he values those who procure him money, lower than those who content his ambition and desires. Since he is always in need, those who have engaged themselves or been chosen to minister to his necessities, cannot do enough for him, and yet stand lower in his favour than they feel should be their deserts. He does not require that money be furnished him by unlawful means, but if it be so furnished, its acceptance causes him no discomfort, and if he can put the blame of it on another he feels himself free of all reproach. His ambition and his thirst for the world's admiration and applause have sometimes

tempted him to shine by displaying his knowledge of
trifling matters, whereby State affairs of great moment
have often been retarded. Among his pleasures it is
gallantry that has most enthralled him. But even there he
has not found that bliss of which he boasts. He has had,
it is true, sensational intrigues, which in the beginning he
pretended to clothe with secrecy, but he is not the daring
gallant he would have himself considered. Indeed he has
scarcely ever exposed himself to the risk of a rebuff. He
has had many adventures, and although most of them
were very tame, he has always pretended that there were
romantick obstacles in his path. He has acted the part of
a jealous lover, but in reality he has not been very nice in
his intrigues, which have usually been with women who
had been first handled by others. In fact, he has not even
disdained to consort with publick women of the town,
sometimes even of the lowest degree.

Next to gallantry his greatest delight has been in
military and civil architecture, and as to his cognizance
of this art, there can be but one opinion. Even here however he has never carried anything to completion, because
his weakness for universal applause causes him to make
such frequent changes in the design, that in spite of many
and various commencements nothing is ever concluded.

In a sense he is good-hearted. For example, if someone
has won his favour or even persuaded him of his utility,
such a favourite is not easily displaced by the envy of

others. But if someone who has been of service has fallen out with his fellow then he will give no help to either, but let them fight the matter to a finish without his interference.

The less he be involved in the affair, the better is he contented.

This strange attitude has often enough driven his mistresses and other ladies to despair, and many times even his ministers.

In many things he cannot be persuaded, particularly when he is once resolved. If one does not then yield to his wishes, it makes him irritable and sometimes the more obstinate. He himself, however, often changes both his purpose and his resolution: when the weightiest reasons have failed to move him from a disastrous decision and he is left to act according to his choice, he is sometimes of his own accord converted to what he had before opposed. He likes men to tell him the truth, unless it be done in publick or with a schoolmaster's air. Despite the popularity for which he strives he stands more than is common upon his dignity. At banquets, though he take no open offence, much displeases him, and though he be deep in his cups nothing escapes his notice. He likes to jest and does it with a ready wit, teasing his courtiers unmercifully. Since he knows his Court well, he fits his talk to the character of his hearers. To one he says what he believes him to think of his fellow, and to his fellow what the latter thinks of the former, so that each finally believes he knows his Sovereign's opinion of others but not of himself.

He can refuse nothing, particularly if he be trustfully entreated, and therefore is more of service to rogues than to honest men.

When it is a question of giving a direct answer or deciding what measures or decisions should be taken, one can be sure of him, but if it be desired to go into matters with more particularity, he is quite capable in all good faith both of giving others the lie and going back on his word. This leads many astray who cannot perceive his true character.

He is not malicious, but can be made so. He is tender-hearted though unwilling to avow it. He is envious of the fame of others. He does not lightly forget an injury, but he forgives it. He acts as though he were dissembling, but it is clearly only a pretence. Nonetheless it is just this which has done him harm as a Statesman, since he would have fared better in his politicks had he played a different part with certain persons.

Often he has spoilt his mistresses and favourites by letting them perceive those weaknesses from which no man is free. For them the consequences have been disagreable. For after having known the weak side of a prince who far surpassed them in his talents, they assumed a superiority over him and imagined now more than ever that their place was supreme. This madness made them high-stomached and arrogant, and after, when their fellows would not brook it, ridiculous, contemptible and ungrateful to their prince.

The King would fain be a second Alcibiades, famous alike for his virtues and his vices. He loves to give feasts and entertainments, in which he is well versed. As, however, he insists in interfering with the smallest details, his presence hinders many in their work. Further, since he is not equal to every task, confusion often results, and the labour is fearfully increased, both for himself and for those whose province it is. I have already said that he cannot dissemble though he attempts to do so. I should like to add that this transparent hypocrisy springs from his desire to have the applause of all with whom he has to do.

Hence it is that his utterances are often contradictory. Earlier, when he had no permanent Ministers, this damaged his repute in affairs of State. He was wont to send envoys to foreign Courts with instructions agreeing only in part with those given to others, so that in the negotiations their voices were in conflict, and while in a particular matter an envoy was treating at one Court, his efforts were being thwarted by his fellow at another. Since, however, the Council has been formed he has abandoned this method of conducting affairs and a uniform policy is followed. He possesses qualities which are most admirable in so considerable a prince. He is noble, full of sympathy and of heroic courage. His mind easily grasps the whole of a situation and penetrates to the root of the matter. He desires that men should have perfect trust in him. If someone had mortally offended him but were to throw himself at the feet of the prince and acknowledge his guilt, I think he would first treat him with great harshness but soon abate his indignation. A pity it is that he was not reared as a prince should be, but lived with wasters and prostitutes whose outlook he has made his own.

He is polite and courteous as a private gentleman, and nothing exceeds his chivalry to women. Formerly he could not tolerate bawdy talk in their presence, but of late he has somewhat relaxed in this regard. Of his mistresses and ministers the most are disappointed in him. His mistresses think he loves them as he professes. In reality he does but hold them for his delight, and since a lust for pleasure is his master passion, he is ready to endure much rather than forgo it. When, however, his mistresses grow overweening and mistake his patience for a proof of his affection, then he bids them a prudent farewell.

It is just for this reason that they call him fickle. He behaves in exactly the same way with those Ministers whom he has appointed to relieve him of his burdens.

When his confidence lets them think that they are

indispensable and they govern more in accord with their humour than with his desire, he allows them to observe his mistrust.

Thereby those who have founded their place on his favour are disillusioned. To those ministers, however, who studiously carry out his intentions and found their place not on his favour but on his interests, without regarding themselves as irreplaceable, he gives back his confidence, even after, owing to lying reports or some other reason, it has once been withdrawn.

The Countess of Orzelska
Pastel by Rosalba Carriera

EPILOGUE

It is now (1929) almost two hundred years since *La Saxe Galante* was first published. Of how many books which appeared about that time can it be said that they are still read with undiminished zest? Must there not lurk in this volume an unusual vitality? Merely to ask the question is to answer it. It is the work of a man essentially akin to the Saxon prince, who conscious of his strength, exuberant and daring, moulds the world to his desire, and since the powers of an absolute Monarch are not to his hand, launches out at times into the entrancing worlds of adventure.

Pöllnitz knew many a tumble from the heights to the depths, on the path of his destiny, but always found his way back to the world whence he sprang. Owing to the changes in his fortunes, he probably endeavoured in his autobiographical writings to cast a veil over much, so that even now there are long periods of his life which remain in obscurity. Born in 1692 at Issum, in the Electorate of Cologne, he became on the early death of his father the playmate of him who was later to become King Frederick William the First. He was thus early at home in the Court of Berlin. After 1710 his lively "wanderyears" bore him for more than a decade over the greater part of Europe, where he sought and found fortune alike in love and play. Can we believe him when he assures us that he was Chamberlain in Berlin, Brunswick and Versailles, that he served the Duke of Weimar as Ensign, the Kaiser as Major, and the King of Spain as Colonel? Hard it is with him to separate romance from fact, since his memoirs are purposely vague. Into this epoch falls his conversion to Catholicism which postponed for years his return to the Prussian Court. With the year 1723 the fountain of his autobiography runs dry, and for ten years all trace of Pöllnitz is lost, until need drove him to earn his daily bread with his pen. In a short time his books in the French language brought him a European reputation. After several unimportant preliminary efforts, appeared in 1734 the work which made him famous, *La Saxe galante*.

Augustus the Strong was just dead, and his entertaining love affairs, written in the polished, fascinating style of Pöllnitz, won him world-wide renown. But the unscrupulousness of the author is shewn by the fact that in the same year he published a most decorous account of the Saxon Court in order to win the favour of the new Elector.

His plans went awry, but in Berlin he prospered. Frederick William the First had forgotten his old grievance and made him his Chamberlain, for he saw in him an admirable jester for his Tobacco-Parliament. This, however, did not prevent Pöllnitz from occasionally furnishing the Saxon and Austrian Courts with political information.

HIS DESCRIPTION

Into these years fall the many volumes of his memoirs, which in what was then the popular epistolary form relate his tour through Europe and his experiences at the Court of Berlin. They were eagerly devoured, despite their mixture of truth and falsehood, and provided the information which to-day one looks for in a guide-book. But despite his successful authorship, Pöllnitz was hard pressed by his creditors. Frederick the Second on ascending the throne in 1740 created him Supreme Master of the Ceremonies. As such his activity continued with a short interruption in the year 1744, save that the demands on him for any of the duties of his office, steadily diminished. In 1775 he died, mourned by none, as Frederick the Great sarcastically observed, save his creditors.

The following description of him is not unjust: "A gentleman of genius and fine breeding, but a first-class adventurer, a regular Proteus, courtier, gamester, author, scandalmonger, Protestant, Catholic, Church official, and God knows what besides." But you cannot dismiss Pöllnitz with a word to-day. The world ever grasps his book, on which his queer life, with all its passionate intensity, is stamped. Life was a joy to him, a game lit with bright and sparkling colours, and in Augustus the Strong, he mirrored his own existence.

This won his book a European public. It is easy to-day to affirm that Pöllnitz only sees the King from one side. We must ever reply that he had not the slightest intention of kindling a discussion on the character of the King. That even in his own day the King was quite differently regarded, is proved by the character-sketch of Count Jakob von Fleming, which is included in this volume. Its author was a man who cleverly removed all dangerous competitors from his sovereign's neighbourhood, and for ten years maintained his position in highest favour as civil and military adviser. Where the one seeks to read the riddle of a man's character, the other is content with the lighter task of the story-teller. A strange chance has decreed that Fleming's observations, which bear the date of January 16, 1722, were lost for nigh on two hundred years; but even if Fleming's incomplete sketch had been available, would it have interfered with the success of *La Saxe Galante*? Pöllnitz remains the amusing jester who never "writes himself out", the witty story-teller who can discuss even the most hazardous subjects with charm, and for whom the stimulating excitement of his narrative is far more important than a scrupulous adherence to facts. It is not his intention to give a historical picture, he desires to relate what pleases him, to entertain. He belongs to that group of witty gossips who, particularly in Germany, are so rare and who, on that account, always succeed in making their readers their vassals.

O.B.

www.ingramcontent.com/pod-product-compliance
Lightning Source LLC
Chambersburg PA
CBHW032243010726
47494CB00002B/609